Toby: A Man

Toby: A Man

A NOVEL

TODD BABIAK

HarperCollins*Publishers*Ltd

Toby: A Man
Copyright © 2010 by Todd Babiak.
All rights reserved.

Published by HarperCollins Publishers Ltd

First edition

HarperCollins books may be purchased for educational,
business,or sales promotional use through
our Special Markets Department.

HarperCollins Publishers Ltd
2 Bloor Street East, 20th Floor
Toronto, Ontario, Canada
M4W 1A8

www.harpercollins.ca

Library and Archives Canada Cataloguing in Publication

Babiak, Todd, 1972–
Toby : a man / Todd Babiak.

ISBN 978-1-55468-439-7

I. Title.

PS8553.A2435T63 2009   C813'.6   C2009-905711-5

Printed and bound in the United States
HC 9 8 7 6 5 4 3 2 1

PART ONE

One

East of boulevard Saint-Laurent on the island of Montreal, it was ungracious to speak the language of the sovereign. If one were forced by circumstance, one whispered. Yet under the society's current leadership, on the eve of the federal election, they finished nineteen bottles of the second-cheapest Bordeaux on the menu, twenty plates of duck confit, and shouted at each other in English. Toby had admonished them several times, to kindly respect the dignity of the bistro. After all, dignity was the reason they had chosen it. His admonitions had been received with mockery. And since his fellows felt no shame, he resolved to feel it for them.

Despite the late hour, Toby had not yet addressed the membership. The Benjamin Disraeli Society was his creation, and he continued to prepare monthly speeches to be delivered during the dessert course, but he enjoyed no administrative power. He looked at his watch, sighed, apologized to the staff whenever possible, and tapped a small glass jar of unmolested tabletop cornichons while staring across the table at the president. "Perhaps we could order crème brûlée for everyone, and move on with—"

"Perhaps we could stop bothering me." The president, Dwayne, was also the station manager and, by some definition, Toby's friend. He sat with his chin aloft, as though he were straining to see over a shelf. It caused Dwayne discomfort to sit in a chair for long periods, due to a car accident when he was a boy. At one time, Toby had known the details of this accident. Now he did not. "And while we're perhapsing," the president continued, "maybe I can introduce you to this little thing called the present tense."

Toby looked up at the maître d'hôtel, who stood against the zinc bar with enviable posture. A handsome and elegant man in his sixties, wearing a pressed dinner jacket. The only one in the room who understood.

"It's happening all around us," said Dwayne.

The server opened another bottle of wine at the opposite end of the table. He presented the cork to one of the new members, who pushed it away as though he were a life peer and said, "I'm sure it's fine, *garçon.*"

Toby balled his serviette and dropped it on his plate. "Did you hear that?"

"He doesn't know."

"But isn't that the point of all this? To know? We're devoted to knowing. Who is he, anyway?"

"My lawyer."

"Discipline him."

Dwayne lifted his wineglass off the agenda Toby had created for him as a non-administrative courtesy, and flicked it onto the floor.

Dwayne was a tall, thin black man with a cleanly shaved

head, a diamond stud earring in his left lobe, and a panhandle of deep acne scars on each cheek. He had unreasonably long eyelashes and a voice so rich he could have anchored the six o'clock news for twenty years, were it not for those cheeks.

None of the eighteen moneyed drunkards before him had thought to wear a dress handkerchief, despite his arresting demonstration of folding techniques in June. Toby accepted that spit-shining shoes or ironing shirts could be burdensome. But choosing and folding a handkerchief was an adventure, really the only radical act of the imagination open to a man of style. He had executed a perfectly imperfect fold at Alicia's house some hours earlier, as a sort of challenge to his fellows.

Of course, the absence of handkerchiefs was the most subtle of their errors. The Disraelites were loud. They cussed. The four lawyers, new members who had recently moved to Montreal from the west, seemed to be comparing snowmobile vacations. *Garçon.* The wise maître d'hôtel had placed them in a tight agglomeration of marble tables near the window so the traffic and rain on Saint-Denis would mitigate any damage to the sensitivities of his regular clientele, the sorts of upper-middle-class Québécois who still believed in the transformative power of the theatre. Toby had been monitoring further acts of barbarism among the membership that he might detail as a preface to his remarks on the bow tie: rubber-soled shoes, poorly woven shirts imported from Asian free-trade zones, improperly fitted jackets, garish timepieces, cellular phones in bulging pockets or—worse—attached to belts.

Dwayne's cellphone was attached to his belt.

Toby tried not to look at it. "I really thought I'd sold them on the handkerchiefs."

"Stop saying 'handkerchief.'"

"You want to be in a frat, don't you? You didn't bother in university, but now you're thinking, *Hey*."

"Can you at least call it a pocket square?"

"Chug, chug, chug. Cuss, cuss, cuss. Rape, rape, rape."

Dwayne stood up, beckoned Toby up, and pulled him in for a hug of malice. "Please, Tobe. Please just be anyone but yourself for the rest of the night."

Toby's phone vibrated inside his suit jacket pocket. For hours his mother had been leaving messages about his father, whose erratic behaviour, in her estimation, had stopped being at all charming. Toby excused himself, but Dwayne did not acknowledge him. The president of the Benjamin Disraeli Society was already deep into a cross-table discussion of Las Vegas with the loudest of the western lawyers: the strip or old Vegas? Which kicks the other's ass in terms of gentlemen's clubs?

He stood under the soaked awning on rue Saint-Denis and phoned his mother.

"I can't just leave. It wouldn't be right."

"Didn't you invent the club?"

"It's not a club. But yes, I did invent it."

"So?"

"So the burden of respect is heavier for me. It's the third anniversary meeting. I'm making a speech and, if I dare say it, setting an example."

"Why do you do this to yourself?"

"The society's at a fragile point. If I abandon it now, even for a moment, it'll degrade into malt liquor, whoring, video games."

His mother breathed.

"You should really be sleeping," he said.

"And goddamn it, Toby, you should be here. I wouldn't ask if it weren't serious."

This was untrue.

"Tomorrow's the election. I have to be up terribly early."

"Fifteen minutes. You want me to beg?"

"Put Dad on the phone."

"He's out."

"Then how do you know he's acting up?"

"Just . . . What's your speech about?"

Toby had worked on it for several hours, on paper and in front of his bathroom mirror. The health of a nation, its hope for progress and the power of its collective dreams, are contained in the manners of its citizens. Their capacity for empathy and compassion, their curiosity and creativity, their intelligence, their education, all of their most haunting secrets live in gestures—smiles and nods, introductions and pleases and parting words, the sincerity of their apologies. Handker-chiefs, bow ties.

"Bow ties."

"Excuse me?"

"Bow ties, Mom."

"For Christ's sake, bow ties."

Toby looked in at the historic photographs on the walls of the bistro, of waiters and managers shaking hands with presidents of banana republics, a few prime ministers, an impossibly old Charles Trénet. Yellowing photographs that Toby had avoided all night: mortality, pretend smiles, failure dressed up as success.

"You allowed your dad to stew in his own miserable . . . miserableness for hours here. Hours. And for what?"

"Mom."

"Bow ties."

"Bow ties are never just bow ties."

"What are they, then?" The click of her lighter. He could see it: a Zippo engraved with a cheetah and her name: *Karen*. "You know what? Don't even tell me."

"I have a compromise. Tomorrow, when the election is over, I'll pick up some Bombay Mahal. We'll play Boggle."

She had already ended the call.

The traffic lights leading to the autoroute flashed green, allowing Toby a rare opportunity to do what the turbochargers in his car—a black sapphire metallic BMW 335i sedan—demanded of him. His twenty-minute speech, in French, about the lost majesty of the bow tie had been ill received.

Dwayne, who had not bothered to restrain the membership, had walked him to the door. "You're off home?"

"To my parents' place, actually."

"Then home?"

"I guess so."

"In case I need to hunt you down in the morning."

"When have you ever hunted me down?"

"Hot speech, by the way. Beautifully composed."

"Mock on."

"*Moi?*"

"The whole point of the society, Dwayne, is to make gentlemen of ourselves. There are rules of order. And you, as president—"

"Next time, you can talk at nine." Dwayne opened

the bistro door, placed his hand on Toby's back and lightly shoved. "I promise. Good luck with your mom and dad."

Dollard-des-Ormeaux was tranquil. All the airplanes had departed. Toby turned onto rue Collingwood and removed his foot from the gas pedal. It was as though he had taken a wrong turn into a queer replica of his street. The house of his childhood glowed orange, almost prettily, with flashes and retreats against the white vinyl siding that suggested, somehow, a circus. He parked across the street and looked around for neighbourly confirmation, but it was eleven at night and there were no people and no sounds on Collingwood. Only the heavy breath of the fire.

Toby could see, from the sidewalk, a man in the driver's seat of the burning Oldsmobile. He sat with impeccable posture as flames rose and crested over the hood. The man appeared to be meditating or chanting, drawing strength from God or some station of his heart. Strands corkscrewed from the tight black base of his hair—it was confirmed, his father's hair. Toby ran toward the car and stopped. The stateliness of the man in the driver's seat, the dignity about him, had fed Toby's instant hope that the Oldsmobile held an imposter, his parents' house randomly selected suburban geography. Its origin was the engine, his father's fire. Melted plastic rotted the air; black smoke purled within white.

Toby watched his father from a point where the flat driveway sloped down to the street, and waved his arms. He waved Edward out. He screamed, though he knew he would not be heard. "What are you doing?"

Edward stared back at him.

"Are you trapped?"

Edward continued to stare. He was not trapped.

You must run to the driver's-side door, open it. Carry him to the brown lawn. Speak to him. Only it was hot, even at this distance. Toby had placed his hand on the red element of an electric stove at one of his parents' dinner parties in 1977, and the scars remained. From a lifetime of cinema and television, he knew that a burning car was always one moment away from blowing up. He was already too close. He did not want to die. He did not want to watch his father die. Toby called out to Edward, jumping-jacked, gathered a handful of dry cedar chips from under the silver maple, and pitched them at the Oldsmobile. The chemical smell, the heat, the image already formed of the red hood twisting up, up, in slow motion, and landing on the roof of a nearby bungalow. *You must run to the driver's-side door.* Patches of vinyl siding dripped. Toby pulled out his phone and dialled 911. The woman, a Québécoise, asked his name, asked if he had a fire extinguisher, access to water. She switched to English, then baby talk.

Toby dropped the phone and read his father's eyes in the stillness.

Flame, and then darkness entered the car. Toby started to run, to run away, but he was interrupted by movement. The Oldsmobile shook and the door opened. A puff, an exhalation, and Edward fell onto the driveway on his hands and knees. The arms of his flannel shirt smoked, the back of his hair. He wailed and rubbed his head vigorously, rolled into the grassy ditch that separated the driveway from the front lawn. It had rained that afternoon, and the grass was blessedly wet. It squished under Toby's brogues.

He pulled his father by his feet, by his baked leather sneakers. His father's eyes were closed now, and he winced and shouted in pain, just once. When they were installed on the neighbour's lawn, away from the inevitable explosion, Edward said, in a voice that was not his own, "I am sorry."

The grass would surely stain the knees of his suit, a three-week-old blue pinstripe Hugo Boss, so Toby crouched. Sirens. He crouched and slid close, put a hand on his father's blackened face. A door opened with an echo, more doors, chatter. He whispered, "What were you doing?"

"A bow tie."

"Dad."

"You've joined a think tank."

"Dad, I promise. I was just about to—"

"Shh."

Men and women everywhere, thick uniforms, *joual,* water, his mother shouting. A small crowd separated him from his father, and Toby called out, vowed to meet him at the hospital. The *beep* of a vehicle in reverse. A fireman close, hands on Toby's hands, yellow in the whites of his eyes, grey in his trim beard, sausage on his breath: "Monsieur Ménard?"

⌒

His legal name was Toby Mushinsky. Producers at the television station had insisted he Latin up shortly after he had been hired as a City Hall reporter in 2001.

"Mushinsky's not Pepsi enough, what?" His father had sprawled in the navy recliner, purchased with a couple of fortunate income tax returns in the latter years of the twentieth century. "What's the source of their hatred for the Semites?"

"And we're off!" Karen had stood behind them, wiping dust off the succulent leaves of her aloe vera plants

with a mixture of milk and water. They had almost finished the bottle of Veuve Clicquot Toby had brought home
to celebrate.

"How can we live here another minute, in this weather,
among these cultural fascists?"

"That's not even a thing, Ed. You're ruining Toby's most
special day."

"Dad, you're right. I'll speak to them."

Shortly after his fiftieth birthday, Edward Mushinsky
had learned he was one-eighth Ashkenazi, on his father's
side. An aunt with an interest in genealogy had discovered
Edward's purchase on Judaism, along with a break in the
family tree initiated by a great-grandmother's dalliance with
a gypsy. Edward, who had been without religion and without any recognizable ethnic community, treated the news like
a conversion miracle. One-eighth chosen. Somehow he had
known it all along. He began sending cheques to the Jewish
Defense Fund and B'nai Brith, volunteering at the Jewish
Eldercare Centre in Westmount, and visiting the rabbi at
Temple Emanu-El-Beth Sholom to discuss worldly and spiritual matters. He appeared on a database of Israel supporters
and received piles of pleading junk mail from charities and
neoconservative political parties every month. He signed up
for Hebrew classes but realized, after the first couple of evenings, that it was really just too hard.

"Let's at least admit, before we roll over, that it's an
insult to you, to me, and to our heritage."

"Ed. Ed, I'm pleading here. We don't have a heritage."

"I'll tell them Mushinsky or nothing, Dad."

"Oh, this is just fantastic." Karen walked into the
kitchen and tossed her milky cloth into the sink with a slap.

"Ménard." Edward Mushinsky finished his champagne in two gulps and said it again, "Ménard," as though he were saying "Intifada."

⌒

In Emergency, the ill lay asleep or moaning lightly on stretchers in the old hallway, and in the examination rooms there were grunts and flashes of torn flesh that Toby hoped had nothing to do with his father. The floor was built around an island of nurses. They had nearly completed a revolution around the island before his mother, wearing red flannel pyjama pants with white bunnies on them, rubber boots, and a puffy black winter jacket, declared she needed to sit down.

Toby unfolded a wheelchair and eased Karen into it. They reached a windowless rectangular room with eight beds. Edward Mushinsky was in the corner, asleep with an oxygen mask over his mouth and nose. A blanket covered his torso. His arms and legs were bare, and glistened with a clear gel that had been slathered over blisters and colourful sores. His face, neck, and hands were swollen and, in the fluorescent light, dead grey.

"You said he was okay, Toby."

"He seemed okay."

"You said he was for sure okay."

"He's just sleeping."

Karen hopped up out of the wheelchair and said, into her hand, "Someone's going to prison for this."

"No."

"Attempted murder. This shall not stand."

"Mom."

"You want me to be quiet? *They* want me to be quiet."

"Who?"

Karen bowed over her husband. Her hands were open to him and quivered as though Edward were the fire.

"I wouldn't touch him just yet." A short, wide-eyed doctor introduced herself, and Toby immediately forgot her name. Her shirt was too large, and she wore an unfashionably wide, clown-like tie under her green scrubs. She explained about his sedative and the burns; the nasty-looking ones were third-degree, on his shins and arms, a spot on his head. Most of the others were second- and first-degree. He had taken in a lot of smoke. A room was being prepared for him on the burn ward, but she could not say how long he would remain in Emergency. He would be perfectly fine, in time. The doctor placed her hand on Toby's arm, just above his elbow. "What you did was very courageous."

Toby continued to look down at his father, and at the oxygen mask clouding and unclouding.

"One of the paramedics told me." The doctor squeezed his arm. "It's no small thing."

"What the hell is she talking about?"

The doctor tsked, shook her head. "Your son didn't tell you."

"Tell me what? Tell me what?"

"Toby pulled his father, your husband, from a burning car."

Karen did not respond. She had made her feelings clear on the drive to the hospital.

The doctor led them down a long hallway to a consultation room with safari-themed wallpaper and a large wooden IKEA box of forlorn toys. A toilet flushed nearby, only faintly muffled by drywall. A uniformed policeman with a goatee sat in a swollen leather chair across from a matching chesterfield, flipping through an issue of *L'actualité*. Céline Dion's polar bear of a husband was on the cover. Edward's charred blue jeans and flannel shirt had been stuffed into two clear plastic bags, which sat at the policeman's feet like little dogs. Everyone shook hands, and the doctor congratulated Toby again for pulling his father out of a roaring fire, for risking his life. She stood for a moment in silent tribute, as though waiting for the final notes of the national anthem to finish, then excused herself.

Toby focused on the fountain of black hairs bursting from each of the detective sergeant's nostrils. The questions were neutral, at first. Edward's work, his age, what he had been doing that night.

He cleared his throat, the detective sergeant, and changed his tone. "Had Monsieur Mushinsky been acting at all oddly?"

Karen sat upright in her wheelchair. "That is an insult."

"Pardon me, Madame."

"Pardon you? Pardon you? I know what you're suggesting and it's . . ." She slapped Toby's arm. "Shit, help me out. The snowman. He's the *what* snowman?"

"I'm sorry, I don't understand."

"Come on, Toby. Not terrible, but really terrible." Karen reached up, in apparent desperation, to her hair. She had been endowed with thick, curly blond hair that in recent years had blended delicately with strands of grey. It was tangled from the pillow. Vanity struck her, and she hunted in her purse for a makeup mirror as Toby and the detective sergeant waited. "The snowman . . . he's the *blank* snowman."

"Frosty?"

"No. Christ, Toby."

"Abominable?" said the detective sergeant.

"Abominable! It's *abominable* what you're suggesting, Monsieur."

"An investigator must ask questions."

"Who dropped my husband off, in the middle of the night, in his car, and . . ." Karen found the mirror, opened it, and considered her reflection. "Who? Goddamn it. He could have been killed."

The detective sergeant allowed several moments of silence. Toby was afraid to touch his mother.

"I have been on the force many years now, Madame." The detective sergeant spoke quietly and evenly. "Seventeen years. And I have never seen—"

"The last I spoke to him was before he went off to his meeting. I hope you'll be speaking to his 'friends' in the Optimist Club. They're boors. You can write that down. They take advantage of his good nature."

"He was his normal self, then? Nothing out of the ordinary?"

"Nothing whatsoever." She struggled with "whatsoever." Karen wore satsuma perfume oil. This scent, and the residue of Old Port cigarillo smoke on her clothes, battled for supremacy in the consultation room. "He listens to the oldies station. A Joni Mitchell song comes on. He loves it too much to turn it off, maddening habit, and parks and waits for the song to finish. Closes his eyes. The engine's running."

The detective sergeant had stopped taking notes. "And?"

"He revs the engine, in his sleep. And something goes, I don't know, haywire. You're the investigator. Investigate, why don't you. That Optimist Club, begin there. Maybe he *knew something.*"

The detective sergeant turned to Toby. "You were at a formal event tonight?" He swished his index finger from bow tie to handkerchief.

"Not formal, no." Formal would require a dinner jacket, entirely different footwear, and a bow tie devoid of whimsy. "I was at a restaurant."

"And what do you do, Toby?"

He was midway through the first sentence of his explanation when the detective sergeant stopped him. "Of course. Of course! I was wondering where I'd seen you before. You're *that man.*"

"Yes."

"You do those things."

"Those things, yes."

"How to be polite."

"*Toby a Gentleman.*"

"Last week I didn't stand up when the wife stood up from the table, at this Greek restaurant. It used to be okay, you know? We live in Saint-Henri! And so—"

Karen, fully awake now, cleared her throat. "What are you doing with my husband's clothes?"

"Lab analysis. As you say, investigating. It's pretty standard."

"Why 'pretty' standard?"

"Sometimes a thing makes sense. Sometimes it does not."

Her breaths, slightly rasped, quickened. "My husband burned up in a fire, Monsieur, a horrible, accidental fire. That is, unless one of those Optimist freaks—"

The detective sergeant slipped his notepad into the pocket of his polyester shirt and stood up. "I am sorry for your husband's suffering, and for yours. If I have any more questions I'll phone you." The detective sergeant pulled two cards out of the same shirt pocket and gave one to each of them. He lifted an eyebrow and asked if he might speak to Toby in private for a moment.

"Divide and conquer," said Karen, just loud enough for the policeman to hear.

Toby followed the detective sergeant into the adjacent examining room. The bed was dishevelled, and next to it there was a puddle of clear liquid on the white tile floor. The man pulled out a third business card. "Could I trouble you for an autograph, for the wife?"

In the black leather satchel he carried, Toby kept a number of four-by-six black-and-white photographs in a protective case. He pulled one out. "What's her name?"

"Angie. No, write *Angela*. I'm sorry about this. But it'll make her so darn happy."

Toby wrote what he always wrote.

"All the best." The detective sergeant inspected the photo, sighed. "Thank you."

"Without viewers, we are nothing."

"When you pulled your dad out of the fire, Toby, did he say anything?"

"He was unconscious."

The detective sergeant held eye contact. "*Évidemment,*" he said, and wished Toby and his parents *all the best*.

A series of announcements, barely audible and entirely incomprehensible, filled the ward. Charred bits of his father's shoes, and his father, had passed to the cuffs of Toby's white shirt and, when he inspected it closely, the Boss. If he had run to the driver's-side door and opened it forcefully, manfully, the fire might have at that instant entered the engine. His new suit, and his entire bloodline, would have been eliminated. There was a pain in his chest, above and below his heart. It was almost three. He could not remain. His heart hurt. The air was thin, contaminated, his lungs filled with melted plastic and now this—this place. Super-bacteria, bird and swine influenza, tuberculosis, norovirus. A clown doctor.

An orderly wheeled Edward away, to his room on the burn ward. He passed and they could not touch him. Toby blew a kiss and Karen embraced her son, slapping him on the back of the head.

"Now do you see? Now do you finally *see*?" There was only a hint of moisture in her eyes when they parted. It would not take exhaustive research for the detective sergeant to discover she had made a false statement; prison would not suit his mother's temperament. "It's my fault."

"How, Mom?"

"And *you*. Mr. Hero. If you'd been there, instead of celebrating the bow tie. Which looks pretty stupid."

"You want me to stay?"

Karen took a step back, as though Toby had pushed her. "You're going?"

"Tomorrow . . . no, today is the election. I'll be up till midnight, on camera. Dad's sleeping." Toby stopped rationalizing, because Karen had stopped listening. They stood in a wide corridor, at the entrance to the room where Edward had been. Five patients remained. Three were asleep, hooked up to machines. One man, an old man in a sweatsuit, sat on the edge of his bed and wheezed through his open mouth. "I'll come back."

She stared into the room, at the old man in the sweatsuit. He slouched, his pale neck drooped. He gripped a metal pole with wheels, a bag of fluid hanging from it like a giant plum. His lips were enormous. Karen's pyjamas were half-tucked into her rubber boots. "What am I supposed to do now? What do you do when this happens? Shouldn't someone be telling me?"

Toby tried to pull her in for a hug, but she resisted and walked slowly back to the consultation room. Giraffes and elephant cartoons decorated the upper third of the wall, faded by time and surely by sadness. Toby nearly jogged to his mother, to help her onto the chesterfield, to apologize some more. But a toxic, painful soup bubbled in his lungs. He would not say goodbye twice; in a week or two everything would be back to normal, and they would no longer visit or think of hospitals. Toby would buy his mother a scarf at Holt Renfrew, where he received a significant discount.

An orderly was in the examination room where Toby had signed his photograph, mopping up the puddle. The reassuring scent of chlorine. Like Karen, he wore rubber boots, this small man from a less prosperous corner of Asia.

The moment Toby passed from the hospital into the cool, wet, early autumn air of Montreal, his breathing improved. His heart untangled. He jogged to his car, which shone mightily. The rain had left tiny spots of dust on the door panels, but they were invisible in the streetlight. Toby had just picked up a pair of lambskin driving gloves, tight and deliciously brown, and he squeezed the leather steering wheel until they squeaked. He squeaked the day away.

He drove south to the Faubourg Ste-Catherine for spiritual renewal. A twelve-foot Toby leaned over the city in his grey Prada, a black vest and tie, with that winning yet predatory rise in his upper lip. "You own this town," the photographer from Chicago had said as he snapped the pictures. "You own it. This town wants to fuck you." The billboard-and-bus campaign had coincided with the season launch, and Toby knew that one cold morning—if not tomorrow, the next day or the next—his colossal selves would be replaced by an enticement to savour rotisserie chicken. Tonight, the billboard over the Faubourg was his cross on the mount. No matter what might happen to him or to his family and friends—fire or flood or lawsuit—he could always retreat into the cozy celebrity quarter of Greater Anglophone Montreal. Biweekly notices in the alternative press, Web chatter, awkward eye contact, and whispers in malls that he would pretend not to notice, in restaurants and nightclubs, the sidewalks of Saint-Laurent: his angels of encouragement.

A few blocks north, Sherbrooke Street was deserted but for a man on the steps of the Musée des Beaux-Arts, clothed in layers and layers of grey, rocking forward and back like a madrassa student. Toby's chest went infuriatingly tight again, and the air inside the car transformed from leather to melted plastic, seared skin. He pulled into the narrow roundabout at the grand entrance to McGill, exited the car, and told himself it was good, it was healthy, it was right, he was strong. He paced on the concrete, in shallow, shining puddles, his shoes clacking in the night. "I am good. I am healthy. I am right. I am strong." These were games he played with himself before he went on camera, to avoid stumbling over words— confidence games. Healthy, right, strong. Then, as though he had stood up too quickly, stars and the scent of blood in his mouth. He bent over, willed it away. He leaned on a stone column and retched, slid down it.

There were footsteps, two sets, behind him. Two women, by the rhythm of their heels. He buried his chin in his chest as they passed, so they would not see his face. His eyes throbbed. To be discovered here.

⌒

He lay awake on his organic cotton mattress for more than an hour, unable to escape the driveway and Edward, Edward's eyes on him. There were two and a half ounces of NyQuil in his medicine cabinet, and at four o'clock, raging against his inability to sleep, he finished the bottle. Still he lay awake, now in drowsy sleeplessness. A series of buyouts and layoffs had eroded the size and integrity of the news team; for election day, he was being temporarily seconded from etiquette to politics. This sort of work required little in the way of cognitive analysis, but late results and victory parties would keep him up. His eyes were liable to darken, and the makeup woman would be too busy with the anchors to daub foundation on him every forty-five minutes.

Only one person had the authority to ease him into sleep.

Toby arrived at the semi-detached house on Strathcona Avenue at five thirty. He stood on the carved stone of her front porch in the dark, NyQuil stirring his vision. The heavy blue door framed with ornate bricks, the perfectly clipped apple tree on the little patch of grass in front. Had he really noticed all of it before? Any fruit that remained on the tree had turned. Most had fallen. The aroma of the rotting apples natural, the scent of wealth and abundance. He pulled the key from his satchel, opened the door and stepped inside, removed his shoes on the mat so they would not echo off the tile. He hung his suit and shirt in the cloakroom, and nearly fell in. Steps creaked on the old floor above, from her bedroom to the hall—Alicia in her bare feet. A giant pink bouquet burst from a white vase in the foyer.

He had always been in awe of her family's money. It was audible in every word she spoke, visible in every wave of her long fingers, yet there wasn't a flicker of self-consciousness about it. Alicia had never seen the Mushinsky house in Dollard, by design; she genuinely feared that failure and mediocrity were viral. Two housekeepers from the Philippines spent three hours every Friday afternoon scrubbing and polishing away the small messes Alicia allowed herself to make in her five-bedroom house, and she refused to speak to them. She had been raised some blocks up the mountain from here, in a mansion with three full-time staff members: a cook, a housekeeper, and an au pair. Alicia had never had to learn the rules, or pretend, or convince anyone that she was an extraordinary and powerful woman. It was a perfume she could not wash away. And she was his.

It was dark in her room, and the NyQuil had plucked away at his equilibrium. He slammed into what she called the "Napoleonic bench" at the foot of her bed and apologized.

"What are you doing here?"

"I couldn't sleep."

"It's not even six, Tobe."

"I was at the hospital."

Alicia rustled in her sheets and turned on the lamp. Her hair and the bed were disasters. There was no sleep about her eyes. "What happened?"

He explained to her about the fire, how it had reminded him of the really frightening moments during a circus.

Alicia said she had never found circuses frightening. "You pulled him out?"

"I did."

"It could have blown up!"

"I know, right?"

"And your suit?"

"There's some damage on the cuff, and the shirt might be ruined from black stuff. Skin, maybe."

"Skin. My God."

"I'm a hero."

"Do you want to sleep?"

"I've been trying all night."

"Get in here, brave boy."

A pillow, his pillow, was on the floor. Even Alicia's room seemed new and strange, as though it had been ransacked by detectives or the mob and put back together carelessly. It was his world, and he trusted it, but someone or something appeared to be moving things around just slightly, to disorient him. His father, his mother, Alicia—and Alicia's bed had been picked up, shaken vigorously, and replaced.

Alicia asked no further questions. She wrapped her long legs around his and was soon asleep, a mist of red wine about her. The sounds of the Victorian house settling were like sneaking footsteps, so much so that Toby was tempted, once or twice, to get up and look around.

Begging and praying for sleep, willing himself to think about anything but his father and hospitals, had dammed him shut. By the time Alicia's alarm went off, at seven, the sun was already up and so was Toby—hunting around her medicine cabinet for a headache drug that might also counter the NyQuil. It was a stunning bathroom, larger than his parents' kitchen, with a Jacuzzi and a multiple-head shower and a bidet, ornate tile work, and leaded windows. A large skylight had been cut into the ceiling. There was an empty bottle of wine on the edge of the tub, and two glasses.

"Who was over?"

"What do you mean?" Alicia was making the bed.

"The wineglasses."

"Mom and Dad were here earlier."

"In your bathtub?"

"They couldn't bathe at home, could they? We had a broken water main down the street." Alicia walked naked into the bathroom, hands on her head. "Why do we do this to ourselves? It's not rational to celebrate *before* election day. We're going to look like a pack of serial killers."

"Television is not rational."

"The girls and I, we watched *The Secret* and drank Prosecco."

Toby was accustomed to seeing Alicia naked, but it had been some time, a year or longer, since he had seen her in sunlight.

"What?" she said.

"You're gorgeous."

Alicia looked in the mirror. "That's the NyQuil talking."

He put his arms around her, her skin still warm from the bed, and kissed her neck. He reached down.

"No, no, no."

"Just half an hour. It'll make me feel so much better."

"There's this taste in my mouth, like I ate a chipmunk."

"I'll go down on you for as long as you want. I'll meditate on your sweet spot."

"How about tonight, as a reward for our—"

"There's these thoughts of my dad, in the fire. I need the full treatment."

Alicia wiggled out of his grasp and stepped into the shower, closed the door.

Her father was a corporate lawyer downtown, an Old Liberal from a line of Old Liberals, and her half-Japanese mother was the only living heir of a developer with significant trust accounts and real estate holdings in the Pacific Northwest. There was never any risk that Alicia would end up in an aluminum trailer on tornado alley, picking Rottweiler hair out of overcooked macaroni and cheese. Yet she did have every opportunity to be ordinary. Alicia might have taken her master's degree in history and accompanied her mother in the Westmount world of charity, benevolence, art patronage, event planning, and non-profit board membership. She might have followed her father into the law. Instead, at twenty-four, Alicia had joined a crew of ignorant yet attractive teenagers for a two-year diploma in broadcast journalism. Toby hadn't known Alicia at the time, but he had seen photographs of her with her classmates—Cleopatra posing with the slaves.

By the time she joined the most-watched English-language television station in Quebec, shortly after her twenty-seventh birthday, Alicia had already read and underlined key passages in Machiavelli, Sun Tzu, and hundreds of instructive biographies of powerful men and women. She kept a black moleskin notebook of collected aphorisms and truths filtered for a career in broadcasting, and read from it in bank lineups and on other occasions when regular people turned to mobile communications devices. A few months after they'd begun dating, she had allowed Toby access to the small book. Alicia had determined the rules for advancement in the television industry by studying the men and women who had thrived in the television industries of the past, people like Galileo, the courtiers of King Louis XIV, Mata Hari, and P.T. Barnum.

> *Do not outperform middle managers or make your boss look lazy or ignorant, particularly if your boss is lazy or ignorant.*
>
> *Act dumb when you must, and make deliberate errors from time to time so that your boss can correct you.*
>
> *Keep your intentions secret. If you are forced into the subject of your future plans, express prosaic hopes and a profound disinterest in quick advancement.*
>
> *Never talk for the sake of talking. Only display rhetorical superiority with a leader who can benefit financially from your skills.*
>
> *Always allow, and subtly encourage, your boss to take credit for your work.*
>
> *Never discuss your accomplishments or quote from literature.*

In her time as the most-watched English-language broadcaster in Quebec, Alicia had progressed from intern to senior reporter, to backup weathergirl to weathergirl, to morning anchor to noon anchor. Only one step remained, to six o'clock, and she was desperate to make it in Montreal, then Toronto, then New York, to establish her brand before the traditional media went Tower of Babel.

The plan was for Toby to mirror her progress, every step. A writer at one of the alternative weeklies had written an article on them, had referred to them as a power couple.

This popped into his head from time to time, in the baritone of God: POWER COUPLE.

He pulled down the seat and sat on the toilet. "We could die, any time."

"What?"

"All these dangers. Physical, mental, emotional. Something could just swoop down and take us."

Water slapped on the floor of the shower as she washed her hair.

"Let's get married."

Nothing.

"Alicia. Let's get married."

Again she did not respond.

"I know you don't want kids right away. Not right away, that's fine, fine, but someday. We're almost forty."

The cleaners had not been doing a thorough job. Where tile met wall, worms of mould.

"I love you. You love me. If we want to move to Toronto or New York, we should go. We should just get married, have a party and do it. And be happy. I just want to be happy."

The shower doors were glass. Alicia was shaving now.

"Are you listening to me?"

"I was waiting for you to break into song."

"Come on."

"Is that your proposal, sitting on the toilet?"

Toby opened the shower door and dropped to one knee.

"You have a ring?"

"I'll get one."

"Leave me alone for five minutes, please." She stood under a shower head, a razor in her hand, one foot on a white plastic bench. Water cascaded off her black hair. "Please?"

"You want me to leave?"

She looked up into the water. "We'll talk tonight, when your drugs wear off."

Toby closed the shower door and changed into his suit. He began to preen, but the look of himself, in the mirror, was unbearable.

The front door was unlatched, though Toby was certain he had locked it. The morning was sunny and warm, typically windy. Two blond girls in uniforms passed with their father, who wore a camel-hair overcoat. He had time, the father. He had been born into timelessness. His children were lovely and his shoes were well polished. Toby greeted them as they passed, and stood next to his black car, recalling the white Lexus SUV that had been parked in front of him a few hours before. A miniature tornado blew a mass of leaves and a potato chip bag down Strathcona Avenue; it stopped and settled before him, as though ashamed.

Two

To distract himself, Toby opened the passenger window a crack and turned up the music, a satellite channel specializing in edgy but not too edgy pop. This was what every smart commodity, cultural or otherwise, strove to be in the ascendance of his generation: edgy but not too edgy. Revolution light. It was the sound of The Man smashing himself with a hollow plastic mallet.

The city and its fading graffiti of despair, all that he had seen before and dismissed, clawed at him. Dirty white steeples peeked up from the crusted neighbourhoods south of downtown, vainly now in the continent's most statistically godless major city. Warehouses and factories of an economy that had gone trite, home to pigeons and the schizophrenic.

He had come to believe that the white Lexus SUV parked in front of him on Strathcona Avenue at five thirty in the morning had been Dwayne's. In the underground parking lot, south of René Lévesque, Toby inspected the vehicle to be sure. He was tempted to ascribe his suspicions to a cocktail of shock and guilt and NyQuil and sleeplessness, to a manufactured paranoia that would seem ridiculous in the arc lamp of sobriety. But the scenario fit, from Dwayne's line of questioning in the bistro to the state of Alicia's bed-clothes. He sat on the rear bumper of the station manager's Lexus until the garage door opened. A Honda Civic passed, a production assistant waved. She opened her window. "Big day!" she said. "Hey?"

Toby drew upon all his strength and managed a thumbs-up.

He had twenty minutes before he was set to leave, with Bruce the cameraman, to interview the Conservative can-didate in the riding of Westmount–Ville-Marie. Instead of researching the hopeless candidate and his curriculum vitae, Toby hunted for Dwayne in the offices and corridors of the station, which occupied three floors of a brutalist structure in the southeast corner of downtown. Every fluorescent light had been removed from the hall of anchors. The pimple-, scar-, and wrinkle-revealing tendencies of the cheap tubes made them a grave danger to newsreaders, who share one essential and essentially dangerous trait: equal parts self-love and self-disgust. The walls were decorated with inspirational poems—*If I have faltered more or less / In my great task of happiness*—and faded colour photographs of sunsets, sport-ing victories, lone wolves, and tall poppies. Dwayne's corner office, at the end of the hall of anchors, was empty. It was inhabited by his collection of African art and a fresh dose of his musky cologne. From his small stereo system, Marvin Gaye. The blinds were pulled down and the room was lit, tastefully, with a couple of antique lamps. Nausea swept through Toby. He had to eat.

"Mushinsky."

Toby turned slowly. His hands quivered and he was certain that if he spoke his voice would be worse. His lips were electric.

"You ready?" Dwayne carried a muffin and a giant coffee. "A real journalist again, after all these years. Let me see your journalist face."

Cuckold. Cock.

"I wouldn't call that a *journalist* face. Say, 'Toby Ménard, Century News, Montreal.'"

He had not prepared himself. Hitting Dwayne was out of the question, and he had no basis for a legal challenge. Nothing he had read in the classics of etiquette suggested the correct course for a gentleman in this situation. Pistols at dawn. Toby was certain, now, that if he were to speak he would actually begin to cry; perspiration flashed across his lower back. They had been out together as a foursome, he and Alicia and Dwayne and Dwayne's wife, Kathia, over twenty times. Dwayne had two sons in elementary school, private school, well-mannered boys. Toby had bought them presents for their birthdays, three years in a row. Most recently, he had bought the older one a set of harmonicas in a handsome silver case.

Dwayne sat in his leather desk chair and put his boots up. The only black man on the island of Montreal to wear cowboy boots. "Say it."

"Toby Ménard, Century News, Montreal."

"I don't believe you! Where's the ancient spirit of blood and fire?"

"Toby Ménard, Century News, Montreal."

"One more time, brother."

"Toby Ménard, Century News, Montreal."

"Slightly better." Dwayne looked at his watch, a marvel

of multi-functionality designed for triathletes and Green Berets. "Did you need something?"

In the studio, as he waited for Bruce, Toby was nearly overwhelmed by an urge to break a pane of glass. In one of his *Toby a Gentleman* segments, he had asked a professor at the Université de Montréal for insight into why youngsters destroyed newspaper boxes and bus shelters and, in the middle of a hockey riot, storefronts.

"Because they have failed," the professor, a bird-like woman with enormous spectacles, had said, "and because they know, in their hearts, they will always fail."

Bruce chatted with his wife on the cellphone all the way to Roslyn School, in Westmount, where the Conservative candidate planned to vote for himself and speak to the media. Bruce and his wife talked about their children. One had the flu. Three times he told his wife he loved her. Toby had planned to buy a muffin at the convenience store next to the station on their way out, but he had been too focused on the possible etymology of the word "cuckold." A Chinese girlfriend at McGill, long ago, had said that in her language and in her country a cuckolded man "wears a green hat." She did not know why.

The scrum was to take place on the front lawn of the school. Toby had forgotten the name of the Conservative candidate, and no other media outlets had shown up to speak to him. Bruce had finished his call, but he didn't know the man's name either. It was not his job to know.

Toby practised his introductory stand-up while Bruce adjusted the camera for the harsh morning light.

"You don't look so good," Bruce said.

"I didn't sleep last night."

"There might be some makeup in the bag."

"I am good. I am healthy. I am right. I am strong."

"Okey-dokey."

Toby said his mantra again, and again, walked in a tiny circle to banish the fire and his father, Alicia and Dwayne, to *appreciate the present tense*. Bruce spoke to the station through an earpiece. Their live window was only a few minutes away, so Toby had to be ready. Was he ready?

"Ready."

"Did you eat anything today?"

"Not really."

"I have a cookie in my bag, if it's an emergency."

"Thank you, Bruce. It isn't. We'll be done in five minutes."

"It might put some colour in that bean of yours."

"I was wondering if I could ask you a personal question."

"Me?"

"Has your wife ever, by chance, slept with another man?"

Bruce stared at Toby for a moment, long enough to blink twice. He lifted the camera to his shoulder as a handsome black man in a suit approached, smiling artificially. He was the same height as Dwayne. A young red-haired woman hustled beside him.

"No one else showed up?" The candidate's teeth had been bleached for the campaign.

His handler adjusted the Conservative Party button on his lapel. "What he means to say is thank you so much for coming." The woman caressed her leather portfolio as though it held her up, and shook her head with affectionate exasperation.

Bruce mumbled into the small microphone on the collar of his Century News leather jacket. He kept one eye on Toby, and it was squinting.

"I'm fine, Bruce." The old trees in the schoolyard, with their naked branches, beckoned. To climb the closest one, to be caressed by its fat limbs and there to sleep. He introduced himself to the candidate, a Conservative running in a safe Liberal riding. A sacrifice of some sort, to demonstrate loyalty and sincerity. It was a non-story, filler. Not long now.

"Thirty seconds," said Bruce.

Isidore. The man's name was Isidore. Toby meditated on it, so he would not forget in the middle of the interview. Dwayne and Alicia, images of them entwined in her bed, in the Jacuzzi—wet!—in his office, *on his desk*, that striking skin contrast, poked through his fatigue. *Good, healthy, right, strong. Isidore, Isidore.*

An elderly couple, the last of the true democrats, clutched each other for support as they took tiny steps toward the school. "Are you well, Mrs. Twiss?" said the gentleman. He wore a thick, bread-coloured three-piece suit for the occasion. It had surely fit him, once.

"I am well, Mr. Twiss. This breeze is something."

"Ten seconds."

Toby watched the Twisses all the way to the door, as Bruce counted down. He turned back to the candidate, who suffered from razor burn in the same manner as Dwayne. Dee-wayne, a hillbilly name. Under what circumstances had his parents found it appropriate?

"Five." Bruce counted down silently to one with his fingers.

Toby introduced himself to the camera and briefly described his location. "I am here with Stéphane Isidore, the black candidate for the Conservative Party of Canada in

Westmount–Ville-Marie." Toby put on his smile. "Monsieur Isidore, whom did you vote for this morning?"

"Uh, can we start over?"

"Actually, we can't. We're already in the living rooms of Montreal."

"Well, then. I voted for myself, of course. A Conservative candidate who *happens to be black*. What you said—"

"It's interesting you bring that up, Monsieur Isidore. This is a great time, I would think, to be black and in politics. Or African-American. African-Canadian. Do we say African-Canadian?" The words arrived before Toby had a chance to filter them through the tiny engine of blandness, of artificial enthusiasm, that a television reporter cultivates. That engine, and the tone it created, was the source of his only relevant talent. And it seemed to have shut down, along with his short-term memory. Who was this man again, and why were they here? Toby was, briefly, freezing cold. Then hot. He struggled to remain standing. A squirrel flitted about on a nearby maple. To be a squirrel, just now. Looking for a nut. Dwayne and Alicia. The first time Toby and Alicia had made love, in the master bedroom of her handsome brick house in Westmount, he was shocked to hear her speak. He was not naturally inspired to speak during sexual intercourse, and up until that point he had seemed to attract only the quiet, smouldering ones. But he did not want Alicia to feel he was ignoring or abandoning her. On that first afternoon, skylight sun lent an auspicious golden tone to her skin. Toby's skin against her skin. An unidentifiable streak of bodily fluid shone on her stomach.

"Give it to me hard," she said, at approximately the midpoint of their activity.

The polished bed frame was clearly an antique, and it groaned beneath them. Toby wanted to match Alicia's vigour, to engage her in a spirit of competition and fellow feeling, yet he struggled to find the words and the intonation. It had to be more than appropriate. This was their first time, and all they said and did would resonate with them later that day, in the ensuing weeks, for the rest of their lives. Toby worried that he would seem arid or Belle Époque if he remained silent. He continued along for some time, and his mute lovemaking acquired a colour and a density. Then, just when he thought it would never arrive, the perfect phrase came to him. He summoned all his actorly vim, and manufactured a sneer that he hoped would render him both serious and surprising. He said, "Oh fuck, yeah, baby, you want me to fuck you hard?"

Either Alicia didn't hear it, caught up in her own reveries, or she was too embarrassed for them both to respond. To his relief, she soon began speaking again, making demands and stating conclusions, but it was thereafter clear to Toby that Alicia was not trying to make conversation. She was a sexual monologist.

What did she say to Dwayne?

Candidate Isidore looked at him with both confusion and mild rancour. "What are you talking about?"

"Being black, and in politics." Toby had to keep talking. Somehow, the tiny engine of blandness would mulch through all of this misunderstanding. "What's it like? I mean, historically speaking."

"What do you mean?"

"I mean . . ." To lie down now, to lie in a bed of soft, red, dead leaves. The hibernating squirrel. "Look at you. You're a handsome gentleman. The world is yours. Yours to seize."

"Mine?"

"You people. All of you."

Candidate Isidore looked away from Toby, straight at Bruce and the camera.

"Barack Obama, right? Rejoice. In the context of."

The candidate shifted his weight from one foot to the other. "I don't get this." He looked about the schoolyard, dished a smile that was not a smile. "Can someone help me here?"

"Election day!" Saying the words with authority summoned Toby's engine back to life, if only on auxiliary power. His voice returned. "It's election day here in the federal riding of Westmount–Ville-Marie. Conservative candidate Stephen—"

"Stéphane."

"Stéphane Isidore just voted for himself."

"I should say that I don't have a people, Mr. Ménard. I don't think in those terms. My family, I suppose, my friends are my people. Canadians. My parents are from Haiti. But if you don't mind, I'd rather not talk about that. I'd like to talk about the Conservative plan for—"

"Splendid! Tell us all about it."

The way the word "Splendid!" had exploded from him, automatically, almost involuntarily, awakened Toby to what was really happening here on the grounds of Roslyn School. The last of the blood and warmth threatened to leave his face and hands. His legs tingled. He shook off the sedative, and as Candidate Isidore began speaking of the Conservatives' plan to battle the effects of the recession and to work for regular Canadian families, Toby interrupted him to put a hand on his shoulder. His viewers had to know. "I have black friends."

"You have . . ."

"Dozens of black friends, whom I love dearly. We've only just met, but I like you, too, Stéphane. I believe in equality. Racial equality. Other kinds, you can't really force those. Social equality, economic equality. But we're not so different, you and I. We look different. People can see that at home. Sure we do. Why pretend we don't? Personally, I think it's something to be celebrated, our looking different and living together in relative harmony, wearing fine suits, both of us, despite the colour of our skin. Don't you?"

"What's happening?"

"No misunderstandings, that's what's happening here. I adore black people, basically, is the message."

Bruce held up his left hand and began counting down from five. There was just enough time for Toby to mention Candidate Isidore one last time and to sign off. Toby Ménard, Century News, Montreal.

The camera came down from Bruce's shoulder, which usually signalled relief. This morning Toby felt like he had jumped a fence and landed in a backyard full of angry, and very hungry, boars.

"Motherfucker," said Bruce.

"I really don't know what to say," said Candidate Isidore. "It was certainly a unique experience, Mr. Ménard."

"Call me Toby, please."

"Why in hell would I do that?"

The handler, who appeared to have drawn a fake mole on her cheek, leaned on a tree and said, as she dialled a number, "I'm sure it's already on the Web." She placed the phone to her ear. "Hey. There's a situation in Montreal. We can own it if we're quick."

Toby thanked Candidate Isidore and apologized, apologized some more, told him about his father and the fire—heroism—and the sleeplessness and the NyQuil and the hypoglycemia. The candidate and his handler made halting eye contact and walked away.

At the van, Bruce continued to cuss and laugh sarcastically as he loaded up. He climbed into the driver's seat and sat, quiet and alone, for a full minute before unlocking the passenger door.

"I regret that, Bruce."

"They're firing people for nothing these days. For pimples."

"No one's going to be fired."

"I should have aborted the interview."

"Nonsense."

"They'll shoot the messenger. They always shoot the fucking messenger."

"I pulled it together at the end."

"You like black people?"

"I'm not feeling well, you see. My father—"

"Please stop talking." Bruce's hands shook as he turned the key. "Please just stop."

"Take me to the Montreal General."

"I'm taking you back to the station."

"You've seen what I'm capable of."

"Do I want to get in more shit than I'm already in?"

"Take me to the hospital. Now."

"I never liked you."

"Now."

The waiting room was equipped with a large-screen television tuned to CNN. Canada's federal election was not the top story, or any story at all. Five patients in monochromatic robes and pyjamas sat in mismatched furniture, watching the progress of a runaway bride who had stolen a white cube van and blown through a border stop into Mexico. American and Mexican officials were struggling to figure out what to do with her, and CNN presenters were struggling to avoid repeating themselves. A helicopter followed her progress into the state of Chihuahua. Toby watched for several minutes, pleasantly hypnotized. A nurse passed, and he inquired about his father.

He passed through a decontamination corridor, where a sign instructed him to wash his hands and apply antibacterial goo. Inside the warm room, Edward looked up from a gossip magazine whose pages he had been turning with his elbows. There was a clarity in his gaze that Toby associated with hangover mornings. His legs were covered in gauze from his knees down, and the random assortment of wraps on his arms, hands, chest, and head suggested an irresolute Halloween costume. "Karen's out getting chocolate milk."

"And you?"

"I'm not so much for chocolate milk."

"You know what I mean, Dad."

Edward turned to a painting of a pond, several ducks. A watery scene for the burned. The room was lightly perfumed. With his gauzy mitt, he pointed to a modest bouquet filled with autumn colours. "From your mom this morning. I woke up and there they were."

"Pretty."

"Did the cops ask you anything?"

"I didn't know what to say. Maybe you could tell me what to tell them."

Edward closed his eyes, and they remained closed long enough that Toby thought his father was drifting off. His girlfriend chattered on a shelf above the door. Alicia McIntyre, Century News, Montreal. Edward opened his eyes and gestured upward with his chin, but Toby did not want to turn around and see her. He didn't want to see his burned father. He wanted to be in his bed, in the darkness, for six to nineteen months.

"Can you help me to the toilet?"

"Now?"

"Please."

"All the way? Right to the toilet?"

Edward placed his mitts together.

"There's a nurse in the hallway."

"Just to the room. To the room, Toby. The things I *did* for you."

"Can't we just have one normal conversation?"

"How? How?"

He helped Edward down, and into a pair of paper slippers. They shuffled to the bathroom like geishas. Edward leaned on the toilet tank and breathed, hunched. Most of the blisters had popped; the gauze had fallen off with the movement, and his bare shins glistened yellow and black.

"You're all right?"

"No."

"Marvellous. So I'll just close the door."

Edward breathed through his mouth.

"Whatever you might need, Dad, just shout. I'm closing the door now."

Edward watched him close the door, his eyes red and wide and wet. Never simply *looking* anymore. This was not a new phenomenon. In the summertime, an intensity was drawn out of him that neither Karen nor Toby had ever seen.

Two months before, in early August, the three had met for dinner in a ballroom of the Ritz-Carlton. The station was celebrating its new season of American reality television and cheap Canadian movies-of-the-week starring D-list Hollywood actors. Back when Montrealers read newspapers, these launches were designed for publicity. Now the station's president, Mr. Demsky, threw them as family parties—in lieu of a Christmas event, which he had always considered depressing.

Toby and Alicia sat at a table of prominence across from his parents, her parents, and a childless VP of advertising and her husband. Edward had laughed at everything, not just the jokes. He had actually booed, in a frolicsome manner, as Dwayne introduced *The Circle of Hope*, a reality show about a town built and administered by the mentally retarded. During the speeches, Edward had whispered insistently about the role television *should* play in our society, as a vehicle of education. Climate change was going to kill us all, to say nothing of illiteracy, crystal meth, and general ignorance. He had made cracks about the wealthy, their shocking selfishness in the face of social and environmental disasters, the moral failure of Montreal's elite—of which Alicia's father was a charter member. He teased Alicia, passive-aggressively, about never coming to Dollard for a family dinner. After three glasses of wine, Edward had touched the advertising VP's hair and made pronouncements about its softness. He had asked Alicia if it bothered her to date Toby, knowing he was part Jew, and elbowed her father in the ribs when he failed to laugh. Then a switch, a physical transformation. His eyebrows lowered, his cheeks sagged. He would not touch his dessert. He accidentally dipped his tie in the chocolate sauce.

"It's no big deal." Karen inspected the tie. "I can get that out."

"I didn't mean to do it."

She laughed. "Of course you didn't."

"I've ruined everything." He looked around the table. "Haven't I?

Edward had explained that these emotional outbursts originated in his solar plexus. It would go mouldy, and the mould would spread everywhere and take him over the way stink takes over a river town.

All evening, Toby had alternated between gripping his serviette and squeezing Alicia's hand. She was appalled, her parents were appalled, Karen was appalled, he was appalled. He *hated* his father for this, and despite his area of expertise it had tossed him into a silent rage. Edward had not seemed mentally ill at the time, only poor and stupid. If Karen had not picked out a tie for him earlier that afternoon, what might he have worn to the Ritz-Carlton?

The plan had been to go for a drink in the lounge of the mighty hotel, just the three of them, after the launch. Instead, the moment Mr. Demsky said his thank yous and goodnights, Toby stood up and said his own thank yous and goodnights. He did not make eye contact with his parents or allow them the time to stand up for a hug. Alicia took his hand, and they walked out of the hotel, straight to her Mercedes, and headed to her house on Strathcona Avenue.

Edward called from inside the bathroom.

"Yes?" Toby placed his ear on the heavy door, opened it a crack. "Let me fetch the nurse for you."

"Just help me up."

"But—"

"Please."

His father was on the toilet seat, trying to lift himself. There were two stainless steel support bars, but Edward lacked sufficient strength. Toby did not know where to stand. In front of his father? Behind him, somehow, straddling the toilet? He held his breath.

"It doesn't smell good."

"No, no, Dad. It's fine."

"Go call a nurse, if you want."

"We'll just lift you up here and . . ."

Edward raised his arms like wings.

Once he was standing, Edward had to catch his breath before he could reach down and pull up the hospital pants that had been cut into shorts. He tried to reach them, but his miniature boxing gloves were too thick, his fingers too tender. Toby did not want to injure his father's pride by lifting the shorts for him, so he waited. He waited out two more unsuccessful attempts.

"I'll just grab those, Dad."

"No. I will. I will when I can." He tried again, squeaked in pain, and failed. He worked his way into a cry. Father crying.

Toby reached back with his free arm and snatched a handful of tissues. For two minutes that passed like twenty, he held his father, naked from the waist down. Though he had only seen glimpses of it in his peripheral vision, Edward's unfrocked, quivering penis might as well have been displayed, by projection screen, on the wall before them. Eventually,

Edward placed all his weight on Toby, and together they lowered themselves to the floor so he could pull up his shorts.

"You did it. You did it, Dad. Way to go."

Edward breathed some more, and stared at him. The fire stare, a toddler gathering secrets.

Once his father was back in bed, Toby collapsed on the adjacent chair. There was a faint burning sensation behind his eyes. For at least thirty years he had gone without seeing his father naked. "I didn't sleep."

"Then sleep."

"You saw the clip. My boss—"

"If you don't want to think of something, you just up and don't."

Already, the pre-sleep nonsense was creeping in. A roller-blader. Scooby-Doo. "Just a few minutes."

"Lie back."

It was a startlingly uncomfortable chair.

"We love you, no matter what you do, or say. Everyone does."

"Thank you."

"You never have to worry."

"Hmm."

"You want me to sing 'You Are My Sunshine'?"

"No, no, no. Shh."

"You are my sunshine."

"Dad, I'm going to buy you a scarf, at Holts."

"My only sunshine. You make me happy."

"Thank you. Thank you."

Sleep came down on him like a mountain of silk.

Three

Toby had met Alicia five years ago, on the day he tried to quit. He had applied for the job of temporary weathergirl, while the weathergirl went in for a tummy tuck. Going weathergirl, even for a week or two, was an indication that management considered you a personality, local celebrity material, the possible subject of a billboard. Dwayne came by the office Toby shared with a rotating series of producers, and together they walked through the studio. He motioned toward Alicia, a new hire, a long-legged, black-haired beauty, rich and reportedly smart, who was taking a lesson on one of the computers. He confided in Toby that he would like nothing better than to *tap that*. Toby thought nothing of this. Dwayne was married, with two sons, yet he often expressed a desire to engage in anal intercourse with interns, production assistants, public relations consultants, and reporters.

It had not been an easy decision, but Dwayne had concluded that Alicia—given her uncommon hotness—was going
to be temporary weathergirl. What could he say? Look at her
for five seconds!

Toby returned to his office, sought his mom's advice, then
his dad's advice, and thundered and flailed briefly in the only
bathroom that locked. Edward had suggested he "harness his
negative energy," and try something wild. Edward had never
forgiven the station's executives for the name change debacle.
"Fuck 'em," Edward had said.

For some time, Toby had been refining a rather wild idea.
The station was overflowing with union technicians working
three hours a day and being paid for seven and three-quarters,
yet they didn't produce anything beyond cheap news. Why
not set up a corner of the unnecessarily vast studio to look
like a cozy living room, and Toby could wear a crisp suit and
interview the fascinating figures of Greater Montreal. It could
be called *One on One, with Toby Ménard*. Or *Toby's People*.
He immediately wrote up a proposal and, with Dwayne's
blessing, submitted it to Mr. Demsky. If Mr. Demsky said no,
he would immediately quit and waltz across town to the CTV
affiliate, whose station manager had expressed interest in him
as a sports guy.

Toby's meeting with the president, to whom he had never
spoken, was scheduled for 3:30 that afternoon. Already he
had summoned the wild fuckemtude to ask Alicia for dinner
at Toqué!, and she had accepted. By the time he knocked on
the heavy wooden door of the executive office, he was quite
certain he could chew through it.

There were five televisions in Mr. Demsky's office, tuned
soundlessly to stations he owned in Western Quebec, South-

ern Ontario, Vermont, Maine, and upstate New York. Pipe smoke hung low and tranquil in the room. There were framed Looney Tunes animation posters and collector cells on the wall, so Toby made a mental note to discuss his theory about Bugs Bunny being the culmination of Ralph Waldo Emerson. A plaque in a place of prominence behind Mr. Demsky's chair recognized his ongoing financial and spiritual commitment to Israel, so Toby made a second mental note to mention and exaggerate his Jewishness.

According to the skin around his eyes, the president and CEO had spent the majority of his youth on stallions and golf courses in Florida, baking creases and blotches into his face. His dry, white hair framed him like an Inuit hood.

"Sir."

"No 'sirs' in television. You can sit." Mr. Demsky waved the three-page proposal for *One on One, with Toby Ménard* over his desk. A snake of blue smoke broke and twirled in behind it. "I'm curious about the city and the world, unlike the majority of my peers and pretty much all yours. But I'm not going to watch you interview a pompous ass about sewer easements in front of a fake fireplace. That's a half-hour of my life I just don't want to give up."

"It wouldn't be about sewer easements."

"Do you know how television works?"

"I should hope so."

"You clearly don't."

"All right."

"We buy prime time from Los Angeles, simulcast it with local news, and invest in some shitty movies-of-the-week set in Medicine Hat to please the communists. We put the profits in businesses that actually make money."

Toby had not prepared for this response. *One on One, with Toby Ménard* had seemed unassailable. The fuckemtude was upon him. "Fabulous." He stood up and loosened his tie, demonstrably. "I'm finished with Century Media. I want to thank you for the opportunity, of course, and I do hope you fail, miserably. And second—second, mind you!—that you and your station manager die a most painful death."

"Sit." Mr. Demsky fetched his pipe from its tray and fixed his tiny eyes on Toby. He pulled one remote control from the regiment before him, a black model, and pressed a button. The humidifier in the corner belched mist in their direction. "That was stirring."

"Can I go now?"

"What sort of a person are you, if you were to sum yourself up?"

"I'm a bit Jewish."

"Listen. I was on an airplane the other night, coming home from a conference in New York. By the way, what the hell sort of name is Toby?"

"Jewish."

"Shut up."

Toby tried to regain his fury. He bit the inside of his cheek, but it didn't make him furious. It only made his cheek bleed a little.

"It sounds like an adjective."

"A Toby, Mr. Demsky, is a coffee mug in the shape of a man's head. With a three-cornered fisherman's hat on it. Now, if you will excuse me."

"Your parents named you after a coffee mug."

"It was coincidental. It's short for Tobias."

"So I'm on the airplane, and the two men sitting behind

me start whining in these battered tones about a meeting they'd just escaped. Some brainstorming session about Internet piracy. They were involved in the music industry somehow; I guessed lawyers." Mr. Demsky reached up and pulled out a pen that had been hidden behind his ear in his wreck of white hair. "How'd that get there? I musta slept with it!" He removed his glasses and tossed the pen at the wall. A rumble started in his chest, like the old Husqvarna chainsaw Edward had bought from a farmer to transform the fallen trees of the ice storm into firewood. It was something between a wet cough and a laugh; Mr. Demsky appeared to levitate out of his chair. The episode went on long enough for Toby to peek down at his timepiece, at his shoes—scuffed—and to think fondly of Alicia's neck.

"Can I fetch you a glass of water, maybe, before I accept a position at your competitor's station? Where I'm treated with respect."

"The in-flight movie comes on and it's some piece of shit about dogs. Dogs and kids in the same movie is always murder. The stewardess is embarrassed, as we should all be, as a species, so she starts handing out magazines. I take a *New Yorker*. Guess what the two music lawyers go for."

The smooth transition from chainsaw to anecdote had paralyzed Toby. The blood in his mouth was surprisingly salty.

"I said guess."

"*Rolling Stone.*"

"Wrong!" Mr. Demsky slid the remote controls down the desk and leaned on his forearms. "Sure, that's the obvious response. Music people read *Rolling Stone* and smart people read *The New Yorker*. But no. No, these two choose a magazine called *Gentlemen's Quarterly*. You heard of it?"

"I have a subscription."

"Tobias, it's a whole goddamn magazine about *being a gentleman*."

"I've learned quite a lot from it over the years."

"Etiquette."

"Yes, sir."

"And men's clothing and perfume and spa treatments. Book clubs. How to please women orally. It's fat with advertisements. There were a couple of recipes inside. One was for brioche! It's a girl magazine, but for men. Men like you, Tobias."

"Like me."

"You ever been in a fist fight?"

"No."

"Ever built a garage or shot a handgun?"

"Oh no."

"Play any sports?"

"I go to the gym."

"At first I thought the music lawyers were a couple of Kansas City faggots. But when one of them went to the can, I spotted his wedding ring."

"Well, it *is* legal now to—"

"Can you believe it?"

"I have a subscription, Mr. Demsky."

"You know what these two talked about for the rest of the flight home?"

"No."

"Guess, Tobias."

"Rap music."

"They talked about the decline of good manners." With some cussing in a language Toby took to be Yiddish, Mr.

Demsky stood up out of his giant leather chair and sauntered to the window. "You been overseas?"

"No, but—"

"A man must go overseas, Tobias. This isn't an actual *country* we're living in; the sooner you understand that, the better. It's a big, big suburb. It's a place you graduate from."

"A suburb."

"If we didn't have oil, we wouldn't exist."

"What does that mean? We wouldn't *exist*?"

"Wood hewers, water carriers. That's all we can do. And we're impolite. Litterers. Spitters. We dress like hobos, most of us, and drink shit coffee. *Toi, toi, toi.* And *One on One, with Toby Ménard*—no offence—that's the best you could come up with?"

"I don't even know what a sewer easement is, Mr. Demsky."

The president aimed his pipe like a rifle. "Where are we living?"

"In a place you graduate from."

"Sterling!" He lowered his cigar. "Now, Tobias, can I ask you a personal question?"

"Go ahead."

"The sort of question you can't ask an employee anymore?"

"Certainly."

"Are you a homosexual?"

"No."

"Come on."

"I'm not."

"So I suppose you like women."

"Very much."

Mr. Demsky looked down at Toby's grey wool pants and shiny black oxfords with that regrettable scuff. "You like suits?"

"Suits are my favourite."

"And unless I'm mistaken," he leaned over Toby, sniffed, "you're wearing perfume."

"Cologne."

Mr. Demsky returned to his chair, sat back, snorted. "Ever go to a dinner party and think, sweet Christ, should I bring wine or champagne?"

"Red wine or flowers, depending."

"Wish you had your own herb garden at all?"

"I have one."

"How about vacuuming? You like to vacuum?"

"There are some delightful vacuums on the market."

"Decoupage?"

"If only."

"You ever been afraid?" Mr. Demsky bit down. The joy had departed. "I don't mean movie afraid. Afraid, *afraid*, for your life or the lives of the people you love?"

"Well . . ."

"A generation of pussies. Shoppers, who haven't even been overseas."

"I intend to go very soon."

"How would you like to develop and host a series of segments on how to be a gentleman? Manners, etiquette. But with shared concerns among the ladies and the poofs? We'll produce them here and broadcast them on all the stations. What do you say?"

"I would adore that, sir."

"One more 'sir' and you're cleaning my shitter. Write up a proposal and slip it under my door."

"When would you like it?"

Mr. Demsky examined his cigar. "I'm due for a Vietnamese massage in an hour and a half."

"I really didn't mean what I said about you failing and dying painfully, Mr. Demsky. My father gave me bad advice. I have only the fondest thoughts."

"Mention, as a postscript, some businesses where Kansas City faggots like yourself shop for clothes and perfume and flowers and, you know, ceramic pots and garden tools and scarves and serviettes with roosters on them. I'll meet with the advertising knobs on Monday."

⟋

That night at Toqué!, Alicia wore a white top that wrapped around her like silk bandages on a mummy. Between the wrap and the skirt, an inch of her stomach was visible. Her dark hair was tied up in the back with an intricate arrangement of clips, and it shone in the candlelight.

Toby was making $38,000 at the station before he became an etiquette commentator, a personality, a person. He could not afford a $298 dinner. Yet Alicia stared over the candles as though he were the most significant man on the island, and feigned fascination as he told her about his family, his meeting with Mr. Demsky that afternoon, and the proposal he titled *Toby a Gentleman*. "You think it's gauche, to make my name the title?"

"How else are you going to be famous?"

The *plat principal* was *canard aux framboises*, and Alicia claimed she had never eaten duck, a claim Toby would realize, some months later, was grossly false. She thanked him more than twenty times: for asking her out on this special day, for ordering food and wine so commandingly—in French!— for being adventurous and knowledgeable about duck.

Toby wanted to ask if he could move into her house. He wanted Alicia to be his before she realized she could be a movie star, a pop icon, a network anchor. The desire to lock her in a kitchen for forty or fifty years of olde-tyme afternoon-sex-on-the-table marital solitude nearly burst out of his chest and onto the expertly unpolished table before them.

⁓

He had framed the bill from that night at Toqué!, still the most magical night of his life. It hung on the wall in his kitchen, where he made an Americano and watched the morning summaries of the federal election. The Conservatives had prevailed, with a minority, but Westmount–Ville-Marie had gone to the Liberals. He wrote a note of condolence and fond wishes to Stéphane Isidore. His neck was stiff from sleeping in a hospital chair for six hours, but with medication, yogurt and granola, and a redemptive session at the ironing board, he was ready to return to work. His phone had been flooded with data, but he could not sufficiently steel himself to hear or see any of it. Instead, he simply dialled his father's cellphone number. To his delight, no one answered, so he left a rather long and inspiring message. A poem, really. "We'll all soon see, Mom and Dad, that this accident was really the catalyst for so much positive change in your lives."

The black sapphire metallic 335i sedan was his super-hero phone booth, spotless and dark, filled with the scent of triumph and, this morning, baroque chamber music. He pulled over at the congested corner of Roy and Drolet to mail his letter to the Conservative Association of Westmount–Ville-Marie. The morning wind was warm and cool at the same time, and smelled of bakery. His decision to forget the fire, Alicia, the on-air gaffe, his naked father, had cleansed him of anxiety. Montreal opened to him, as it always did. He said, "*Bonjour, Monsieur*" and "*Bonjour, Madame*" to the francophone media workers who passed, in black boots or shoes, on their way from renovated houses on the Plateau to the game show studios on Saint-Laurent. He complimented a retired gentleman in mustard slacks on the splendour of his poodle.

A woman on an old bicycle, with one speed and a basket, waited to cross Drolet. She ventured too far into the street and tried to steer back onto the sidewalk, but she caught her skirt in the gears. The bicycle wouldn't move. Gingerly, she tried to tug the fabric out. He shouted for the woman to get off her bicycle and carry it to the sidewalk, to safety, and she turned to him. "*Quoi?*" she said.

"*Allez à la . . .*" Toby was too far away from her, in the wind, to be heard.

A taxi with its light off sped southward on Drolet. The woman looked at Toby instead of the traffic and did not see it. "*Quoi?*" she said again.

Toby gestured madly toward the bank of cars, led by the green taxi. As the woman shifted her attention back to the traffic, her heavy bicycle rolled forward slightly and the taxi clipped the front wheel. She cried out and at once flew sideways off the bicycle and into the pile of dust and decomposed leaves that had gathered at the mouth of the storm drain. The contents of the basket, her handbag and its secrets, lay strewn about. Cars behind the taxi had stopped, though it had continued along. Toby ran to the woman and helped her up onto the sidewalk. Then he pulled her bicycle to safety and gathered up pens, tissues, an address book, a tiny photo album, three blank postcards, her bulky wallet, one condom, and a set of keys.

Back on the sidewalk, he asked the woman, in French, if she was injured. She listened, with large green eyes and thick lips slathered with gloss, but did not respond. Toby wiped the dust from her arms and shoulders. She was pale and thin and agitated, the uncharismatic daughter of Mick Jagger and Carly Simon. On her feet, she turned around as if before a mirror and felt her body quadrant by quadrant until she reached her right leg. She lifted her torn red skirt to reveal a pair of black nylons. They had ripped in three vertical strips above the knee, and tiny bits of gravel and sand were embedded in the wound. She wept briefly, with one hiccupping sob.

A gentleman is obliged to carry a dress handkerchief, along with a square of white linen, for emergencies. Brooks Brothers manufactured lovely linens for this purpose, with just-detectable fleur-de-lis embroidery. She wiped her eyes and blew her nose, then stuffed his linen into her bag without taking even a moment to consider its astonishing beauty. From time to time, in moments of crisis, moments like these, Toby questioned the rewards of his behaviour. He understood why so many of his peers cussed in public, why they spent more time in restaurants and cafés looking at their iPhones than into their lovers' eyes.

The woman removed her helmet. "He was a murderer."

"No, Madame." The taxi had long gone. "He was just an idiot."

She rubbed her shoulder. The sturdy bicycle had survived the impact, but the chain had fallen off. Toby took her bag and walked her bicycle one block east to the gas station on Saint-Denis.

"It's another awful day. Another ridiculous, monstrous day." She sobbed again. Toby pulled the linen out of her bag and gave it to her demonstrably, so she might notice the fleurs-de-lis. Traffic was light suddenly. The sun was warm on his face and the wind had calmed. No one was honking.

"The day will surely improve for you, Madame. I have a feeling."

She pointed to her ripped nylons. "I'm already late."

"You were hit by a car."

"There is a recession, you know."

"My name is Toby Ménard. I'm enchanted to meet you."

"Catherine Brassens. I've seen you on television." She attempted a phrase in English: "I practise sometime to hear correct."

"*Parfait.*"

"It's normal, I suppose, that you'd stop for a woman in distress."

"I suppose it is."

In English again, she ventured, "A gentle man."

"A gentleman and a gentlewoman."

Catherine went into the washroom, and Toby waited for one of the gas station attendants to make eye contact with him so he might ask for some assistance. Eventually, he gave up and replaced the chain himself. Now there was grease on his hands, plenty of it. He hopped on the bicycle and pedalled in a small circle in the gas station parking lot.

"Like it never happened," he said, when Catherine returned.

She had three wet paper towels. "The mirror in the washroom's too small and too high. Will you?"

Toby crouched and inspected the wound on her upper thigh. She had done a thorough job, but islands of dirt and debris had been hidden by her nylons. "May I?"

"Of course." Catherine lifted her skirt a few inches higher.

He pulled the fabric away from her skin and reached in through a hole, gently dabbing the dirt and bits of gravel away. The skin of her leg was not as pale as her face and neck, and she was muscular: the advantage of bicycle commuting. He looked up, for an instant, when he was finished. She watched him. The colour had returned to her cheeks. Neither of them spoke until a dump truck passed, rattling him to his feet.

"You're going to be all right, Madame Brassens."

"Thanks again, Doctor Toby."

"I shouldn't have shouted."

"The murderer shouldn't have hit me with his taxi."

They shook hands. His grease transferred to her, and he apologized. She pulled a small package of damp wipes from her pocket and offered one to Toby. Together, they wiped the grease from her hands, and Toby wondered about the damp wipes: Who carries such things?

"Can I do something for you in return?" Already she referred to him as *toi*.

"Madame Brassens, it was my pleasure to help."

"I'll make you dinner."

"It's not necessary."

"What's necessary? I just want to make you dinner." A strong gust came up Saint-Denis, without any bakery in it. She shifted the bangs of her blond hair from her eyes. "You're a gentleman. You can't refuse. I have you."

Toby pulled a calling card from his stainless steel Frank Lloyd Wright holder, a gift from Alicia. "My number is here, and my e-mail."

"Friday night. Six thirty."

Catherine wrote her address on the back of a crumpled receipt. He watched her go, on her ugly bicycle. The receipt was for a thirty-six pack of Huggies.

Now, on top of everything else, he was late. The phone buzzed in his satchel, his parents, no doubt. First he would deal with Dwayne, then he would call his parents with more late-night infomercial philosophy. *We are indeed the architects of our own lives.*

There was enough traffic on René Lévesque to allow him to work his strategy into a baroque chamber composition, with dramatic pauses and hand gestures. He rehearsed, imagining his meeting in the office of the station manager, his friend, the president of his society. Humility, first, and an acknowledgment of one's failings. Then a stunning declaration of grievances, leading to eloquence and great wit, historical allusions, mastery of the room. All of it set to the fifth Brandenburg. Toby was not the first man in history to be cuckolded by a member of a visual minority, and father-burnings must be quite common, statistically. If anyone had actually heard the interview, other than his father and Bruce, he had a footnoted speech prepared about the public's short attention span.

He used his electronic card to enter the parking garage, and remembered to be comforted and delighted by the sound of the driver's-side window snapping shut. In challenging times, times like these, it was essential to return to a place of sumptuousness and strength, a small victory, rather than succumb to self-doubt.

In the elevator, Toby pulled his shoulders back and raised his chest; he thought of Jacques Chirac's moving retirement speech in front of *le drapeau tricolor*: "*Mes chers compatriotes de métropole, d'outre-mer, de l'étranger . . .*"

The elevator opened onto the dark studio, and Toby stepped out as though passing through saloon doors. The writers, producers, on-air talent, and interns stopped speaking for a moment, in what Toby first took to be stunned reverie. Most of them had been to his parties at the converted candy warehouse. He had taken baguette lunches with them on the port, as the long-legged rollerbladers zoomed past. He had briefly dated one of them, before Alicia, but she had smoked the same brand of cigarillo as Karen—they were surely the only two women on the island with a cigarillo addiction—and the sex had made him thoughtful. Toby greeted those with whom he shared friendly relations, with whom he had made sarcastic remarks about Ed Hardy T-shirts. "What's up?" His friends and acquaintances and Sandra from Poland, the former girlfriend, responded with barely perceptible nods. In his office, he dropped his satchel. The orange light on his telephone flashed.

There were six voice messages from Dwayne, four e-mails from Dwayne's secretary, and a yellow sticky note affixed to his keyboard: *Come see me NOW.*

He took the circuitous route to Dwayne's office, bypassing the studio, blowing on his hands to keep them warm. On the way, he ducked into a washroom, made certain it was empty, and practised his speech in front of the mirror. He had faith in the universality of human compassion. Dwayne, for example, had always wanted to be in front of the camera. Acne scars had made a lesser man of him. It had been entirely beyond his control. Poor Dwayne. Toby meditated on this to gain an understanding of his boss: poor Dwayne, and his cowboy boots.

There was another voice in Dwayne's office, laughter. From time to time, when she allowed herself to relax, Alicia's laugh degraded into a snort. He had grown to love this rare flaw in her, as it was inspired by joy. Joy. Compassion. Cowboy boots. Good-healthy-right-strong. It was marvellous that Alicia and Dwayne were in the office together—destiny.

"Good morning to you both," he said, at the doorway.

Alicia was enthroned in one of the fake antique chairs that faced Dwayne's desk, in a dark blue dress that tied around the waist and a pair of long black boots. She looked at Toby as though he had traded faces.

"Before you say anything, allow me to—"

"Alicia." Dwayne stood up. The tone in his voice was entirely new. "Please excuse us."

"What happened yesterday?" she asked.

Toby had not imagined Alicia would be here. He had over-rehearsed his address, and now his starting place was hidden from him. Like finding the right key, he could not choose the right tone of voice without plinking a few notes. "I . . ."

"Alicia, please," said Dwayne.

She moved in to kiss Toby on her way out, and he backed up to block the doorway.

"Actually, Alicia, would you mind staying?"

"Well . . ." She looked at Dwayne.

"I have a couple things I need to discuss with you, Toby." The morning sun shone down through Dwayne's tilted blinds and highlighted his scars.

"Please sit, both of you," Toby said. "Just give me a moment."

They sat.

"Exceptional." Toby rubbed his hands. He had rehearsed hand-rubbing. "Exceptional."

Dwayne looked at his watch. "There's a conference call in half an hour."

"This won't take long." Toby sat in the matching chair, next to Alicia. He crossed his hands in front of his chest. "I know about your affair."

A glance between them. "There's no affair," said Dwayne.

"Toby, that's insane."

"I'm not here to condemn you or break into tears in public. What can I do? I've been through it in my mind, a thousand times. You obviously love one another. Why else would you forsake an epic romance, a powerful friendship?"

Alicia stood up and sucked in her cheeks. "'An epic romance, a powerful friendship.' With your Lord Rector voice on. We both know where you grew up." Then she walked out.

"Wait. You had better . . ."

She did not wait.

"Come back here, Alicia, or it's over between us. It's over between us forever. You can't . . . Guess what, I mean it!"

She did not come back. Toby and Dwayne looked out the door as the sound of her heels on the thin carpet faded below the low hum of the computer. One of Dwayne's eyes appeared swollen. His children brought legions of viruses into his house.

Toby pulled out a sheet of paper, upon which he had made notes earlier that morning. All of his rehearsals in front of the bathroom mirror and in the car were now entirely wasted. His soundtrack had gone silent. "Well, that was unnecessarily awkward."

Dwayne closed his blinds.

"I apologize for that," Toby continued. "And for yesterday. I'm prepared to take blame where blame is due. However—"

Dwayne turned his monitor around. There was Toby in front of Roslyn School. He had not noticed yesterday how handsome a building it was—multicoloured brick, turn-of-the-century design. His suit, a brown Canali, had been a perfect choice, given the architecture, the late-morning sunlight, the autumn leaves. The image was frozen until Dwayne sniffed, hit a key, and leaned back in his leather chair.

Dwayne played it once, and again, and once more. Then he slid a sealed envelope over his desk. Toby opened it and skimmed the letter from the human resources director, outlining his severance package.

"You can gather your stuff like a grown-up and leave. Or I can have Security escort you out."

"You know the situation I was in yesterday. My father—"

"I have one letter from Mr. Isidore and another from the president of the national council of the Conservative Party of Canada. I have one from the Council of Canadians of African and Caribbean Heritage, and one very long letter from the executive director of the African Canadian Heritage Association."

"I'm not a racist."

"Of course not."

"We're friends, you and I."

"Friends."

"The Benjamin Disraeli Society."

Dwayne massaged his jacket pocket to emphasize the absence of any dress handkerchief.

"I hadn't slept. I hadn't eaten. I was on a lot of NyQuil. I'd just learned that my trusted friend, my terrific pal, was sleeping with my—"

"There's nothing we can do."

"I'll go to Mr. Demsky."

"It was his decision."

"Liar."

Dwayne shrugged. Before the first segment of *Toby a Gentleman* launched, he had customarily worn jeans and wrinkle-free khakis with a series of checkered, unironed shirts. He had cussed and slouched. Now he had six Chester Barrie bespoke suits and flew to Jermyn Street once every two years to have new shirts custom-made with hand-sewn button holes, removable collarbones, mother-of-pearl buttons. But no handkerchief! And why he had held on to the cowboy boots was mysterious and regrettable.

"I have a proposal for you." Toby stood up and placed his hands on Dwayne's desk. "I have a counter-proposal."

"I'm not accepting any proposals or counter-proposals. I have to prepare for a conference call, as I mentioned. All this is a real shame, damn it to hell. But you, of all people, will understand how this racist business reflects on the station."

"I'm not a racist."

"You're preaching to the choir."

"You do have a choice, Dwayne. Stand with me."

"Just relax."

"I am relaxed. I'm relaxed!"

"Just rewind a little."

"Yes. Let's. Back to the good old days when I had a job."

"I am sorry. Sorry for everything. Really. Just calm down, be calm, and give me the knife."

Toby didn't understand. He looked down. In one hand, he held a pewter letter opener designed to look like a dagger. Dwayne had received it as a Christmas gift from his wife, and occasionally swung it about during conceptualization and strategy sessions. Toby dropped it on the desk.

Dwayne slid the dagger out of Toby's reach and stood up, a layer of perspiration where his hairline used to be. "This is a real shame for all of us."

It seemed Dwayne expected Toby to leave now, to walk down the hall of anchors to the loop of middle management. There was nothing left to discuss.

"Do your wife and children know about Alicia? Did you tell Kathia about her?"

The station manager made a fist and chewed on his thumb knuckle for a moment, a tic. He walked around the desk and approached Toby, said gently, "Maybe you have a tape recorder in your pocket."

"No."

Dwayne reached up with one hand and pulled Toby by the tie until he fell to the ground, bouncing his forehead off the wooden arm of a chair. Simultaneously, Dwayne slammed his door closed with his other hand. Toby could smell a blur of chemical in the carpet. In school, drama class and membership in the debating club had formed a shield of preciousness and, in the constellation of high school brutes, pointlessness around Toby. He did not have a brother.

With sinister tranquility in his voice, Dwayne whispered, "I don't want to hit you."

"Don't hit me."

"But if you ever, *ever* so much as hint at hurting my family, I'll find you and I'll fucking hit you. I'll hit you hard."

"You've been abundantly clear, Dwayne."

"Hard."

"Clear and merciful."

Dwayne pulled Toby back up to his feet, again using his tie. He then loosened Toby's tie and fixed his left lapel. Opened the door. "You know, it's been a real treat working with you, Toby. A real treat."

The lights were off in Alicia's office. She sat in a wicker chair near the window with a cup of coffee and Lawrence, her stuffed owl. All he had really wanted, down the hall, was to make her feel ashamed and to draw something—anything—for himself from her shame. Now he just wanted her.

She looked at him and looked away.

"You might have apologized, Allie."

"I might have."

"Never once did I cheat on you. Never once did I consider it. Not that I didn't have opportunities."

"My sincerest congratulations."

Toby knew she was not in love with Dwayne. It was not in her to fall in love with a married man who occasionally contracted pink eye from his children. It did not work that way for her. "If you promise, and I mean really promise, to stay loyal to me, Alicia, I'd be willing to give you another chance."

She blew a burst of air out her nose.

"There's enough money in my severance for a trip to Paris. First-class flight, a week at the Four Seasons. We could get married at the Hôtel de Ville. If one of us has to be there for a month before they'll do it, I'm willing to make that sacrifice. I can plot the next stage in my career."

"Toby."

He went down on one knee, again.

"Still no ring."

"We can go together, right now, to the Tiffany counter. Whatever you want."

"Say goodbye to your parents for me. My best wishes to poor Edward."

"No."

"Toby. You don't even have a job."

"I'm not leaving." He thought he detected a smile. Something. "Tractors couldn't drag me away now, my darling."

"You have nothing."

"I have love."

"Not that."

His right knee began to hurt, so he switched to the left. "'Love does not rejoice at wrongdoing, but rejoices with the truth.'"

"You really don't understand."

"I do understand. I do. I know why you were with Dwayne. But if you stick with me, I can take you ten times farther. I can—"

"No."

"I'll do anything."

"This is a real spectacle."

Toby crawled across the floor to her chair.

Alicia produced her iPhone. "You're humiliating yourself, and I can't watch it. What's the number for Security?"

"What can I do?" Toby stood up. "What can I do?"

"Go."

"I'll show you, Alicia. You'll see."

She looked at him, but also past him, as though most
of Toby had already left the room. "We try to hide it, but it
shows in a moment like this. Where we come from."

He wiped the dust from his knees and tried to formulate
a response. His father with the mitts on, his mother with her
chocolate milk and her cigarillos, the pile of scrap wood in
the backyard. "This isn't finished."

Alicia followed him to the door and pushed it closed
behind him.

Half an hour later, he was in his own office, adding four new
Toby a Gentleman segments to his demo reel. He phoned
Anton Beauchemin, station manager of the CTV affiliate, and
said he was available.

"What? Have they gone shithouse rat over there? You're
still on billboards."

"Craziness is a pretty good summation, Anton."

"Well, of course, we'd love to have you. Not sure what's
available at the moment. We're officially in a hiring freeze,
like everyone else. But we're retooling the morning show.
How'd you like to wake up at four every day?"

"I would like nothing better."

They exchanged numbers and addresses, made plans to
meet for drinks at the end of the afternoon. Toby packed

a wine box full of awards and books and photographs. He printed off several copies of his C.V. and burned ten discs of his updated demo reel. The studio was half full, with a meeting of the morning show host and producers. Sandra from Poland said, flatly but not quietly, "Nazi."

He drove north and west toward the Montreal General. His phone vibrated. At the next red light, at Sherbrooke and de la Montagne, Toby checked and discovered an e-mail from Anton Beauchemin.

> *Dear Toby,*
> *Heard about the thing. Can't do it. No point meeting.*
> *Apologies, regrets.*
> *Anton*

For the past year, Mr. Demsky had lived and worked in a Victorian townhouse on Elm Avenue, two blocks west of the Forum, Montreal's factory of half-remembered sepia dreams. He might have lived higher up the mountain, in the detached stone houses of multi-generational business-class travellers, but he had chosen to stay close to his audience, whom he both adored and despised. Elm Avenue was tranquil despite its proximity to a shopping mall, a synagogue, the college Toby had attended after high school, and the twenty-two-screen cinema complex that was once the Forum. It was a Wednesday, and therefore difficult to find a parking spot. Bits of dust blew up and settled on the lapels of Toby's suit and on his violated tie, and with this wind came nostalgia for the early 1990s: kisses, European coffee, thunder, marijuana.

Personal assistants never lasted long with Mr. Demsky, and when he hired someone new he would seek an untried nationality: Chinese, Ukrainian, Thai, Caribbean, Pakistani. Toby couldn't pick out this latest woman's accent, at least not on the intercom system. There was a breathlessness about her. "The door is open," she said. "Just enter."

Mr. Demsky kept several residences in North America, France, and Israel, and in the midst of his semi-retirement he moved from house to house to avoid extreme cold, extreme heat, and boredom. According to the October chill Toby felt as he entered the townhouse on Elm Avenue, Mr. Demsky's time in Montreal would soon come to an end for another year.

There was a dark wooden arch in the foyer and complex geometric shapes on the tile floor. Over the neoclassical violin music that issued from tiny speakers bracketed to the ceiling, Toby could hear Mr. Demsky and his assistant arguing bitterly. On his way up the stairs, Toby stomped his feet so they might hear him and quiet down. Of course, they knew their visitor was not a former prime minister; Mr. Demsky worked before a bank of LCD screens that displayed shots of the perimeter of his townhouse. The giant master bedroom, transformed into an office, had a bay window overlooking Elm Avenue. There was nothing on the white walls but a single art deco cowboy poster advertising canned tomatoes. Toby knocked on the door jamb; again, they ignored him.

The woman was stout and wore a dress and stockings inspired by a Bavarian beerhouse. Her hair was red and tightly curled, flecked with grey.

"I don't want bulgur wheat salad."

"Vegetables, Adam, vegetables."

Mr. Demsky shook Toby's hand, though he hadn't yet made eye contact. "Go cook me a steak."

"You had red meat yesterday."

"And while you're at it, open a bottle of Chablis and order us up some hookers."

"You would not know what to do with a hooker."

Mr. Demsky looked down and shook his head. "And now you emasculate me in front of my protegé."

Protegé. Hearing this word, Toby knew that Dwayne had gone too far. He would be back on the air before the end of the week. Until now, he had been an external presence in the room. With "protegé," a word of infinite hope, he settled into the triangle. The violin music, Mr. Demsky—his hero, really—the ornate features of the townhouse.

"I quite enjoy a bulgur wheat salad, with lots of parsley," Toby said. "It's cleansing."

"You see?" said the Bavarian.

"Oh, betrayal." Mr. Demsky squinted at her. "Tobias, wait downstairs for twenty minutes. I'm about to strip this woman to her underclothes and teach her a lesson."

"You are too old."

"I have drugs."

A stalemate ensued, until the assistant walked out. Toby watched her go.

"She humours me." Mr. Demsky sat in his leather chair and wheeled back behind his desk.

"Mr. Demsky, I'm here because—"

"When my wife died, Tobias, I was miserable. Couldn't see a way out of it. I gave myself two years, tops. It's been eleven." Mr. Demsky pulled a pack of Marlboro Lights from underneath a hollow Bible, selected one, and lit it with a match. "She throws a fit when she catches me smoking."

"Of course."

"In the midst of my misery, eleven years ago, I sat down and made a list of my final goals. How old was I? Not so old. All I *really* wanted, at that time, to cap off my life, was to fuck a robot. I still do, but technological innovation has been moving slower than I anticipated." He took a drag on his cigarette and blew it straight up with his eyes closed. "But I refocused. I refocused. I took my hit, and I refocused."

"This morning, Dwayne fired me."

"He called for permission."

"But—"

"I've been working for the past two hours with a couple of my lawyers, threatening to sue anyone who distributes the video. It's been halted on the sharing sites, but it did spread quickly. The damage has been done. I can't afford to piss off the Conservatives right now."

"But—"

"But nothing. Nothing, Tobias. What you are in that video is the one thing we cannot be. The station is dead to you, like my wife and my robot."

"He's sleeping with Alicia. He wants to destroy me."

"Sentimentality."

"I'd been up all night, with my dad. He was burned in a fire, and I was on a lot of NyQuil."

Mr. Demsky walked to a tall wooden bookshelf stained a deep burgundy. He pulled down a leather-bound volume with gold-embossed pages and placed it open in Toby's hands. It was a long poem, in English on the left side and Latin on the right, "On the Nature of Things," by Lucretius. Toby read the first few lines in English without really concentrating.

"Wow. That's really pretty."

"Out loud, for Christ's sake."

Toby put on his broadcaster voice and read slowly. "'Therefore death to us / Is nothing, nor concerns us in the least, / Since nature of mind is mortal evermore.'"

"Lucretius was a brilliant old atheist. Whenever I'm tempted into sentimentality, I like to read him. You can borrow that if you like."

"Mr. Demsky, I'm—"

"You're serious about this business."

"I am."

"You made a mistake and you want to make it go away."

"Yes."

"Well, you can't. But starting right now, you have to see the lesson in this. It's time to grow up, yes? To forget about your mother and father, your friends, your girlfriend, your wife, strangers who can do shit for you. If it isn't sleep they're taking, it's your centre of gravity. Your calm. Your gift, Tobias. Everything you've earned. You don't have to be an asshole, but you do have to be discerning with your time and energy. Ruthless. Dwayne succeeds, you see, because he genuinely does not care about displeasing his wife and breaking his children's tiny little hearts. He never cultivates friends who cannot help him. It all comes naturally to Dwayne, as it comes naturally to me."

"That goes against pretty much everything I've ever taught my viewers, Mr. Demsky. What about the breakdown of morality? The spiritual crisis in America? What is etiquette, if it isn't—"

"It's irrelevant. It's an effect, and men like us, we have to be in the business of causes. There is success, Tobias, and there is nothing else. It's very, very simple. You and I can share a bottle of wine and talk about making every man on the East Coast a gentleman, but there is only one reason, one, to do it. To create wealth for ourselves, and honour."

Mr. Demsky sat down across from him again. They remained silent as Toby went through a mental roll call of great men and women.

"This is why we are here, why the universe was created for us." Mr. Demsky butted out his cigarette. "At first it's difficult, but slowly, as with everything else, you develop your muscles. It becomes routine, and you begin to notice the people around you responding submissively. Because they sense a beast is among them, a beast of ambition."

"A beast."

"Of ambition, Tobias."

"I'm not young anymore. This is serious. I could be unhappy for the rest of my life, all because—"

"You're not sounding beastly."

"What should I do?"

"That's for you to decide."

"This isn't fair."

Mr. Demsky sighed and spun his chair away from Toby—toward his desk.

"You can't help me?"

"Not now."

Toby said goodbye to Mr. Demsky and thanked the woman downstairs. She was frying a steak. On the counter beside her, as she spiced the meat, sat a photograph of Mr. Demsky on a beach somewhere, smiling, a beast of ambition in a cheap black frame.

Four

In the car, Toby completed a mental calculation of his financial health. With the mortgage on his condominium and the lease payments on the BMW, taxes and utilities and clothes and restaurants and shoes and organic food, he had lived paycheque to paycheque with either a small surplus or a small deficit each month, based on travel. His severance package from the station had not been generous. Once he paid off his credit cards, there would be very little remaining in his account.

He drove north to his dealership, where an open parking stall lay enticingly before him. It was one of his favourite places on the island, this showroom, and he knew it would be good to him today. Storm clouds were moving in, deep grey and purple, and a rare flash of October thunder shook the car. Toby rubbed a few crumbs from the passenger seat and picked one of Alicia's hairs from the headrest. He put the long, wavy black hair in his mouth, tasted it, then removed it.

The floor of the dealership gleamed with promise. A titanium silver 7-series with tinted windows and tires so shiny Toby wanted to bite into the rubber murmured to him from the centre of a faux-marble floor. He leaned inside an open window, inhaled the off-gassing of success, and stored it in a special corner of his right lung.

A salesman in his late twenties put his hand on Toby's upper back. "I am such a fan of your work!"

A Mozart concerto emanated from hidden speakers. Toby adjusted his posture and took a step back to tread on the outer layer of the salesman's cologne field. Behind him, modest signs on the wall advertised monthly interest rates and payment plans beyond the budget of nearly every working household in recession North America. Which was the point, really. "Thank you."

"I heard you were a customer here and I flipped." The salesman had braces and shoulder-length blond hair. There was a faint orange to his tan that blended unsuccessfully with his beige suit. "My hard drive tapes your show for me. I have a collection."

"Really, thank you so much. I'm Toby Ménard."

"I know!"

"Good."

"Oh, what crap etiquette of me. Gary Dunlop, sales associate." He extended his hand for a shake and left his business card in Toby's hand like a gangster dropping a Benjamin. He pulled back his left cuff to reveal a round watch with a faded leather band. "Recognize this?"

"I do."

"You wore this bad-boy on your show about the classics. I had one of those stupid save-the-day watches, and after I watched the show I pitched it into the river. I actually did!"

"I'm sorry, Mr. Dunlop. But may I speak with the sales manager?"

In the span of three seconds, Gary Dunlop appeared to go through a series of emotional and psychological changes. He was trained for this moment—to capture his commission despite all impediments. "I can help you, Mr. Ménard. I can. I know I look young and whatever, but I'm empowered to help you."

"Well."

"You must be here to upgrade."

Mozart crashed deeper and louder toward an ancient climax of orchestral doom. There was no point waiting for the sales manager if Gary Dunlop was sympathetic. Outside, another gust slapped a layer of dirt from the roadside flower beds into the window. Toby did not know if he could say it out loud. "It turns out I've lost my job, Mr. Dunlop."

"You?"

"Very soon my lease payments will be prohibitive."

"Pro—"

"I can't afford the car, for now. What I'm hoping for is a reprieve, Mr. Dunlop, a break from my payments. Just while I find a new, and better, position." He adjusted his posture, strained for belief. "It shouldn't take longer than a month or two."

The salesman slouched, ever so slightly. He took a couple of steps to his right and leaned on the 7-series. Moment by moment, as Gary Dunlop adjusted to this knowledge, Toby felt his social superiority float up into the artfully exposed ventilation system and away.

"How long you had 'er?" Gary Dunlop said.

Toby supplied the relevant data, and Gary Dunlop frowned. He informed Toby that interest payments were top-loaded in lease contracts. "You gotta wait for Donny."

New customers, actual customers, an Asian boy and his parents, entered the showroom. Gary Dunlop corrected his posture and strode toward them with such relief it verged on a sprint. For almost half an hour, Toby flipped through pamphlets and compared himself to images of authentic BMW people as the boy's parents argued rancorously about the appropriate options on his graduation present.

The manager, Don Chana, walked into the showroom with a Starbucks coffee. He was tall and thick, with a red tie turned around in the wind to reveal the word Togo—a former house brand of the Hudson's Bay Company. He spotted Toby and feigned a stagger. His black loafers squeaked on the faux marble. "About time you came back to see us. How long's it been?"

"Some months."

"God*damn,* it's good to see you."

In the manager's office, which was decorated with BMW posters and sales awards and icons with Punjabi script, Toby discovered that the story of his dismissal was a common one. Don Chana looked up at the beams and ducts and asked God to commit an act of violent yet creative sexual assault against Toby's boss. He vowed never to watch the television station again and mimed a spit on the floor.

"That is really too kind, Mr. Chana."

"It's the least I can do." He put on his reading glasses, looked up Toby's file. "Well, I'll be damned. That can't be right, can it?"

Toby recalled thinking, less than a week before, that he would never again need to send out a C.V. The next stage of his career was supposed to be in Toronto or New York or London, with Alicia, as soon as the headhunters noticed them.

"This is not what you wanted to hear, my friend, but with your down payment, if your car is in utterly pristine condition, utterly, I can release you from your contract. That is, if you write us a cheque for $1,500. Of course, we can go to the used lot and see if we can't somehow help you out of this damned carlessness."

"So I can't keep the 335?"

"No. No, you absolutely cannot. If you stop making payments, we will take it from you and destroy your credit rating, my friend."

"I was hoping, Mr. Chana, that given my high profile in the community . . ."

"But you have lost your job, sir."

"Just temporarily."

Don Chana sipped his Starbucks.

One hour and $1,800 later, Toby pulled out of the BMW dealership in an orange 1980 Chevette. Don Chana had just received the car and the "union fucks" in the service department had not found the time to clean it out or inspect it. Toby stayed off the autoroute, fearing a breakdown, but the sun broke through the clouds again just as he re-entered the stable and happy environs of Westmount. Schoolchildren, joggers, the elderly, and new mothers stopped to stare at the Chevette, which growled and farted as he passed Alicia's house on Strathcona Avenue. He slowed and stopped, hoping that she would come running out and restore him to dignity. A smorgasbord of colourful pollution rose up behind the Chevette and filled his rear-view mirror. He had once described car exhaust as "a crime against humanity" in a segment of *Toby a Gentleman*.

A rust-based ecosystem thrived in the Chevette. A

mature spiderweb dotted with mosquito carcasses was on the passenger-side floor. A late-season bee hovered at the back of the car, slamming into the rear window. For the first time in two days, Toby checked the messages on his cellphone. There were a number from Dwayne and his secretary, two from Alicia—pre-confrontation Alicia, pretend Alicia, I love you Alicia—and one from his mother, dated from that morning: Edward was being discharged.

⁓

Karen sat and Edward stood in the waiting area of the burn unit, the television still tuned to CNN.

"Where in hell have you been?" Karen jumped up from her chair, and brown crumbs fell from her shirt. "They kicked him out of his room hours ago. We were just about to hire a taxi. A *taxi*. How much would that have cost, do you think?"

"Forty dollars."

"At least. You have that kind of money to dump in the toilet, but your father and I are in altogether different circumstances."

Edward walked a line of grout on the tile floor, his arms out for balance. His mouth was open, a seven-year-old at his birthday party five minutes before he opens his presents. Every ounce of yesterday's dourness had been drained away, replaced by delight. His hands and arms were free of bandages now, but a large rectangle of gauze remained on his head. He wore a pair of mauve hospital pants that covered the burns on his shins. "I'm a tightrope walker," he said.

Karen spoke through her teeth. "Do you see what's happening here?"

"Dad?"

"Embrace me, my son." Edward jumped off the tightrope and hugged Toby, gingerly. He whispered, "We're just so blessed to be here together, the three of us. What's the magic number? You remember the song. What is it?"

"Three."

"It's the magic number." He broke out of the hug and raised his fist in victory. "Can I get a witness?"

A number of the burn victims had turned away from CNN to watch and listen to Edward.

Toby addressed his mother silently. She shrugged in response.

"*Three is a magic number,*" Edward sang to his fellow patients. "Everybody now."

The patients backed into their chairs.

"I left messages at home and at Alicia's, on your cell, at work," Karen said.

"It's been quite a day."

"You've had quite a day? You? Well, sonny, you missed your dad being Barry the Butterfly for the apprentice nurse."

"Oh, Toby, you have to meet her." Edward returned to them. "She could be a model."

"It made her plenty comfortable when Cary Grant over here told her so. And that was *before* he did Barry."

Toby picked up his father's belongings, in two white plastic bags, and his mother's small leather valise. He led them to the elevator and began planning his afternoon. The bank would not immediately foreclose on his condominium. There were still two English-language stations on the island to phone—then Toronto and Vancouver, where they knew nothing of what he had said in front of Roslyn School. A beast of ambition.

For the first two floors, they were alone in the elevator. Karen continued to poke him about all the better things he had done today, in his family's time of need. She counted each of his imagined exultations on her long fingers. "You went to a nice café on the Plateau, I would think, for a late breakfast. Perhaps you signed autographs for some teenage girls with their underwear showing. Oh, then what? A massage."

"I was fired this morning. And Alicia and I are finished."

"Finished," said Karen. "What does that mean? Finished?"

"Is there a clearer word for 'finished'?"

"You're being funny."

"I wear the green hat."

Edward looked up at the fluorescent light on the ceiling of the elevator car. "Like father, like son."

Karen pressed her fingers to her forehead.

The elevator stopped, and two women, doctors, stepped on, each with a cup of coffee. They whispered.

"Is there anyone I can phone?" Edward poked Toby when he did not answer. "To make this right?"

The elevator stopped again, on the mezzanine level, and a woman helped her one-legged husband into the car.

Edward's voice trembled. "Do they know who you are? Do they even *know*? Your boss, the Jew with the hair. He knows. He must!"

There is a spiritual component to etiquette, an instinct that precedes and supersedes the most comprehensive book of rules. Toby could practically hear the doctors, the unfortunate couple, bursting with perspiration. The car reached the lobby, and it seemed to take several lifetimes for the doors to open.

"Do they?"

The man with one leg murmured a plea in his wife's ear. "*Let's go. Quick, quick.*" One of the two doctors looked back at Edward as she walked out, more curious than afraid. When they were alone, Toby answered his father. Yes. They knew exactly who he was.

In the lobby there were stand-up signs carrying bilingual public service announcements about sexually transmitted diseases, as well as two tables where it appeared a miniature craft sale was imminent. A woman and two men organized a collection of crocheted and carved goods, and chatted with Gaspé accents.

"You're my genius boy," said Edward. "It's so clear."

"Dad. Wait until we're in the car."

Toby and his parents stopped near the tables to put on their jackets. "You're the best. You're my boy, and you're the very best, and that's the truth. Since the fire, I have resolved to speak the unvarnished truth."

"Oh goody," said Karen.

"Look at you: pure frustration." Edward, in the black overcoat Karen had packed for him, opened his arms to her. His voice echoed in the hall. "Release it. Release!"

The sellers of crafts looked over. Three elderly women, nuns, sitting on a bench, slowly turned their heads in unison. Toby reached out to quiet his father and whisk him out the doors, but Edward broke away. The burns on his shins extended to his knees, so he walked stiffly, pelvis forward, Chaplin-esque. He pointed to Karen with his left hand and

placed his right hand on his heart. "*Deep river,*" he sang.
"*My home is over Jordan.*"

Three young men passing through the lobby stopped
and smiled. One of them laughed. All other discussion in the
room stopped.

"*Deep river, Lord, I want to cross over into campground.*"

Karen pushed Toby. "Stop him."

It was, at first, exquisite. The fire, or something, had
added a dimension to Edward's voice that Toby did not recognize. Singing, at home, was quite natural for Edward—in
the shower or in the yard as he cut the lawn. Never in public,
though, and never anything holier than classic rock and R & B;
his oeuvre had consisted primarily of Credence Clearwater
Revival and Otis Redding.

Edward repeated the first two lines of the song, and one
of the nuns stood up and joined in, quaveringly. At the second
"campground," his voice rose beyond his ability to hold the
note and passed into the grotesque.

"*Oh, don't you want to go to that gospel feast? That
promised land where all is peace?*"

There was aggression in his interpretation now, rock and
roll, as he moved through the rotunda. Karen began to cry.

"*Oh, deep river, Lord, I want to cross over into campground.*"

The nuns applauded as Toby guided Edward tenderly
through the doors, saying, "Bravo, Dad, bravo," and into the
parking lot. One of his segments, on how to deal with beg-
gars, had touched on insanity and how one must confront it.
Karen followed them, several paces back, blowing her nose
and delivering sarcastic thank yous to no one.

"What's this?" Edward stopped a few paces away from the Chevette.

"My car."

"No, no, no, no, that isn't even close to your car."

"I was fired today, Dad. I can't afford seven-hundred-dollar lease payments anymore."

"But all morning, all the way down here, I was figuring on the Beemer."

Toby opened the doors, with a key. He reached in to move the seat forward so Karen might climb into the back, and he snagged the empty breast pocket of his first real suit, his third-favourite suit, an Ermenegildo Zegna, on an apparently pointless hunk of jagged metal in the doorway. The pocket flopped open, and Toby's muscles went limp with it. He leaned into the car, resting one knee on the back seat, and closed his eyes.

Mountains and forests bordered the small northern Italian village where Toby's first real suit had been designed and manufactured, and a fragrant wind of sophistication and virility blew through the pines. The sleek appearance of his shadow, in the Zegna, had always been a comfort to him. He wore it only on important days. When Toby had bought the suit in the late 1990s, on a one-year payment plan that amounted to $195 a month, he could not justify it. He had kept the purchase a secret from his parents. They were hosting him in their basement at the time, buying his organic food—which they could not afford—and providing an occasional allowance so he could attend all critical social functions in Montreal and carouse as necessary. It was not possible, after all, to exaggerate the importance of networking.

It had rained on the day he bought the suit. For months Toby had feared Boutique Jean-François, near Université de Montréal, assuming it would be full of business professors and lawyers already wearing Zegna and Armani, established francophones who would recognize him as the beneficiary of a weekly allowance, and as someone who could never say *je vous en prie* quite right. It was a Saturday. Toby had borrowed his father's Oldsmobile. He loitered under the black awning of Boutique Jean-François and counted the soaked red cobblestones between the avenue and the store. The sidewalk, it turned out, was fifteen cobblestones wide. Clover grew between them. Chopin played on small outdoor speakers, and the composer's sensitive genius only ripped deeper into the membrane of timidity that had grown around Toby's heart. But once he had gathered the courage to step into the store, everything changed. The other customers in Boutique Jean-François were strivers in Polo and Club Monaco button-ups, working out the payment plans in their heads. He had discovered a secret.

"You all right?" Karen placed a hand on his back. Her voice had returned to normal.

He calculated how long he might last, given his monthly responsibilities and his cash flow. The BMW was gone, but the Visa bill remained, along with payments on his last renovation, his furnishings, his electronic needs, his last two suits. An avalanche of what the newspapers called consumer debt, which until recently had seemed normal. Then the mortgage, utilities.

Toby backed out of the car. "Just super!"

She climbed into the back seat, tended to her eyes in the rear-view mirror. "You could definitely use an air freshener in here, son."

Toby eased Edward into the passenger seat. Even with

the painkillers, the process was clearly agonizing for Edward, bending and stretching his charred skin. For a month or longer, he would have to return to the hospital twice a week for day procedures and therapies.

"So what are you going to do now?" Edward's old tone had returned.

Both of his parents struggled with their seatbelts. He drove slowly out of the hospital parking lot, slowly west. "Look for a new job."

"You have money saved?"

The autoroute appeared on the horizon like an advancing army.

"We can help you, son."

"No, we goddamn well can't, Edward."

"We can help."

"With what? With what, exactly, can we help him?"

How long, realistically, could he last? A month, maybe two. There were layoffs and hiring freezes across the country, in television and in newspapers. He had heard it was even worse in the U.S. Potential employers would round his age up to forty. His bald spot wasn't getting any smaller. His salary expectations were his salary expectations. Would he hire himself?

"The boy can move back home, where he belongs."

Toby caught his mother's eye in the rear-view mirror. "I can't move back home."

"Think how much you'll save. You can sell the place in the gay village."

"It's not the gay village."

"Or rent it out. And move back in with us, where you belong. Three is the magic number, after all. Think of the Scrabble alone!"

He was thirty-seven years old.

"Name one reason why not."

Toby could name thirty-seven reasons. His mother reached up and poked him in the ribs as Edward broke into "Deep River" again. They were on the autoroute named after a folk singer now, rumbling west into the archipelago of parking lots. She cleared her throat as Edward sang, and again Toby met her eye in the rear-view mirror. The sarcasm had passed away. All that remained was fear.

"Please," she mouthed. "Will you please?"

Warehouses. Unkempt yards. Big-box retailers. Minivans. Identical houses. Fewer and fewer pedestrians until, as they neared his hometown, the *pays natal*, there were none. To his knowledge, he had never before suffered a real anxiety attack, with all the trimmings. He opened the window for some air. Dollard-des-Ormeaux stretched out before him.

PART TWO

Five

There was a fire department SUV parked in the steep driveway of the house on rue Collingwood, behind the carcass of the Oldsmobile. One side of the house, the white door of the garage, and a swath of lawn had been scorched black. Toby could not look for long at the remains of his father's fire in the afternoon light. It exposed Edward more fully, more intimately, than the flourescent bulb in the hospital bathroom.

Toby guided his parents out of the car, and Karen ran interference between Edward and the Oldsmobile. Two men in jeans and matching red bomber jackets sneaked about the car, performing a silent ritual. "What are they doing here?" said his father.

"Investigating."

"Investigating what? Hey! Fellas! This is private property."

Toby asked Karen to lead Edward into the house and make him a tuna sandwich.

"Don't you refer to me in the third person. Two will be the magic number pretty damn soon."

Once his parents were in the house, Toby introduced himself in French. Both investigators, who wore polyurethane gloves, waved like drowsy men swatting at flies. One bent under the melted abstract sculpture that had once been a hood. The other was on his knees in front of the driver's-side door.

"Have you determined the cause?"

The one addressing himself to the engine scratched his orange beard, looked at the other and sighed.

"We're not supposed to say anything," said the younger man at the door.

"Do you always investigate so thoroughly?"

Orange Beard said to his partner, "You deal with it. I want to be home for dinner. We're having ribs, and I like them hot."

The younger fireman removed his right glove and shook Toby's hand. His name was Gregoire. It struck Toby that he had never met a Gregoire or Gregory who referred to himself as anything but Greg.

"There are irregularities."

"Like what?"

Gregoire looked up at the house. Toby followed his gaze. Edward was looking out the picture window, his cheek pressed to the glass. "There was accelerant on your father's pants."

"Accelerant?"

"Gasoline."

"Perhaps he had been mowing the lawn."

"In October?"

Toby beheld the Oldsmobile with Gregoire. It was set to rain.

"And if you discover he's done something preposterous here, what then?"

"We inform certain agencies. The police, the insurance company."

"So you're working for insurance companies?"

Orange Beard cleared his throat. "Back to work."

"We won't be much longer," said Gregoire.

The house smelled faintly of rum-and-wine-dipped tobacco, as it always had. Officially, Karen only smoked outside, on the back patio, but unofficially she indulged in the living room whenever it was cold, whenever she felt lazy or drowsy, and whenever smoking guests visited. Her collection of ashtrays was formidable and, along with the standard black glass pieces, included representational pottery stamped with images and logos from Hawaii, Paris, San Francisco, Puerto Vallarta, and Buckingham Palace. Edward and Karen had not visited these places; their friends, knowing Karen's penchant for collecting, had found ashtrays a simple and rewarding Christmas gift.

His parents were at the kitchen table. The chairs, covered in peeling vinyl, had not been updated since the late seventies. But for the two navy recliners, the furniture in the living room was only a few years younger; furniture had never been a priority. The lampshades had gone faintly yellow from a combination of nicotine and sun bleaching. Toby had been in elementary school the last time the walls had been painted. Yet when he had neared graduation, and had veered toward the prep-school aesthetic, Edward and Karen had found room in the budget to keep him in the West Island uniform of Polo and Lacoste shirts, Sperry Top-Siders, white pants by Yves Saint Laurent, pastel Givenchy shaker knit sweaters, and Ray-Ban sunglasses.

"There's no tuna, it turns out," said Karen.

Edward's forearms were on the table. He stared down at them.

Toby hunted in the fridge and cupboards and found little but pasta, canned beans, condiments, and discount beer. "Is everything all right? Financially, I mean?"

Karen looked in the pantry, where they traditionally kept large and bulk items purchased at the discount mega-stores. "Well," said Karen.

"The Chien Chaud?"

"I don't know."

"Answer him, Karen."

"He just walked in the door. He lost his job."

Toby regretted the initial question and nearly suggested a game of Boggle, to divert the energy in the room. "You don't have to talk about it, Mom."

"It's never been good, as you know, in the 'making money and getting ahead in life' sense of good. We've been beavering away, good little entrepreneurs, sure it would turn around, a time would come when we wouldn't have to work so pissing hard, when we could take vacations, when some half-assed reward would come. Then it never did. And now it won't."

Shortly after moving out of the city, his parents had quit their government jobs and opened a hot dog shop called Le Chien Chaud. It did well enough in Dollard to support two more shops on the West Island. Toby had worked at the Chien Chaud until he moved into an apartment in the McGill ghetto when he was nineteen, where the contents of his refrigerator were eerily similar to his parents' fridge today—five years from their planned retirement.

"But they're making money?"

"Well," said Karen.

"No." Edward had not yet looked up from his hairless forearms, glistening even in the flat light of early dusk. "Not even close."

"Couldn't we have waited till he sits down?"

"It's getting late." Toby had intended to stay in Dollard for the night, for a week, to help with his father's recuperation and to stew noiselessly in his shame. But now that he was here, really here, it appeared quite impossible. "I think I'll head back to the condo."

Karen shoved a kitchen chair into the table, pulled it out, and shoved it in again. "You get yourself fired, you do hell knows what with Alicia to push her away, and now you can't even talk to your parents for five minutes?"

Out of habit, Toby looked down at Edward. It was father-son eyebrow-raising time, a well-honoured tradition in the Mushinsky household. He might have reminded Karen that, less than thirty seconds ago, she had not wanted to talk about the Chien Chaud. But that would have inspired a dangerous escalation. A slammed door, at least. This time Edward did not look up for the eyebrow raise.

"Poetry," Edward said. "I think Toby might feel a heck of a lot better if he had a hobby like poetry."

"Let's stop talking about me."

Karen said, "Ha! You see. Here's the heart of it."

With a series of surprising grunts, Edward pushed himself up from the kitchen table, a solid maple gift from Toby's paternal grandparents—both dead now, drowned. He stood before Toby and said, "Son. Listen to me. I know your pain."

Toby turned to his mother. "Aren't we here, together, for *his* pain?"

"We all have our pain," she said.

"Life as I know it has been destroyed, *in two days.*" As his parents watched, Toby slowly drew and drank two glasses of water, to prevent himself from making an untoward emotional display. He wanted desperately to shout at his parents, to splash their faces with cold water and rush out of the house, back to the city and his condominium, his computer and his ironing board. But etiquette was about using beauty and grace to restrain one's passions. Outer dignity reflected inner peace. "'Pain' isn't the right word. My state of mind is *completely* under my control, as yours should be."

Now Edward and Karen stood together, against the stove. "Toby, we saw what happened. On TV. We're worried about you," said Karen. "Really quite worried."

"About me?" There were so many things Toby could say about their house, the contents of their refrigerator, the burned-up car in the driveway, the whole idea of a business, in the twenty-first century, devoted to poor-quality beef slipped into a flour-sprinkled white bun. Karen's cigarillos. Edward's impromptu performances of Negro spirituals. The family portraits from the late eighties, in which they represented the Platonic form of Unhappy. He corrected his posture and said none of this. He said, "I'm going to buy you two some groceries."

In the IGA, after-work singles picked through last year's Halloween leftovers, many of them speaking cheerlessly into cellphones. None of the brand-name chocolate bars and chips were out yet. Crates of molasses candies, Rockets, lollipops, jujubes, and marshmallow treats were priced to sell, and the young citizens of Dollard went through them like runt hyenas looking for a slice of organ.

"Marshmallows. Do they take us for morons?" A slightly taller man in khakis and a nylon jacket with a Tommy Hilfiger logo on the breast stood next to Toby. He was familiar in a misty way, like a backbench politician or the general manager of a lesser sports team. His watch was of the G.I. Joe variety; Toby wondered if, after damning the Halloween candies, the gentleman was planning to dive to the bottom of the St. Lawrence and save a damsel. He did not know whether to reinforce the man's efforts at geniality with his own remark about the marshmallows. They had not yet made eye contact. The man inhaled and spoke again, his words married to a sigh. "How is your dad?"

Steve Bancroft: former neighbour, industrialist, villain. "He's home already."

"How'd it happen?"

"Just an accident." Toby poked through the Rockets as he debated whether to ask what Steve Bancroft had heard on the street. "He's absolutely fine. They're both terrific."

"Well, isn't that terrific."

Brown loafers with tassels. Steve Bancroft was a wealthy man: Why would he choose to diminish his humanity with tassels?

"So, Karen. Karen's holding up, with the shock?"

"She really couldn't be better. Thriving, Mr. Bancroft."

"Tell her I said hello, will you? I've been thinking about those hot dog joints of hers."

"Theirs."

"Theirs." He pulled a card out of his pocket. "Pass this on, will you?"

Toby pocketed the card and walked away, toward the cut-flowers section. He had already picked up the fruits and vegetables, but he could not have stood next to Steve Bancroft any longer. A real man, his father's son, would have at least made a sideways comment about those loafers.

To avoid returning immediately to rue Collingwood, Toby wandered the aisles and played the game he played in bank lineups, in the waiting room at the dentist, and on park benches as the camera operator set up the shot: he appraised the sandals worn with socks, fleece mountain jackets, jeans that did not fit, flip-flops, and sweatpants of his peers. His parents' generation had done this to America with their pretend revolution and the ensuing after-school specials and desperate self-help philosophies. The inner world was the realm of truth.

The goal of *Toby a Gentleman* had been to prove the baby boomers wrong, to demonstrate the enduring links between traditional manners and success, between clothes and the soul. Did a man not feel more serious and thoughtful, more worthy of respect and social acknowledgment, when he wore a well-fitted suit? When he spoke in full sentences, instead of belches and grunts? When he said please and thank you, *vous* and not *tu*, Monsieur and Madame? When he allowed a woman to pass through a door before him? How did it feel, truly feel, to wear bicycle shorts, a fanny pack, and a gigantic T-shirt advertising a sports conglomerate? In the early days of the show, Toby had flattered himself with fantasies in which the male populations of Quebec, Southern Ontario, and northern New England were transformed.

Contrary to his critics' suppositions, Toby had not set out to reinforce class differences. His broad social goals were to encourage men of all salaries and births and tastes to see that dressing like a superhero, a hiker, a homeless person, or a sideshow performer were acts of cruelty—to oneself and to others. It was not a frivolous notion. Every day, a man ought to wake up and consider his behaviour and his wardrobe gifts to the community and to the world. Now, what sort of offering is a snort at the checkout while on a cellphone? Camouflage short pants and a Yankees jersey? Why did the man of today spend two hundred dollars a month on satellite television and high-speed Internet access, yet only thirty dollars on clothes from a big-box discount retailer headquartered in Arkansas? Did the man of today not see that he was doomed by this behaviour, that the outer life, contrary to what he might learn in a romantic comedy, had a direct and enduring effect on the inner life? And vice versa? An effect so powerful that a Harley-Davidson shirt might actually erode some of the brain's higher functions?

Karen had asked him to pick up a frozen pizza for dinner. Toby worried that a week or two of heavily salted prepared food would do further psychological harm to everyone in the house, so he bought the ingredients for his specialty: blackened cod with spinach and mushroom risotto. Steve Bancroft was in the checkout line, flipping through a celebrity gossip magazine, so Toby lingered in the aromatic bulk section until the villain was gone.

⁓

In the mid-1990s, his mother had endured a cancer scare. A checkup had led to a chest X-ray and what appeared to be shadows in her lungs. She quit smoking her long miniature cigars for three weeks, until she learned it had been a mechanical error.

The scent of Old Port through the heavy front door, upon his return, extracted and diffused a fraction of the world's hope and beauty and reminded him that soon, very soon, they would all be dead. As he opened the door, however, his mother's tobacco took on a depth and texture he did not recognize. American cigarettes. Gasoline.

Two men sat on the chesterfield. Both of them smoked. Toby recalled seeing a bright red Cadillac sedan and a tow truck parked across from the house, both of them outside the norm of rue Collingwood. He peeked out before he shut the door. PILE TOWING: THE TRUSTED NAME IN TOWING. And here was Randall Pile, all six foot seven of him, in a suit that was at least two sizes too small. Toby recalled, as he approached Randall, that his old friend would have been taller if the doctor had not used hormone therapy to slow his growth. He had matured so quickly in grades six and seven that the muscles, tendons, and bones in his ankles had never fused properly, so he walked with a limp. In high school it had been faint. Now he was in his late thirties, hard living etched around his eyes and the limp more fully—yet lyrically—pronounced.

Randall extended his hand for a shake. "Let me get this right. Remember that show you did on handshakes? Eye contact." Randall took Toby's hand and stared down. "Forward thrust, to avoid having your fingers squeezed. Firm, firm."

"Not too firm," said Garrett Newman, Randall's best friend since grade three, who remained seated.

"No, no, not too firm. Then what? Oh yeah, stand not too close but not too far. I know we've already been doing it way too long. No more than three seconds, right?"

"Ideally."

"He has a library of your tapes." Now Garrett rose and stepped in for a shake, more natural in his suit. Like both of his parents, Garrett had become a lawyer. He was completely bald and fat in an old-fashioned, hereditary manner. There was an attractive, ancestral essence about his cheeks and neck, the way his eyes were set in his face; it was impossible to imagine Garrett any other way. In high school, at the worst possible time in his emotional development, a girl on the volleyball team had come by his house on a Saturday morning, raising funds for a trip to Hartford. The entrance was on the side of the house, so visitors passed the basement window. The girl peeked in and made eye contact with Garrett, on his knees, naked, masturbating in front of a mirror. By ten o'clock on Monday morning, everyone in school had heard the story of Garrett's shame. Before that Saturday, his bons mots in social studies class had been widely appreciated by preps and punks, headbangers, jocks and debaters. No one could tear apart Bill 101, the failures and contradictions of the Pepsis, like Garrett. Yet he never recovered. Even though every teenage boy on the island of Montreal abused himself merrily, an air of lonely perversion attended Garrett for the rest of his formal education.

In the forty-five minutes since Toby had left for groceries, the adults in the bungalow had apparently taken two or three stiff drinks each. Their eyes were covered in a cozy film. Classic rock played on the kitchen radio. His high school friends and his parents dished glances at one another.

Toby sat on the footstool. "What?"

"Nothing," said Karen.

"My birthday's not for a while."

"It's nothing!"

Randall walked to the picture window and looked out. An inch of his right pant leg was tucked ever so precariously into his sock. "Your mom and dad called us, Toby."

"I didn't. I did not call you." Edward poked Garrett. "Did I?"

"No. You're right about that. It was Mrs. Mushinsky."

Randall cleared his throat. He continued to look out in a tsarist fashion. "She called us, Toby, because she's nimbly worried."

"Nimbly? Mom, you're nimbly worried?"

"Actually, no," said Karen. "But it's close."

"I'm not sure that's what you meant to say, Rand," said Garrett.

"It's precisely what I wanted to say."

"'Nimbly' doesn't mean what you think it means."

"What?"

Edward opened his palms to the ceiling. "We're all worried. Toby's worried, Karen's worried, I'm worried. Some nights, when it's quiet, I can hear the earth murmuring. Listen. Just listen for a moment, all of you, in the silence. Listen for the message."

They listened for the message. The clock ticked. From the kitchen, "Takin' Care of Business."

"Am I right? I mean, come on."

Karen cleared her throat, demonstrably, and Edward followed her into the kitchen. He said, enunciating every syllable, "We are going to put the groceries away."

This allowed Toby another opportunity to listen for the message. He struggled for an acknowledgment or an explanation of Edward's words. Silence did its subtle work, and soon the conversation in the kitchen, which sounded sane enough, inspired Randall to turn from the window and fuss with his Asterix and Obelix tie, which he had mangled into a four-in-hand knot with no crease.

"Your mother said you lost your job and your lady in the same day. Believe you me, I understand."

"We saw the video," said Garrett. "My secretary is a big computer girl."

"Intervention." Randall lifted a handful of jelly beans from the decorative bowl on the bookshelf, and before Toby could tell him they had been there for over a decade, he popped a couple into his mouth. "A laying on of hands. That was my first thought when Karen gave us a shout this afternoon. We grew up together. This suit? This tie? It's all you."

"An Asterix tie? I don't think—"

"I haven't spit outside—except on grass when nobody's looking, and that's only on hot days—in probably five years. That's all on you. We care about you, buddy. We love you. We've got your back."

"I do appreciate that, Randall, but my back is just marvellous."

"That's what I told him," said Garrett.

Randall pointed to his mouth. "Is there a garbage somewhere? These jelly beans don't taste right at all."

"Kitchen or bathroom."

He rushed off and Toby was left with Garrett. "I am sorry about this. Your mom and him got each other excited about the idea of an intervention. She said you'd gone off a bit. They both watch that show, I think, about interventions. I'm more interested in Edward and his car. What happened there?"

"It's under investigation."

"Damn."

"I wish I knew how it happened."

"Damn." Garrett swirled his highball like cognac. "You know, Randall bought that suit at Sears, on the way here. The woman clipped his pants, in lieu of hemming."

"It's the wrong size for him."

"She wasn't very good at her job, per se."

Randall returned to the room, talking. "This love, Toby. It's unconditional. All right? It surrounds you, from every corner."

"That's incredibly thoughtful."

"I do not. I do not want to see you go down that road. I just don't."

"What road?"

"Don't burn too brightly, Toby, because falling stars always . . . no, no, no, wait, hold on. If a star falls, and is bright, and then it burns. Something."

"We thought maybe the three of us could go out," said Garrett. "Get some hot wings."

"I'm making fish and risotto. Really, you guys, there's nothing wrong with me. To answer your question more fully, Garrett, I'm here to take care of them." Toby nodded in the direction of the kitchen. "I don't know what's happening with my dad, with the fire. And the hot dog shops are dying. It's true I've had a pretty terrible week, but—"

"That is a falsehood."

"Just talk normally, Rand. He knows you drive a tow truck."

"Oh. Oh, now *I'm* being attacked!"

"And I really have to get to work on my C.V. I'd like to send out some packages tomorrow, to Toronto and Vancouver."

"It's one night," said Garrett.

"An hour. I'll go for an hour."

Randall high-fived him.

"An hour. And only if I can have assurances, from you both, that sharing hot wings isn't a laying on of hands in any way."

Randall and Garrett looked at each other and nodded, somewhat grudgingly, it seemed.

⌒

Half an hour later, Randall, Garrett, and Toby were at a corner table in La Moufette, near the deserted dance floor and the women's washroom. A fresh pitcher of beer sweated on the table, next to a salt shaker. Lights flashed in time to "Good Vibrations" by Marky Mark and the Funky Bunch, and a server leaned against the empty DJ booth with her eyes closed. Three ageless men in jeans and T-shirts sat at the bar, looking up at a television on mute, tuned to sports highlights.

It occurred to Toby, as Randall talked and talked, that all of his adult companions had been couple friends, shared with Alicia. He spent time with almost no one, singly. In the wake of his misfortune, he could not imagine phoning any of his couple friends. Staying in Dollard would have financial benefits if he were forced to sell the condo, but it would also allow him to avoid humiliating chance encounters in Square Saint-Louis.

The conversation had focused on Randall and his children, Dakota and Savannah, six and four, "life's chiefest pleasures." Their sleeping patterns, their favourite toys, the boy's first year of hockey. "He doesn't take any lip. There've been a few incidents, let's just say, when some other kid makes the mistake of fucking with him."

Garrett leaned over the table. "Hear how proud he is, raising a bully?"

The ashen men at the bar did not speak to one another or move except to lift beer bottles to their mouths, to cough, to retreat to the washroom or to the sidewalk for a cigarette. There were five other single men scattered about La Moufette, eating fries or dry ribs, drinking beer, looking up at one of the mute televisions. Men without couple friends.

Randall pulled out a cigarette and drew it under his nose. "I love it when they're like this, all clean. You coming?"

"Next round," said Garrett.

The beer had begun to warm its way through Toby, and it reached his brain like a flower unfolding its petals. Their waitress walked past and held eye contact.

"He was so nervous about seeing you," said Garrett. "That tie. He really agonized over it."

Toby wanted to go outside and phone Alicia; the notion had struck him, here in La Moufette, that he had not been the most attentive lover. Their sexual relationship had fallen into a comfortable pattern. Perhaps there were moves she had wanted to try, cues he had not picked up on. It had never occurred to him, until now, that she might actually *enjoy* anal sex. He wasn't against it! Who knows? It could be quite bracing. There were instructional videos one could order.

For several minutes they sat quietly, looking about La Moufette. It surprised Toby that he did not feel uncomfortable in the silence. He did not feel the need, with his old friend, to bring up hockey or the weather or leaving. Then he did. "I should get going, Garrett. I have a phone call to make."

"We just got here." Garrett waved the waitress over and ordered three shots of tequila. Four, if she wanted to join them, he said, winking in Toby's direction. She nodded and sashayed to the bar. "I think she likes you."

"I really appreciate that, Garrett."

"Things haven't gone well for our Randall as of late, either. Romantically speaking."

"With his wife?"

Garrett looked over his shoulder, as Randall was on his way back to the table. "She kicked him out."

"But the kids."

"It's killing him."

There was a commotion at the bar. One man had accidentally knocked over another's drink, and threats were being flung about. Toby was pleased to have something to watch while he finished his final glass of salty beer.

Randall retook his seat, a breeze of cigarettes about him. "So what have you decided? Are we gonna join the space program or what?"

"I was just saying I really should go."

They announced toasts to Edward, to Toby the hero, and to Randall's children before suffering through their cheap tequila shots. Randall ordered six more. The new tequilas arrived, and with each of the two shots they toasted Edward, his goodness, his resilience, a new spook about him that Randall and Garrett had both noticed. Toby told the version of events he had come to accept. He had run to the driver's-side door.

"Weren't you worried it would explode?" said Randall.

"Of course I was worried."

Garrett leaned back in his chair and squinted both drunkenly and suspiciously.

"Now what about Alicia?" said Randall.

She was probably the most famous woman in anglophone Montreal—an anchor and an omnipresent spokeswoman for charities related to cancer, children, and children with cancer. "The station manager, he cuckolded me."

"No!" said Randall.

"He's married. With kids."

"No," said Garrett.

"His name is Dwayne."

"You know, I hate that name, and not only because of the cuckolding." Randall filled their glasses, emptying the second pitcher.

"Dwayne means 'poem' in Gaelic," said Garrett.

"For me, it's not the name so much as the cuckolding I object to. We were friends of a sort."

"It goes against everything you've tried to do, Tobe, to improve our lot."

"Thank you, Randall." He checked his watch. "I really should—"

"And Garrett, old boy, since when do you speak Gaelic?"

"I knew someone."

"Who?"

"Does it matter, Randall?"

"Someone Gaelic?"

Apparently it did matter, for an ugly instant, as Randall stared at his much smaller friend. Then he turned away from Garrett, unfolded his arms, and slammed his fist on the table. The empty pitcher fell off and bounced, hollowly, on the concrete floor. "Where does this cuckolding bitch live?"

"Dwayne?"

"Yes."

"The south shore."

"I say we go, right now, and teach him a lesson in gentle-manly behaviour. I say we go to his house, pull him out of bed, strip him naked, and packing-tape his cuckolding ass to a tree on Saint-Catherine. Let's go. Right now. It'll be an adventure! We deserve this."

"Well . . ."

"Come on, Toby. I'm wearing a suit, for fuck sakes! We can be gentleman vigilantes, righting wrongs. Like thieves in the night! Only not thieves."

"I'm really tired, guys."

Randall stood up and marched out of La Moufette. "Let's move!"

Something had malfunctioned in the PA system, and a sad violin song played, with Sarah Brightman singing along in an insistent vibrato. The ashen men of La Moufette looked around, searching for the source of this perversion. Garrett insisted on paying the bill.

"He started drinking pretty early. I'll get him home and put him to bed."

"Where is he living?"

"He has this house in Westpark, with Tracy, but he's staying with me for the moment. It's only been a couple of weeks since she asked him to leave."

"Why?"

"She doesn't love him anymore is the foremost reason."

Outside, Randall paced in the strip mall parking lot, shadowboxing with a limp that seemed to have worsened over the course of the evening.

"Hang back here a second," Garrett said to Toby. He approached his friend like a crocodile wrangler. He bent his knees, even though Randall was nearly a foot taller. "Let's just talk through this."

"I'm sick of talking. That's the trouble with us—talk, talk, talk. We get cuckolded and fired and kicked out of our own houses, where we pay the mortgage. The Frenchies make us call skunks *moufettes*. Where does it end?"

Garrett placed a hand on Randall, and Randall pulled away. He opened the door of the tow truck and started the diesel engine.

"You're drunk!" Garrett knocked on the window, and Randall unrolled it to listen. "Let's call a cab."

"I'm coming for you, Dwayne. Gaelic!" Randall closed the window and put the truck in gear.

Garrett opened the door of the red Cadillac. "You coming?"

"Not really comfortable with this, Garrett."

"We'll get him and I'll drive you right home."

Moments later, they were on boulevard des Sources, going north. Up ahead, the tow truck did not swerve. The smell of leather remained about the black cabin of the muscular sedan.

"I had a BMW until a couple of days ago."

The road thinned as they neared the riverfront park. Garrett breathed furiously through his nose and did not speak. Up ahead, the tow truck careened to the right and into a ditch. Then, with a jerk, it went left, crossed the road, and entered an open field. It bounced over a deep hole and puttered, slowly, into a glade. The trees stopped the truck. Randall opened the door, stepped out, limped about in a wide horseshoe, and collapsed, bawling.

Garrett stopped the Cadillac on the shoulder, and they walked across the field of low grass and wet leaves. Randall lay in the glow of the headlights reflecting off the old bark. The smell of fish and mould in the air was strangely pleasant. Beyond the trees, there were metallic cusses and whoops. Twenty years after Toby's high school graduation, the teenagers of Dollard continued to build illegal bonfires on the same beach, a wonder he had never seen, except from afar. Preppy or not, all Toby had ever wanted when he was seventeen was to roam through Dollard with the heavy metal boys and girls, smoking cigarettes and kissing in alleys, lighting fires on the beach and drinking lemon gin, and, just maybe, sliding his hand down the jeans of some troubled French girl.

He had met Randall and Garrett in grade ten, during mandatory gym class. Randall was uncoordinated, Garrett was fat, and Toby was both pimply and timid—fearful of breaking his nose or touching another boy's moist armpit during a flag football game or wrestling match. The teacher, a cynical bodybuilder and amateur cartographer from Switzerland named Urs, was entirely cooperative. Urs allowed Randall, Garrett, Toby, and three other misfits to play table tennis in a corner of the gymnasium.

In the riverfront park, Parc des Rapides-du-Cheval-Blanc, Garrett commanded Randall to get up.

Randall stayed in the weeds. "What are we supposed to do now?"

Garrett sighed, rolled up his slacks, and crawled on his bare knees to Randall. They muttered softly and embraced, in their business suits. Randall's silent weeping intensified, and he grabbed the back of Garrett's collar and grimaced. They bumped heads, awkward but tender. Toby walked away. The moon and stars were obliterated by the lights of the island.

Kids laughed on the other side of the trees, and the river rushed demurely over the rocks. It had been a wilder river in 1660, when Adam Dollard des Ormeaux, the twenty-five-year-old missionary, passed on his way to meet the Iroquois—who tortured, killed, and devoured him. In the intervening centuries, the men of Quebec had not significantly improved their prospects for success.

Toby returned to darkness and silence in the house on rue Collingwood, the smell of furnace and cigar smoke, steamed vegetables. Karen was asleep in her navy blue recliner, her head drooped forward like a wet flower. She wore pyjamas and a white terry cloth robe with a heart sewn on the breast.

She mumbled that she had just been dozing, not sleeping. The news had been on. News of tremors on the West Coast. They had discussed the big one. All those people, she said, punished for living somewhere pretty. She and Ed had honeymooned there, back when they were happy. "No suicides in the hopper." Karen's eyes remained closed as Toby led her down the hallway. "Not back then."

"Mom, shh."

"Just some mountains and some water, really, quite a lot of stucco, and rain, rain."

In the bedroom, the acrid smells of sleep and his father's gentle snores, the puff of a humidifier. Toby said good night and Karen felt her way past familiar landmarks—a table of presents for nobody in particular, purchased at Costco just in case an occasion were to arise, drugs and photographs on the dresser, a dirty clothes hamper. He whispered good night again and closed the door.

In the bathroom of his childhood, he was forced to wash his face with a bar of white soap and water, relics of a more unfortunate dermatological era. His sulphate- and petroleum-free cleansing gel with grapefruit seed extract and pure aromatic oils drawn from birch leaf, burdock, yarrow, and wild peppermint was back at the condominium.

Toby lay awake in his old bed, the door closed. Nothing of the city here: no engines or alarms, no sirens, no howls from the sidewalk. He plotted his reconciliation with Alicia: candygrams and promises and performances, running toward each other through a field of spring flowers. Rings on their fingers. But he returned and returned to the Oldsmobile. The silence, in the end, was too much. He opened his door and his parents' door, and fell asleep to the sound of his father breathing.

Six

Edward had always found uncommon meaning and pleasure in the Halloween season. The year after he had graduated from high school, 1966, Edward and two friends had spent the autumn and winter months backpacking through Mexico. They had spent late October and early November in Michoacán, where they had witnessed the Day of the Dead celebrations around Lake Pátzcuaro. It had been one of the defining moments of his life, a well of dinnertime stories, based around legends of the phantom-strewn lake and the sincere belief, among the people of Michoacán, that they were able to communicate heartily and happy with their lost friends and loved ones.

In the garage there were three grass-fronted black boxes, altars of Michoacán, handcrafted by Edward in 1983. The first and most elaborate represented Toby's paternal grandparents, whom he had never met. Both had drowned in a boating accident on Lake Memphrémagog when Edward was in his early twenties. Toby's grandfather, in the diorama, was depicted as a violin-playing skeleton; his grandmother, a dancer, lifting her skirt. Their black box was decorated with tiny items they appreciated: vodka and border collies, pot roasts and fishing poles. Edward had honoured Karen's parents in the second diorama: a pharmacist skeleton and a housewife skeleton in a long dress and apron. First her mother and then her father had passed away in a seniors' home on the south shore, after an occasionally fraught relationship with their son-in-law. Hence the blandness of their diorama. The third box was empty but for an Edward skeleton and a Karen skeleton standing over a cradle with a baby skeleton inside; this was Toby's younger brother, Ryan, who had succumbed to crib death three weeks after he was born.

Something about that backpacking trip in 1966 had convinced Edward that the personal mastery of death required an openness of spirit. Before he found Judaism, whenever Edward had wanted to feel close to God he spent time among his hand-carved wooden skeletons.

It was late in the afternoon. Toby's network of acquaintances and colleagues at the station and at other stations, even off the island, had been largely silent. They were polite when they answered their phones, and willing to listen as he outlined what he saw as injustices, but no one had called back— not socially and not professionally. Toby had already updated his C.V. and had phoned the television outlets in every major market in Canada. Not one of the station managers or human relations directors had expressed much hope, given the economy and the "failure of the business model."

Karen and Edward had taken the other family car, the Corolla, to bring soda cups to the Chien Chaud. Toby worked with what he considered to be an unfair hangover, placing the Halloween boxes in their traditional positions on the front lawn, setting up the spotlights and sugar skulls. Edward had built square vases into the tops of the boxes for dried marigolds.

To admire the finished product, Toby poured himself a glass of wine, the only reliable cure for a headache he knew. His BlackBerry and the bottle sat beside him on the front porch. Twenty-five kilometres away, in the southeast quadrant of downtown Montreal, someone was doing the five-o'clock weather update on the sidewalk.

The Corolla pulled up as Toby poured his second glass of wine. He took a proud sip. His father walked stiffly up the lawn, his eyes darker and larger than usual, his face thinner. He stood before the dioramas, in a pair of Bermuda shorts and a loose-fitting sweatshirt that said *Gap* on it.

Karen came up behind him in her faded yellow Chien Chaud apron. The hot dog mascot they had dreamed up together, Rover, waved and said, in a bubble, *allez, viens!*

"Oh look, Ed," Karen said, in the voice of an elementary-school teacher, "Toby put up your Halloween display."

The BlackBerry hummed and twirled on the concrete platform. Toby was frantic to pick it up, or at least look at the caller identification, but Edward was a lit match on the brown lawn. "The kids in the neighbourhood, Dad. They'd miss the skeletons so much. I just figured . . ."

Edward looked down at the third box, the baby Ryan box. All the nothingness in the baby Ryan box. He closed his eyes and tilted his head skyward. "Blessed are you, Lord, our

God, king of the universe, who bestows good things on the unworthy, and has bestowed on me every goodness."

"Superb." Karen climbed the porch steps and sat next to Toby, drank from his glass of wine. The BlackBerry buzzed and then settled, miserably, next to her thigh.

"Blessed are you," Edward said. "Blessed, blessed." Like a vintage movie monster, he whipped the marigolds to the lawn. He knocked the candy skull away.

Toby did not know whether to stop his father. A woman pushed her baby carriage past the house. Karen lifted her wine in greeting, then leaned back against the front door. His initial attack at an end, Edward stood before the diorama and breathed. Then he pressed his weight on the box and, with his stiff legs, broke the thin window in the front. He kicked the cradle over. Karen stood up and walked into the house with the wineglass and bottle.

One of the dioramas was now destroyed. Edward turned to the next one, said, "Blessed are you." The woman jogged her carriage away. Toby hopped up and wrapped his arms around his father's torso, where the fire had not touched him, and held him away. Edward reached back and elbowed Toby in the forehead. Toby released Edward and fell onto the cold grass, allowed his father to rip the flowers and skulls away, to break the thin window, to smash the skeletons.

Edward lumbered into the garage and returned with a mallet. When he was finished, the boxes were a black pile of scrap before the innocent hostas. Edward wiped the dust from his clothes and leaned heavily on the mallet, panting like a marathon runner. He looked across the street, over the roofs. Somewhere, a woodpecker went at a hollow tree. Edward walked up the steps, each a trial of unbendable limbs, and into the house.

There was a box of professional-quality garbage bags in the garage. Toby filled five of them with the detritus of the dioramas and left them near the cans at the sidewalk. He swept up the sawdust and glass as best he could and stood on the driveway with a broom in his hand. A flock of geese flew overhead, south to hope.

His missed phone call was from a woman with an unfamiliar, halting French voice. "Good day, Toby, it's Catherine. I'm calling to confirm our dinner at six thirty tonight. I hope it's all right that I can't leave a message in English."

On the second listen, he remembered: the woman whose heavy bicycle had been hit by the taxi. A skeleton from another life. He did not remember agreeing to a night or a time, and had assumed he would not see her again. Any number of people had his business card, had expressed an interest in coffee, or a drink, or dinner. It was five thirty, and this stranger expected him in an hour. He had planned to make the fish and risotto for his parents, but going out for dinner with anyone else, anywhere, was more attractive than spending one more minute on rue Collingwood. His car keys were in his pocket; without a word to his parents, he dashed to the Chevette.

After two nights in Dollard, he luxuriated in the candy warehouse, a physical extension of his personality. Toby had been delaying the call to his real estate agent, hoping a mad mogul of francophone media would save him from the numbers in his bank account. He now knew nothing would save him. Had anyone ever been saved? He showered and shaved, pulled his finest bottle of wine from the electric cave Alicia's parents had given him as a housewarming present, and set off to have dinner with a strange woman.

The route to Catherine's apartment took him past the Olympic Stadium, a grand void, a public error so profound and embarrassing that Edward and Karen Mushinsky had almost moved to Ontario after the 1976 Summer Games. Toby loved the Stade Olympique, as it represented all that was valiant and all that was tragic in his hometown. The stadium had been commissioned and designed with ambition, boldness, and that open-hearted search for particularity that had always made Montreal the only real city in Canada; yet it also represented the naïveté, the political corruption, and the spirit of ruin that hovered over the island.

Plans for Catherine's apartment building in Pie-IX had been inspired by the suburbs of Vladivostok. There was a nearby Dixie Lee, and the combination of wind currents and rotten luck filled the neighbourhood with the smell of fried chicken.

Traffic had been lighter than Toby had anticipated, and his stop at the florist had been uncommonly quick, so he sat in the Chevette and played with the AM radio receiver. A cassette tape was stuck in the deck. He pulled it out with two pens: *Love Gun* by KISS.

In the shower, to batter away at thoughts of his bank account, Toby had decided he would show Alicia. He had received many offers from women over the years—it came with the job—but he had always said no as nobly as he could manage. A gentleman may quietly have a mistress, to protect himself from the spiritual effects of a loveless marriage, but he does not philander.

He was startled by a knock on the passenger-side
window. Catherine was there, in a T-shirt and a pair of jeans.
He reached over and rolled down the window.

"*Que fais-tu?*"

"I was five minutes early."

Catherine stepped back from the door of the Chevette
and bowed and waved her arm in a gesture of welcome. The
small patch of grass in front of her building was decorated
with four non-traditional jack-o'-lanterns. They slumped
like toothless grandfathers at the end of Christmas dinner.
He handed her the bottle of wine and a bouquet of gerbera
daisies.

"They're from Fleuriste Marie Vermette."

"Oh."

"Do you know of it?"

"I don't really buy flowers."

"And I've been saving the wine. Châteauneuf-du-Pape,
2002."

She considered the bottle, without really reading the
label, then his suit. Toby had worn his grey Prada, his slim-
mest and most daring suit, definitely not appropriate for a
corporate event.

There was graffiti on the concrete stairwell leading up to
her suite; the front door of the building had not locked. "You
look beautiful, Catherine."

"Hey, you're lucky. I showered today." She opened the
door into a five-and-a-half with cracked parquet floors and
faux-wood walls decorated with concert posters for Georges
Brassens. The avocado appliances in the open kitchen
were older than Toby and Catherine. Toys and books were
stacked neatly yet randomly. There were abstract crayon

drawings tacked on lower quadrants of the walls and off-white cupboards, and the humming and clicking refrigerator was a tumult of baby and infant photographs. If there was a modern design element in the space, anything that declared "independent, thinking, desiring adult of the twenty-first century," Toby had not yet discovered it.

He developed a short list of illnesses he could immediately fake. "You're a mom."

"I am."

The pictures were of a boy with blond hair and softened versions of her features, a big mouth and big eyes. He had a solemn air. Among all the photos, Toby could not discover one in which the boy was smiling. "What's his name?"

"Hugo."

"Like the novelist."

"No."

"The designer?"

"No, no."

"The president of Venezuela?"

"It was his father's idea, to name him after the world's strongest man, Hugo Girard. He's almost three, Hugo." Catherine opened the wine.

"I've never heard of Hugo Girard."

"You're not Québécois."

Whenever Toby heard a proclamation like this, he was tempted to pull out his birth certificate. "Does your husband live here too?"

Catherine laughed. "He's dead."

"I'm sorry."

"And he was never my husband." Catherine bent down and peeked into the oven. There was a green salad on the counter, a plastic bottle of Italian dressing, and a wooden bowl of tortilla chips. A store-bought mini-tub of hummus.

Nausea was best, for a quick escape. People understood immediately if you complained of nausea.

"They said, first, it was some sort of Taliban attack. It was on the news and everything. Then one of the other men came home and told me he shot himself."

"That's terrible, Catherine."

"We didn't really like each other. He was an accident, Hugo. I thought one thing was happening, during sex, and I guess Hugo's dad thought another thing was happening. You know how that is?"

The only other person on the fridge, aside from Hugo and Catherine, was Georges Brassens. A large, full moustache on him, dark brown with flecks of grey. One of his eyebrows was higher than the other, expressing humour, perhaps, or impatience. A publicity photo. His brown eyes were serious, his ears massive. There was a Mediterranean tint to his skin.

Catherine poured the wine into one Burgundy glass and one sherry copita. She kept the copita for herself and they clinked. The station had paid for him to take a ten-week sommelier course some years ago, for *Toby a Gentleman*. If a camera had been on him now, he would have said that the wine was smoky, with hints of chocolate and eucalyptus.

"Is he here?"

"Who?"

"Hugo."

"He's staying at my neighbour's, one floor up. She's dropping him off early in the morning, though. She works at Subway, and they have to start baking the bread."

General stomach ailments worked almost as well: a bad cramp, with a hint that it could be appendicitis. The wine was open, though, and it was only getting better with each sip.

"It smells wonderful."

"Chicken terrine."

Catherine's red T-shirt was thin. The colour had begun to fade from years of machine washing and drying, and her nipples were visible. Toby had never allowed himself to hold on to a shirt for so long. He would have packaged it up for the diabetes society before it ever reached this state, but there was something admirable about it, poignant. He told Catherine so, and she stared as though his French had suddenly become incomprehensible. He finished his thought and she finished her glass in one gulp, apologized.

"I'm so nervous!"

"Don't be."

"I haven't had a proper date in so long. Since Hugo! When you helped me, I thought . . . I don't know what I was thinking."

"It's my pleasure to be here."

"Is it? Is it really?"

"Of course." Toby wanted to touch the shirt, so he did, in a safe region of her upper arm. Her skin was warm through the thin cotton. "Of course."

"Did you work today?" She pushed the chips and hummus toward him. "On TV?"

"I'm taking a break from TV for a while. I was out in Dollard, helping my parents."

"Dollard is so beautiful. So green and quiet."

Toby poured more wine for both of them. "I grew up there."

"Wow!" Catherine pressed play on the stereo system attached to the underside of the cupboard. George Brassens sang without a prelude, the guitar tuned high. There was a pleasing gargle in his voice. "*Je n'avais jamais ôté mon chapeau,*" he said, somewhere between singing and chatting.

"How long have you lived—"

"Shh."

Her fingers, resting on the white plastic counter, possessed the length and fineness of a more beautiful woman. Plain women, women like Catherine, wandered the world like phantoms. At the end of the song, she lowered her head and sighed.

"He's my father."

"Who's your father?"

She pointed to the stereo, then to the postcard photo on the fridge. A number of questions, ranging from the absurd to the serious, occurred to Toby. Instead of asking any of them, he drank some more wine. It really was spectacular. Perhaps his escape route would be excessive drunkenness. A cab home, then a quiet return in the morning for the Chevette.

"He's dead now too."

"My sincerest condolences."

"You know he died without heirs, my father?"

"Goodness."

"I know what you're thinking."

He had been thinking it must be difficult for the boy, for Hugo, to have a lunatic for a mother. "Oh?"

"But I know he's my father. I hear it in his voice, in the words between the words he sings. My father, he knows the secrets of my heart."

"You must be incredibly proud. He did really well for himself, Georges Brassens."

She began washing vegetables, swaying and singing along to the music, so Toby wandered out of the kitchen and into the hall, with a view into Hugo's bedroom. It was dark, but he could make out a live-action poster of a giraffe eating leaves from a branch. He sat on a grey chesterfield and flipped through a couple of photo albums as Catherine sang and cooked behind him. He had not seen a modern collection of printed photographs in some time, since the people of North America had gone digital. There was something here for a segment of *Toby a Gentleman:* What was the most intelligent and urbane way to steal a moment from the present tense without allowing it to spoil the actual experience? Catherine and a thick man of her height, with a moustache, hiking in the Laurentians. Pregnant Catherine. Catherine in the hospital with baby Hugo in her arms, the father leaning in with a fatigued smile. Shortly thereafter, the man disappeared from the album entirely. Hugo acquired more hair, grew taller, learned to walk, ran, blew birthday candles, built a tower of blocks, surrounded by other toddlers.

Candles were lit and the music of Georges Brassens was freshly chosen, turned down. The terrine was bland. The bottled vinaigrette was a travesty. Catherine opened a second bottle of wine, a cheap twist-off. She asked Toby about his upbringing, which he considered to be entirely normal—lower-middle-class suburban anglo Montreal. The Edward of his childhood was so different from the current Edward, so monumentally different, that as he described him Toby worried for the final third of his own life.

Catherine, it turned out, was adopted. She had tried unsuccessfully to locate the files related to her birth, and the provincial government had determined that the event had taken place outside an institution. The first sign of her was in windy Matane, on the Gaspé Peninsula, where she was abandoned at the Centre Hospitalier in 1972. This is where she was adopted, two years later, by a carpenter and a short-order cook with an interest in weaving by antique hand loom. She left Matane at sixteen and retained only the faintest contact with her adopted parents.

"My first memories are of my father."

"The carpenter?"

"My true father."

"George Brassens."

"I see us—there we are—walking along the beach together. He tells me of the creatures of the sea."

"What creatures?"

"He had a pipe, my father, and he wore rumpled business suits. A great artist, a hero, with business suits and a pipe and a moustache. I know where he lived, in the fifteenth arrondisement. They named a park after him. Once, I believe, it was an abattoir."

Something in her tone suggested he was not to ask about the carpenter and the short-order cook, who, in Toby's imagination, were desperately clad people of the nineteenth century. She spoke instead, with astonishing detail, of Georges Brassens.

He was born in Sète, on the Mediterranean coast, in 1921. So when Catherine was conceived, he was fifty. According to her research, he had arrived in Montreal in 1971 for a series of concerts. Catherine deduced that his romance with her startlingly beautiful but troubled mother had begun in

Quebec City in the autumn, for she was born the following summer. Georges Brassens was back in Paris by Christmas for a famous concert at the Cabaret Bobino. There was no official record of his return visits to North America, but Catherine had her memories.

Memories and ambitions. On top of her bookshelf there were several small manuscripts, bound in transparent plastic. For eighteen months she had saved, sacrificing pleasures that were her due and living in this dump, for a commissioned business plan. A consultant with an office on the thirty-fifth floor of a tower on University Street had written and researched it for her. All she needed to proceed was a partner.

"I know, I know. You're thinking, *She is not Chinese!* But that does not matter anymore, not in this country. The first time I tried it, the black tapioca through the wide, wide straw, I felt it deep inside me."

The title of the business plan was "Bullé Pour Moi: A New Model for Bubble Tea." Toby congratulated Catherine on her cleverness and flipped through the document. The effects of the red wine and the contours of her breasts, through the thin red T-shirt, distracted him. He could only pretend to read it. "Your own shop."

"A nationwide chain."

"You're a mogul."

She shrugged.

"How much do you need, to get started?"

"Half a million at least."

"You're almost there?"

"I have nine thousand. No collateral. And a student loan from my anthropology degree. I make eleven dollars an hour, at a bubble tea shop in the McGill ghetto."

She insisted that Toby take one of the plans, as the consultant had given her seven copies. Midway through "*La complainte des filles de joie,*" he learned that his instincts about Catherine had been wrong. She was a natural beauty of the highest order. Now that she was talking about bubble tea instead of Georges Brassens, she approached normal. The rule about single mothers was clear: Do not hurt them. But he recognized when someone had feelings for him. Catherine did not have feelings for him. She had a scheme.

Her scheme was his scheme: a one-night stand. His first ever. She had not been with a man since the birth of her son. He wore the green hat. The second bottle of wine was nearly finished, and Toby could not imagine learning anything else about Georges Brassens or bubble tea that was remotely illuminating, so he slid his chair around the table and kissed Catherine. It took some adjustments. They apologized to each other for uncomfortable positions, and Toby burned his forearm, mildly, on one of the candles. Catherine had fuller lips than Alicia, and she was hostile with her tongue. By the end of the album, they were in Catherine's bedroom.

Toby knew the right clothes to wear on every occasion, the correct gifts to give, the proper tone of a congratulatory note, the ideal physical and emotional architecture of a dinner party, a wedding, a funeral. The bedroom, however, he had always considered the only room in life beyond manners and etiquette—intellectually, at least. Though he had never built a segment of *Toby a Gentleman* around it, he considered sex the one activity during which selfish impulses, bad language, social experimentation, and carelessness about bodily fluids made life more and not less enchanting.

Sex with Alicia had been a visual feast, and she had learned to heighten and enhance Toby's experience by ensuring that the lights—preferably a lamp—were always on and by writhing about like a trapped mermaid. Her preferred mode of foreplay was the erotic massage, not because it felt good but because her skin glistened. It was never an ecstatic experience, however, as Alicia valued control far more than anything else in her life; the spirit of surrender was something she could only manufacture. Despite her naughty talk, Alicia was, at heart, a conservative. And so was he.

Catherine cried out in apparent agony and in the next moment announced that she had never known pleasure so acute and explosive. She licked him, head-butted him, commanded him to take her like a Viking, asked if she could be upside down, so the blood would rush to her brain during orgasm; she growled and roared and slapped him on the face, twice. She pulled him into the shower so they could do it with the water running. When Toby begged for sleep, she shouted insults at his penis.

Eventually, she grew tired. Toby lay in one of the wet spots, not only exhausted but regretful that he had gone thirty-seven years without a night like this. Of all the women on the island of Montreal, he had chosen perfectly for his first and last one-night stand. The idea struck him with such force that he said it aloud before really thinking about it. Luckily, Catherine was asleep.

He awoke in the dim light of an overcast morning to the muffled sounds of francophone rock from a neighbouring suite. The Québécois were a sophisticated and avant-garde people, brilliant with circuses and abstract theatre, but utterly hopeless with a guitar. He was alone in the bed, which smelled of the previous evening's activities and also, faintly, of Dixie Lee fried chicken. There were dead bugs in the orange base of the light fixture above, cobwebs in the corner of the ceiling.

In the bathroom, plump with the humidity of a recent shower, Toby discovered and swallowed some Aspirin. He wrapped a towel around himself and walked out into the kitchen. No sign of Catherine.

The only cereal in the cupboard was Raisin Bran. Toby splashed milk on it and, as Catherine didn't seem to subscribe to a newspaper, read the back of the box in both of Canada's official languages. The table was still covered in the aromatic remains of their dinner, so he sat on the couch with his bowl. He was in the midst of considering the nine essential nutrients—why exactly nine?—when he heard a coo from the hall. The Aspirin had not yet completed its work, and his entire body thumped. Hugo's bedroom door was open; it had not occurred to Toby that Catherine had sneaked into bed with her son, who would have been delivered by the upstairs neighbour some hours ago.

Another coo, a whine from the direction of the child's room.

Toby squeezed the cereal box.

"*Maman?*"

He stood up and crept around the corner, peeked into Hugo's bedroom like a sniper. It would not do to have the boy see him. There was a layer of aluminum foil over the window, so it remained dark. Cracks in the foil provided just enough light for him to see that Catherine was not in bed with her son. She was not on the floor or in the rocking chair. Toby had been bracing himself on a white IKEA bookshelf, and as it shifted to the right so did he.

"*Ma.*" The boy spotted Toby and sat up on his bed. "*Ma!*"
"*Bonjour.*"

Hugo backed into the corner where bed met wall and began to scream. Toby sprinted into Catherine's bedroom and wrestled into his suit. He opened the window wide enough to crawl out and hop to the fire escape. He folded his tie into the inside pocket of his jacket and pulled the chair over. The trick was to slither out the window without ripping his second suit in a week. Hugo continued to cry. Toby had no idea what to do with a crying child, and Catherine had not left instructions.

"Don't worry, Hugo," Toby called out, in French. "*Maman* will be back in a minute." He stood on the chair, looked out at the gunmetal morning. A raccoon was at the bottom of the fire escape, plucking at an open pizza box. Was it possible that, in a half-conscious state of grace, Toby had agreed to babysit the boy for an hour?

He crept back into the hall and peeked inside the room again. Hugo fell back into a defensive position, arms and legs in the air, and said, "*Non, non, non.*"

Touching the boy at this point would have been illegal. Toby crawled into the bedroom, turned on the lamp, and sat on the floor. Hugo shrieked and covered his eyes. In nature documentaries, animals tend to approach one another with their necks and bellies exposed to display a lack of aggressive intent. So Toby sat with his arms behind him and said, every few minutes, "Shh," in the softest voice he could muster. He hummed the only French children's song he knew, "*Frère Jacques.*" On the fifth go-round, it occurred to him that it might actually be about death.

Eventually, Hugo stopped crying. He sat up on his bed and stared at Toby in an expressionless manner. "*Maman,*" he had said, but that didn't mean he could talk. Could almost-three-year-olds talk?

"My name is Toby." Speaking simple French to a child, he was reminded of the cassette tapes his teachers played to the class in elementary school. "I am your mom's friend."

Hugo wailed again, just once, and lifted a book as a shield. *Le chat chapeauté,* a translation of *The Cat in the Hat.*

"Would you like me to read that to you? I would enjoy it immensely."

Hugo sneaked under the covers and kicked, aimlessly, until he knocked a glass of water off his bedside table and directly onto Toby's exposed neck and belly. Much of the water soaked into his crotch. It was just after eight in the morning. Toby saw a day of this stretching before him, stuck in a rabbit warren, smelling of sex and chicken, with a violently disturbed two-year-old. While he had peers with children, he had always been the adult they avoided. The stubborn ones, who saw a challenge in him, would torment Toby until he performed a lacklustre horsey ride or perhaps an impromptu puppet show, but everyone—including the child—tended to see this as a stunt.

A stalemate was reached. Hugo remained under the covers, peeking out from time to time to make sure Toby had not advanced on him. At first, when he saw the boy's eyes, Toby would wave or nod his head or say something innocuous like "*Salut,*" but this only served to inflame Hugo.

Half an hour passed in silence, though it felt like a full morning of peeking and looking away and smelling stale urine. When the front door of the apartment suddenly opened, they raced to the bedroom door. Toby just about knocked the boy to the parquet floor as they rounded the corner. They rushed into what served as the salon, and Hugo broke into tears again and jumped into his mother's arms.

"You're awake, my darling, awake."

Toby was entirely dressed but for his shoes, so he put them on as mother and son became reacquainted. The boy clung to her like a gibbon.

"Where're you going?"

"Home. Then to Dollard. Then I don't know. Saskatchewan."

"I went out shopping for breakfast. I got bacon."

"Thank you again, Catherine, for a bewitching evening. But I really must go."

She did not seem fazed by this. "Are you and Toby friends now?" Her voice raised an octave when she spoke to her son. "Good buddies?"

"Hugo was terrified, which seems natural. He was left alone with a stranger."

"It was just a few minutes."

"Again, thank you for last night. It was extraordinary." Toby saluted on his way out the door. "And Hugo, good luck to you, my handsome young friend."

Seven

Toby spent three hours scrubbing and cleaning the condominium for a parade of men and women whose most pressing problem, for the moment, was deciding how exactly to spend $450,000. He phoned his real estate agent, a dangerously thin woman he had interviewed for a recent segment of *Toby a Gentleman* on how to remain poised in the midst of financial calamity.

"You're trading up?" she said.

"I can answer that in a variety of ways."

"This is a terrific time to buy, Toby."

"Not to sell?"

"As long as you stay in the market. You're staying in the market. Good lord, tell me you're not fleeing the market."

"I'm not fleeing the market."

"Never flee a down market."

A night of drinking red wine and the stress of babysitting conspired with the cleaning supplies to give him an eye-twisting headache shortly after noon. He boiled a pot of chamomile tea, tried to drink a mug of it, and lay on the chesterfield. Thirty-seven was so close to forty, and forty was practically fifty, if you lay on the couch with chamomile tea and a hangover and really thought about it. He had grey and thinning hair. The skin on his neck was softening. The stock market crash had not affected him because he owned no stock. To be unemployed and unemployable at this age was his most potent nightmare—but it no longer fit the precise definition of a nightmare because he was actually living it. He lay on the chesterfield and came up with a new most-potent nightmare: to be unemployed and unemployable at practically fifty with a palsy that comes out of nowhere and makes one side of your face sag.

Edward had taken the train into Montreal to have dead skin scraped and sluiced from his burns, and had been calling to ask Toby to meet him for a late lunch. To avoid thinking about himself any longer—the possibility that a man without a career was not a man at all—Toby phoned Edward back and arranged to meet him a few blocks south of the hospital.

The bistro was an imperfect choice. Toby had remembered it from his student days as relaxed and affordable, with thrift-store art on the walls and far too much smoke in the air. But the boom-economy sandwich years had inspired an unearned air of formality and tradition in the small room, and several more tables had been squeezed in. The server wore a black polyester suit and tie. A small towel with a Kilkenny ale logo was draped over his arm to complete the picture of near sophistication. It was enough to intimidate Edward, who had worn sweatpants and a black Jazz Fest 1997 T-shirt.

"Everyone's staring at me."

"No they aren't, Dad. But you really shouldn't leave the house in sweatpants."

"I'm a burn victim."

"There is really no excuse. None exists. Maybe exercising—maybe."

Toby had discovered a book called *Birds of Southern Quebec* as he had cleaned, a gift from the president of the Regroupement Québec Oiseaux, whom he had interviewed while filling in for Leonard, the Madman in the Morning. He presented it to his father while they waited for the server.

"What am I supposed to do with this?"

"It's better than praying and taking drugs combined, they say."

"Who says? Birdwatchers? They're hardly neutral." Edward flipped through the book, looking at the colour photographs and illustrations. "I understand birdwatching. I just don't *understand* it."

The server arrived with a basket of sliced baguette, a pitcher of water, and a booming "*Bonjour.*" Edward ordered a litre of house red wine before Toby could warn him against it. If he were capable of destroying his beloved Day of the Dead dioramas while quoting from religious texts, who knows what he might do after two or three glasses of Caballero de Chile.

Edward closed the book. "I'll take a whack at watching birds."

The bistro was half-full of sleepy graduate students and various quasi-professionals in blazers and jeans. None of the men wore ties, yet all but one of the women had scarves, which briefly meant something to Toby. The conversations around them were exactly the way Toby would have liked his relationship with his parents to be: light, effortless, uncomplicated, occasionally ironic. Edward sat like an apprentice spy whose cover has been blown.

"Nothing came of all those resumés I sent out."

"Idiots."

"I picked sort of a terrible time to destroy my life. Economically speaking."

"Problems can be opportunities, they say."

"The real estate agent thinks I'll get four-fifty for the condo."

"How much did you pay?"

"Three-ninety. But I put about fifty thousand into it."

"You could lose money."

"I could."

"Only a Mushinsky."

The wine arrived in a carafe that was once a milk bottle. Toby raised his glass but struggled to find an appropriate toast. He proposed one to a general improvement of conditions. They drank to "anything will do."

"Great wine," said Edward.

It was not great wine.

"Are you ready to order lunch?" Toby asked.

"I'm not hungry."

"But we're out for lunch. Historically, at lunch, people—"

"I wanted to see you, without your mom."

Toby worried that his father wanted to speak to him about moving into the house in Dollard as a sort of long-term caregiver, so he looked around quickly to see if anyone was watching. No one was, so he took a long drink of his inferior wine. "All right."

"Something's wrong with me," Edward said with the uncommon calm in his voice that Toby remembered from the neighbour's lawn on the night of the fire. "Something's wrong with me, inside."

"Nothing's wrong with you."

The server returned and, with his put-on Parisian accent, asked for their orders. Toby chose a goat cheese salad for himself and a bowl of soup for Edward, who either didn't notice or didn't understand. When they were alone again, Edward said, "Don't pretend. You know."

"I don't know anything."

"You were there."

"I was where?"

"You're playing stupid."

"Evidence clearly shows that I *am* stupid."

"We're going bankrupt."

"No, you aren't, Dad."

"But I won't be here to see it through."

"Where are you going?"

"I'll need you to take care of your mom."

"Where are you going?"

"Listen to me." Edward placed his bandaged hand on Toby's. "Look at me and listen to me very carefully. I want you to take care of your mom."

"Dad."

"I want you to fall in love properly, and get married. You need a child to understand life. I know you think you understand everything, but you don't. You don't understand anything yet."

"What is this?"

"And make your name Mushinsky again, one of these days. That hurt me very much, as you know, and I worry that it hurts you. Deep inside. Woody Allen's real name is Konigsberg, and I think the reason his movies aren't for shit anymore is that it rotted him, inside, to be untruthful."

Edward's voice was clear and calm, but too loud and

rising. Toby looked around to see if anyone had noticed.

"You can't be untruthful. Are you listening?"

"No."

"You owe it to me to listen."

"I'll listen to anything about birdwatching or the Chien Chaud, your treatment today, retirement plans. Normal things. But this . . ."

"I'll ask you to look for God."

"Come on."

"If you don't find Him, that's fine. It's the process, I've learned, that's good for you. Rabbi Orlovsky will help. I've already spoken to him about your struggle."

"What struggle?"

"There is no out. There is only the in."

"I'm not Jewish, Dad."

"Just like Woody Allen."

Toby grabbed *Birds of Southern Quebec* with his free hand, as though it were a root that might save him from sliding down an escarpment. Edward pulled it back.

"I've been memorizing things before bed. 'Speak to Him thou for He hears, and Spirit with Spirit can meet—Closer is He than breathing, and nearer than hands and feet.'"

"You're a little loud."

"'Nearer than hands and feet.'"

Toby's heart beat hotly and crookedly in his chest, as it had in the hospital on the night of the accident. The wine was not working.

"One more thing."

"No more things. Please."

The server returned to the table to fill their glasses. He looked down at their hands, Edward's on Toby's, and spent a moment regarding Edward's attire. Toby had worn the Prada again, because only Catherine had seen him in it. He looked up at the lingering server. "*Un problème?*"

"*Pas du tout, Monsieur.*" The server backed away.

Toby took another long drink of his wine and spoke quietly. "There's nothing wrong with you, Dad. Absolutely nothing that birdwatching can't fix. Birdwatching or golf. And you aren't going anywhere."

Edward leaned over the table. "Get Steve Bancroft."

"Pardon?"

"You heard me."

"Get?"

"Get him. He's been coming into the shops the last while. It can only mean one thing." The server propped open the bistro door to let in some air. The air helped. "Let me tell you about the fire."

"You know what, Dad? I don't want to hear about the fire."

"I don't care what you *want*. We're miles past that now." Edward had barked "want" and had shouted the rest. Everyone in the bistro, including the server and the woman behind the bar, looked at them. "There's a crust around us, all around us. And I broke through. Everything else, all of this, all these people, these burns, this restaurant, it's nothing. It's an illusion. I'm after the truth now, before I go. The core of things." Edward looked about. "Drink up, you people. Drink your fucking wine. I'm talking to my son."

It was as though a wave had crashed in the restaurant and they were all waiting for the water to leave. Carrying an empty champagne bottle, the server looked around, perhaps for physical support, as he approached the table, new sweat on his forehead.

"Let's go, Dad," said Toby.

"I'm not going anywhere. We've got wine still."

"We'll get some more on the way home."

"No!"

"You're scaring these people."

Edward looked around, and his eyes filled with tears. He opened his mouth slowly, in what seemed at first a yawn. It was a silent cry. His tongue was stained purple by the Caballero. Toby walked around the table and helped his father up. He apologized to the server and to the diners. "*Mon père est malade,*" he said. "He's really sick, all right?" Toby pulled out his wallet to pay for the wine and the food they had ordered, but the server, emboldened by their retreat, shooed them away.

"*Allez-y,*" he said, raising his bottle.

Edward apologized all the way to the car, and in the car, and with each apology Toby assured him that he need not worry. It was nothing, really. Soon enough, it really was nothing. Edward flipped through *Birds of Southern Quebec* and decided he would focus on ducks, for starters.

Toby's plan had been to drive immediately back to the condominium, but Karen drew him into the basement.

"What happened today?"

"Nothing."

"Your dad's face is a mess. From crying?"

"He was a bit off in the restaurant."

Karen crossed her arms and sat in front of the television. It was cold in the basement, and it smelled as though the carpet had not been vacuumed in three or four years. "This is the rest of my life. Twenty years, or more, of looking after a . . . I don't even know what to call it."

"This is just a phase, Mom."

"You know that isn't true."

"I'm not a psychiatrist."

"You'd prefer not to discuss your father."

"No, no. Let's talk. Please."

Karen expelled a sigh and a sarcastic chuckle at once. "You're heading back to Montreal tonight?"

"I am."

"Well, here's the thing. Nahla's pregnant, so—"

It no longer bothered Toby that his mother expected him to know everyone in her life by first name, even though he had not lived in Dollard in over ten years. "And Nahla is?"

"Nahla. Nahla! From the Dollard location. She just told me, but I knew. I could tell. She's got appointments tomorrow afternoon, the first ultrasound. I was hoping you could cover."

"You want me to work at the Chien Chaud?"

"I know it's beneath you. It's an insult, really. But I have to be at the bank."

"Dad can't do it?"

Karen pulled her hair out of its bun.

"Just tomorrow, Mom?"

"I promise."

Toby did not want his parents to see him doing it, so he flopped in the basement to watch Century—Century News, two simulcast American forensic cop dramas, infomercials, and all-night movies about cops. Alicia and his former co-workers remained special in the only way we can be special, as images replicated exponentially through a marketplace, while he had become normal. The deathly fact of his normalness echoed in his parents' basement. His girl showed up at least twice an hour, promoting herself and her show in a navy suit that worked brilliantly with her eyes, her hair, her skin and the light. He knew the suit. They had been together the summer afternoon she found it, at Max Mara. Later that same soft day, Toby made a Waldorf salad and Alicia swiped one of her dad's serious bottles of wine, and they walked up to King George Park for a picnic dinner. They chatted about a move to Toronto and European vacations they might take, the possibility of children. Several passersby recognized them and complimented them on their work. It was sunny and hot, but not too hot, and the wind did not bother them. After dark, they went to a party for a gay cabinet minister in Old Montreal, and a sweaty, coked-up man with a startling birthmark on his forehead asked Toby if he might join the party one day and run. He was handsome and bilingual, he had "name rec," he had certain attachments to money. On the way home in the cab that night, Toby felt as though he were bursting from himself, as though his skin and bones could not hold him.

When he was sure his parents had fallen asleep, Toby taped one of Alicia's promos and abused himself as he watched it forward and backward in slow motion. Then he went upstairs for some junk food, but all he could find were Fig Newtons.

Shortly after two in the morning, a *Toby a Gentleman* segment rotated through a commercial break, and there he was. The man he knew. He cried a little and stopped eating the Fig Newtons and drifted in and out of sleep with the television on. He awoke to the echo of door-knocking and the theme music for the lunchtime news. His neck was sore. He waited for his parents' footsteps, living room to front door, but there were none. The knocking continued, so he walked slowly up the stairs.

Through the peephole, he saw Catherine Brassens and Hugo. She was in a red dress, with a white scarf. She wore eye makeup and carried a large bag: a diaper bag. The boy wore a tie-dyed sweatshirt with *Ladykiller*, backwards *r*, in giant white lettering.

"I heard something," she said to Hugo.

Toby examined himself in the mirror near the door and fluffed up the hair at the top of his head to enhance the illusion of fullness. His suit was in exemplary condition, despite plenty of rolling about on the chesterfield. But Catherine and Hugo had just seen him in it. He rushed downstairs to change out of the Prada and into his Paul Smith, climbed back up the stairs, gathered his breath and his dignity, and opened the door.

"Hello, Catherine. Hugo."

"It's super-cool to see you again. Isn't it, Hugo?" She chewed at a fingernail, and they both looked at the boy. "No one was home at your condominium. This was the only Mushinsky in the Dollard phone book, so I took a chance."

"And I'm so delighted you did. Would you like to come in for a cup of coffee?"

She asked Hugo. "What do you think?"

The boy said nothing. Something in his little face suggested that he was embarrassed for them both. There was a tiny witch on a broom hanging from a nail near the house number—427—that Edward had not destroyed in his anti-Halloween fury. Hugo reached forward, touched the witch's hat.

Again the fridge was empty. Toby made coffee and determined, upon tasting it, that he would cart his espresso maker to Dollard from the condo that same evening.

Since the moment he had granted her entrance, Catherine had not stopped talking. A crash on the autoroute, controversial claims about Georges Brassens's sexuality in the latest biography, this hormone-twisting chemical they had discovered in baby bottles and cans of soda, Hugo's bum rash, a Québécois hip hop artist she had actually dated in high school, the latest edition of *Tout le monde en parle*. This sort of behaviour was common in the television industry, especially at the end of the day, when staff gathered for drinks. It was usually induced by cocaine, but Toby suspected it also had something to do with profound loneliness. All the while his mother was talking, Hugo swished the milk around in his glass as though it were a rare Bordeaux.

Cod was the last thing Toby wanted to eat for breakfast, but if he didn't do something with the fish soon, it would pass the smell threshold and devour all of Dollard-des-Ormeaux. He cooked and, along with Hugo, ignored Catherine. Every time Toby turned away from the stove, he made eye contact with the handsome boy and wondered two things: How was it, really, to live with a woman like this? And how would he get rid of them?

He served the food at a quarter to one, and she came to the point. "I was wondering if you could look after Hugo for a couple of hours this afternoon."

The boy had already started eating. There was a booster pillow on the chair, but even so, the table was level with his chin. Toby had given him the smallest salad fork in the drawer, but it was too big. At least a half of every forkful fell on Hugo's Ladykiller sweatshirt or on the floor.

"You know, I'd love that. I so would. But I'm helping my mom at her store this afternoon."

"Why not bring him?"

"It's a hot dog shop."

"Kids love hot dogs." Like every other francophone on the island, she called them hot dogs—*ot dog-uh*—not *chiens chauds*. "Don't you love hot dogs, Hugo?"

The boy was not deaf. He just preferred not to speak, or look up when addressed, or smile, or play, or anything else Toby accepted as normal behaviour. "Hugo doesn't talk?"

"He chooses not to."

"Can you say something for me, Hugo?"

Hugo lifted a salad-fork full of fish to his mouth and sniffed it.

"I like children. I like Hugo. But to be perfectly honest, Catherine, I have no experience as a babysitter. If I weren't working at my parents' shop, maybe."

"You'll hardly notice him."

"Who usually looks after Hugo when you aren't able?"

"Friends. But they were all busy. It's an opportunity to get to know him."

Toby had already determined never to see her again. "I'm honoured that you would think of me, Catherine. But I'm sorry. We're strangers. It's not at all appropriate."

"We were strangers a couple of nights ago, but that didn't stop you from fucking me."

At the vulgarity, a crucial tendon in Toby's left hand failed and he dropped his fork on the table. Hugo seemed not to have heard, or to have noticed, the word. The moment she and her son finished their lunch, Toby would ask them to leave. He would, very quietly, suggest to Catherine that she never come back here again. In his deeper regions, where he responded to his own secret emergencies, Toby wanted to plop the boy in front of a television station devoted to educational cartoons and fuck his mother again.

Catherine began to cry. Her tears had a disastrous effect on her eye makeup, so Toby directed her to the bathroom and returned to the table. Hugo looked longingly in the direction his mother had gone.

"You don't want to spend the afternoon at a hot dog shop, do you?"

Hugo turned to Toby, blinked.

"I'm a man you don't know. You're supposed to avoid people like me."

The boy had finished all of his fish and most of the risotto.

"You want something more to drink? Water? Another milk?"

A nod, the gentlest and slightest nod in the history of communication, at the word "milk." So Toby poured half a glass for Hugo, and they sat together in silence until Catherine reappeared.

"I'll pay you. How about that?"

"No."

She had not reapplied the makeup. There were faint freckles on the bridge of her nose that he had not yet noticed. "I'll do anything, Toby. What do you want me to do?"

"To go have a lovely day with your son, I suppose."

"If he's not with you, I'll leave him in the car for two hours. Strapped into his seat. You want that? Maybe he learns how to get out, and he opens the door and runs into traffic. Does that sound like a good idea to you? It sounds monstrous to me. Monstrous."

The flagship family hot dog shop was tucked into an old neighbourhood corner without ample parking, a relic of 1960s Dollard, when people still used sidewalks. It was clean inside, even after Toby had switched on the fluorescent lights. The white and black menu sign above the counter, first acquired in 1984 with the participation of the RC Cola company, was the only surface of the store that cried out for a mop.

Nahla, a pregnant woman in a plain black dress and a hijab, whispered advice and suggestions to him before she jetted off for her ultrasound. The soda machine was new, and his mother had engaged in some creative cost-cutting measures, so it was fortunate that Nahla had a few minutes to train him. Most other rituals returned immediately, bursting with the sounds, smells, and recollections of his teen years; all those girls he feared and adored with teased-up hair and Calvin Klein perfume who came into Le Chien Chaud for strawberry milkshakes. For the post-lunch afternoon shift, she suggested he pull only ten dogs out of the freezer. Ten seemed scant, a mistake, but Nahla insisted. Toby placed them on the warmer and brewed coffee in a machine Karen had purchased in 1974 from a Baron de Burger that had gone into receivership; the heating coils inside the machine looked as though jackals had been gnawing on them.

Catherine wrote a mini instruction manual on a sheet of paper she had ripped out of her address book. Toby fashioned a small apron out of a tea towel and some duct tape, and handed it to the boy. Hugo held out his hand as though he were receiving a giant insect. It seemed excessive, all the kissing and hugging and baby-talking, but Toby was unfamiliar with the rituals of parenting in the twenty-first century. Catherine planted one on Toby's mouth and dis-

creetly grabbed his behind, cried a little bit, and departed.
It wasn't until she was in her car and away that Hugo ran
for her.

The boy screamed and jumped at the window, pounded
on the glass. When he could not open the heavy door, Hugo
threw himself onto the white tile floor and shouted nonsense
words, kicked and straightened and rolled. He ripped off
his duct-tape apron and tossed it at the wall. Two men in
coveralls and workboots entered the store and looked down
at Hugo; before Toby could convince them that the tantrum
would soon end, they exited again. It was two thirty.

When a moment of silence arrived, Toby offered Hugo
some apple juice. The boy eyed it suspiciously, nodded, and
sat at one of the four tables with the little plastic bottle and
a straw. He slurped occasionally. Toby sat across from him,
and they held eye contact much longer than allowed by polite
society. This took them to two forty-five.

It was at this point that Toby began to notice the smell.
No one had yet entered the store, save for the two men in
coveralls, but eventually someone in Dollard-des-Ormeaux
would crave a hot dog. According to Catherine's note, there
were diapers and wipes in the bag. There were no further
instructions. He waited as long as he could, hoping Catherine
might arrive early. But the smell advanced.

"Would you like me to change your diaper?"

Hugo shook his head.

"It's unhealthy, I would imagine, to sit and stew in it. It
doesn't hurt or chafe?"

Again, he shook his head.

"Do you do it on the floor or what?"

Hugo looked out the window. "*Maman.*"

"She'll be back soon, but not soon enough, I'm afraid."
Toby worried that the moment he stepped into the washroom
with the boy, a rush of hungry teenagers would walk into the
shop. Or worse, the health inspector. He phoned home to see
if Edward and Karen had returned. They had not.

The public washroom in Le Chien Chaud was equipped
with a changing table that unfolded from the wall. Toby
propped the door open for psychological access to the outside
world. "Are you ready?"

Hugo shook his head.

"I don't really know how to do this. So let's be a team.
If I do something wrong, let me know, please?"

The boy ran out of the washroom and into the restaurant, where he hugged a garbage can. It took several minutes to extract him from the can, as Toby worked through a
number of strategies: asking, then begging, then gently pulling, then less gently pulling, then yanking. He carted Hugo to
the moulded plastic table in the washroom and made certain
the boy was steady. To take Hugo's attention off the unpleas-
antness, Toby pulled a plush panda out of the diaper bag and
bestowed it upon him. Hugo hugged the panda and looked
vacantly up at the fluorescent lights of the men's washroom.

"I'm going to take off your pants now, is that all right?"

No response, so Toby removed them. Winnie the Pooh
and Tigger were imprinted on the front of the diaper, having
a hell of a time with some bees. It lent an atmosphere of levity
to the proceedings.

"It can't be so bad, right, if Winnie the Pooh's involved?"

Hugo swallowed.

Toby unfastened the first of the Velcro strips, and
the smell roared through him. He endeavoured to breathe

through his mouth, but the knowledge that he was inhaling the smell unfiltered was fouler than the odour itself. Toby abandoned the boy on the table for a moment as he walked in a circle to psych himself up, a boxer who knew he was outmatched by the fiend in the ring.

The bells above the front door sounded, and a woman in a beige trench coat walked into the shop. Toby caught only a glimpse of her as she walked straight to the counter. "*Un instant, s'il vous plaît,*" Toby shouted. "I'll be right there."

One had to move swiftly. Toby unfastened the other side of the diaper, and it opened heavily, with an amount of shit that seemed more fitting of a grizzly bear than a two-year-old boy. Hugo shifted up on the change table, to perform some feat with the panda, and a portion of the warm shit rolled out of the diaper and into Toby's hand. Toby unconsciously flicked it out of his hand and, briefly, onto his Paul Smith pants. "No!" he shouted, startling Hugo, who turned onto his front and struggled to his feet. The Lady Killer sweatshirt dangled to its natural length, touching the chunks that had attached themselves to the boy's bottom. Toby lifted the boy off the table and onto the floor while he washed his hands, splashed water on his pants, and gagged in the sink. Hugo scampered out the washroom door. "No, Hugo!"

Toby caught up with the boy in front of the condiment station, busily cleaning himself with the panda.

The woman in the trench coat leaned on the counter as though Hugo were a grenade that might go off at any moment. She wore plastic-framed eyeglasses with a beaded strap, in case she wanted to take them off and let them dangle.

"I'm sorry, Madame," he said. "This isn't at all normal."

"No," she said.

"Do you have children?"

"No."

"I'll serve you in just a moment. I do appreciate your patience."

It was three fifteen. Toby decided that as soon as Catherine arrived to pick up her son, he would attack her with the shitty panda. He spoke sweetly to the boy, who valiantly tried to escape. Toby carried him back into the washroom, closed the door, and removed all of his clothes. The dirty diaper lay on the corner of the change table, threatening to fall off, so Toby snatched it up and, without thinking, tossed it into the toilet. While Toby filled the sink with warm water, Hugo stopped crying long enough to pull the flush handle.

"No!"

"No!" said Hugo.

Toby lowered the boy into the sink water and splashed the shit off him. Hugo kicked at first and then settled in, defeated. It seemed unhygienic to allow the boy to rest in the water, as he was immediately surrounded by floating debris. So Toby unstopped the water, let it drain, and repeated the process three times. Then he held Hugo under the hand dryer, which was at first funny to the boy and then a form of torture. The pants had escaped shitless and there was, luckily, an extra shirt in the diaper bag.

By the time they emerged from the washroom, the customer had departed. Toby plunged the toilet. When the diaper reappeared, he gagged again, an unfamiliar honking noise escaped from him. He tried to fish the diaper out of the discoloured water with a glove fashioned from toilet paper, but it was one-ply and quickly dissolved. Toby threw the diaper into the garbage with the Lady Killer sweatshirt, wrapped the shit-stained panda in a spare diaper, washed his arms as best he could, and walked into the shop to discover Hugo on a chair, eating the sauerkraut from the condiment table.

It was nearly four o'clock. Toby removed his Chien Chaud apron and collapsed into one of the chairs. He quietly watched Hugo eat sauerkraut, and then chopped onions and tomatoes. At ten after four he walked to the window and looked out for some sign of Catherine's white Honda Civic. At four thirty he made a hot dog for the boy, with plenty of sauerkraut, chopped onions, and tomatoes, and began dialling the number she had left. The dinner rush—seven people—began at five o'clock. His replacement, a teenager named Rick, arrived to relieve him at five thirty.

"Is this your kid?"

"No."

"Huh."

Toby phoned Catherine again and left another message, then phoned home. Obviously, her emergency was more serious than she had anticipated, so Toby hoped to leave the boy with Edward and Karen while he drove into Montreal. No answer. And again, no answer on Catherine's phone. He paced. He asked Hugo if he knew where his mother might have gone. The boy stared.

"Um, man," said Rick. "Is there anything I can help with?"

"It's polite of you to ask, Rick."

Rick did not feel comfortable babysitting Hugo while Toby drove into Montreal to meet his real estate agent, despite assurances that Hugo had just shit himself and probably wouldn't shit again for at least a couple of hours. Toby bundled the boy up and led him outside to the Chevette. He was so small that the shoulder belt would have strangled him in a head-on collision, so Rick hunted through the shop and found seven bungee cords in the storage room. Together they strapped the boy to the front seat.

Toby drove cautiously down the autoroute until someone in a minivan cut him off. Sweat burst from every one of his pores. He turned off onto Saint-Laurent and pulled into the parking lot of the Sears at Place Vertu. Hugo would not take his hand, and he screamed when Toby tried to pick him up, so to protect Hugo from elderly, vision-challenged drivers in giant Plymouths, Toby leaned over the boy like the sole member of a presidential security detail.

The department store was bedecked with pre-Halloween Christmas trees, lights, and wreaths. Bing Crosby parumpummed over the hi-fi. It appeared as though a pack of coyotes had recently been through the children's section of the store, as packages had been ripped open and blankets and bottles lay on the brown carpet. The car seat section was small but illuminating. Prices started at $110 and reached $300 for an elite model.

Safety should not be compromised for a couple of hundred dollars in savings, Toby determined. He chose the most expensive seat, the Westchester, even though he worried it would take up most of the space in the back of the Chevette. When Hugo was settled in with the provincial Department of Families and Seniors, Toby would come up with an excuse to bring the Westchester back to Sears for a full refund. But the boy might as well experience luxury before moving into the orphanage.

The Westchester was built for vehicles that were manufactured after 2000, so it took Toby almost half an hour to rig it into the back seat of the Chevette. When he finished, the seat appeared to be solidly in place. Just to be sure, he used the bungees to secure the sides and back of the unit.

Tania, the real estate agent, met Toby in the foyer of the warehouse, where she had been answering e-mails. They were twenty minutes late. He apologized but didn't bother explaining. "You wouldn't believe me anyway."

In the hall, on the way to his suite, Tania acknowledged Hugo. "Oh my God, is he beautiful? You didn't tell me you were a father. I did not know this about you."

They weren't exactly friends. "I'm just babysitting."

"Hello." She bent over. "My name is Tania Miller. And you are?"

"He doesn't speak English. His name is Hugo."

"Like the strongman?"

"Yes, actually."

"A stunningly serious boy. *Enchanté*, Hugo!"

Something about Tania's manner—her loud voice, her overpowering perfume, her unblinking eyes, the plastic surgery, or the inscrutable nature of her black cape and scarf combination—inspired Hugo to take Toby's hand and cry all the way to the suite.

As they moved through the main floor, Toby pointed out all the improvements he had made in the kitchen and bathroom, the faucets and the black toilet. Tania complimented him on his taste and his cleanliness, and made a few recommendations for staging purposes. She had him sign a contract. "So, where are you looking?"

"Looking?"

"For your next house."

Hugo no longer had his hand. "I'm living in Dollard at the moment."

"Oh my God, you're joking!"

"Hugo?"

Nothing. Not a footstep or a squeak. The sleeping quarters and *cave* were on the lower level. Toby ran to the ornamental railing, hand on his heart. He said a little prayer and looked down into the darkness. "Hugo?"

Tania seemed confused by the intensity of his worry and peeked into a couple of closets. She stopped at an open door. "Where does this lead?"

Toby rushed past her and bounded up the stairs to the roof. Three steps from the top, he recalled speaking at a condo board meeting. Half his neighbours in the candy warehouse had wanted to spring for a tasteful cedar fence and some trees and vines on the roof, an $18,000 investment if they hired a contractor. No one had small children, and few of the tenants spent time on the roof, but it was a relatively small sum when split among ten units. Child friendliness would increase the resale value. Toby, and a couple of like-minded neighbours who did not see children in their near future, felt it was a mad waste of an international airplane ticket—especially when the art in the lobby was so pathetic.

Hugo sat on a corner of the roof, facing the mountain. One of his feet dangled over the sidewalk four storeys below. He turned to look at Toby, who crept forward on a carpet of tarpaper, gravel, leaves, and faded chocolate bar wrappers. The cross on the mountain was alight.

Toby spoke flatly, to calm the boy. If Hugo recoiled and slipped, he was gone—and Toby's ability to live and thrive on earth along with him. No one would understand how this had come to be. "Hello, my darling friend."

Three steps away, Hugo appeared to sense the falseness

and the fear in Toby's expression. He eased away. Away was the sidewalk.

Toby stopped walking. If he went back to ask Tania to call the fire department, the boy could slip. If he called for her, Hugo would be alarmed. Toby crouched low and whispered gently, telling Hugo that ice cream and chocolate cake and a pony ride were forthcoming if he agreed to a hug.

Toby looked at Hugo's perfect head, the clarity of his skin, his tiny hands and tiny shoes and tiny khakis. His blond hair shone, nearly green in the cheap, distorting light of the street lamps. Neither of them moved for several seconds, like gunslingers before the draw. Preposterously, the taste of good mustard rose in the back of Toby's throat. Then, with the awkward swiftness of a kitten, Hugo leapt up. Toby screamed. But the boy did not tumble to his death. He ran toward Toby and jumped on his back. A sharp rock dug smartly into Toby's right knee and, he knew, poked a hole in the shit-stained Paul Smith slacks.

"*Poney. Allez, Poney!*"

To prevent any more trips to the ledge, and to express an explosive feeling of relief, despite the mortal damage to a second suit, Toby bucked Hugo off and hugged him. The rapid movement startled the boy, and he began to kick and bawl. Toby kissed Hugo on the forehead and said "Thank you, thank you, thank you" to Whomsoever. He carried Hugo to the stairs. The smell of his blond hair, the warm living body that was its root, inspired more kisses. By the time they reached the bottom of the stairs, and Tania, Hugo had wriggled away from the kisses; Toby appeared to be choking the boy.

"Have you done this before?" said Tania.

The agent departed and Toby called Catherine again. Her line no longer rang; a recording declared it disconnected. Toby sat on the chesterfield with Hugo, who inspected the reproductions in a Chagall coffee table book, and phoned Dollard. Karen answered and Toby explained about Hugo. Something in her tone, or on her face, inspired Edward to get on the other line.

"So she's gone?" said Karen. "Gone gone?"

"She certainly doesn't want to be found. I should call the police, shouldn't I?"

"You don't have a choice," said Karen.

"Who says?" said Edward. "He always has a choice. You always have a choice, Toby."

Karen had evidently been holding a mouthful of Old Port, so there was a faint air of Cheech and Chong in her next declaration: "Stupid choices are always available."

"What's the little blueberry's name?" said Edward.

"Hugo."

"If this lady wanted Hugo in police custody, she would have dropped him off. Isn't it obvious? She investigated you and figured, 'Hey, here's a top-shelf guardian for my son.'"

"An unemployed television reporter, living in his parents' basement."

"The mysteries of the human heart," said Edward.

"Jesus, Ed. Where does this stuff come from?"

"Truth. You know, beauty."

"I can't be his guardian, Dad." Toby stood up, walked into the kitchen, and opened the refrigerator. "He doesn't like me, for one. He's creepy. He's crappy. And I really don't have a clue what I'm doing. How do you even talk to kids?"

"I hope he can't hear you," said Karen.

"He doesn't speak English."

"Bring him here," said Edward.

"No," said Karen, "do not bring him here. Under no circumstances. Take him to children's services, where he belongs. With professionals. French professionals."

"No," said Edward. "No, no, no. My heart tells me no."

Toby hung up and made scrambled eggs with shallots and Gruyère. He liked salsa on the side, and Hugo would not answer yes or no, salsa-wise, so Toby prepared identical plates. He played Mozart—*"Eine Kleine Nachtmusik"*— because he had heard, repeatedly, that it exercises a child's brain.

The boy tried a spoonful of the eggs and made a face.

"What, Hugo?"

He dropped his spoon.

"You don't like it? What do you want?"

This inspired a series of comings and goings from the fridge to the table, until Hugo showed a soupçon of interest in an Anjou pear. The boy mangled the fruit, dripping juice all over his shirt. Toby cleaned the floor as the adrenalin departed his bloodstream, replaced by a powerful desire to cry and then sleep. His shoulders ached. He was beginning to understand how Catherine had been moved to surrender.

They drove to Pie-IX and walked up the stairs of the fragrant building, knocked on the door. Footsteps crackled in the suite, and the door opened to *joual* one-liners and the high-volume ululations of a studio audience. A shirtless man in a Canadiens baseball cap and soccer shorts stood before them, a small pot in his hand.

"*Bonsoir, Monsieur.* Is Catherine home, by chance?"

"No Catherine here."

Hugo broke free from Toby and ran into the apartment. "*Maman?*"

"I'm eating dinner," said the man.

"May I?"

"Go."

Toby caught up with Hugo in Catherine's bedroom and carried him back to the door. The boy had scant fight left in him. He flopped in Toby's arms and moaned quietly. "*Maman.*"

"You're subletting the apartment?"

"Yes."

"Did you speak to the woman who was living here?"

"This is her stuff, I guess." The man gestured toward the furniture with his pot. "I'm renting it furnished, through a management company. You need their number?"

Toby took the number and carried the boy down the stairs and into the Westchester. Before they reached Sherbrooke, Hugo was asleep. Toby drove to an address on de Maisonneuve, just east of downtown, parked in front of the six-storey building and turned off the engine. The windows of the Department of Families and Seniors had been streaked by autumn rain. Dark-haired bureaucrats and public service posters, too-bright lights and grey cubicles were visible from the curb. Toby went through every reason why Hugo could not remain with him for another minute— reasons legal and medical, financial and psychological—and tenderly unfastened the straps of the Westchester. He lifted the boy out of the seat, careful not to bump his head on the front seat or the top of the door jamb. Ahead of him, a few people walked through the emergency door. Toby paced up and down the sidewalk for ten minutes, the sleeping boy heavy and helpless in his arms, before finally entering the building.

The waiting room was filled with what appeared to be recent immigrants, two and three generations' worth of fatigue and frustration. Hugo shivered under the fluorescent lights, buried his eyes in Toby's neck. His breath was warm and smelled of pear. For twenty minutes, Toby sat waiting among the men and women speaking languages that were neither English nor French, wasted by worry, their bright clothes wrinkled and stained. A clerk in a fleece jacket, installed behind a thick pane of bulletproof glass, called him up at last and tilted her head in greeting. She opened her mouth to ask, through the tinny intercom system, if she could help him.

Hugo would soon awaken in the company of strangers.

"*Monsieur,*" said a social worker, who had walked around from behind the glass, "is this your son?"

⌒

Edward and Karen whispered and sneaked about the house, finishing up a frantic, two-hour nesting ritual. The sheets on Toby's childhood bed had been washed and dried. Stuffed animals, smelling faintly of rain, had been drawn from cardboard boxes in the basement. A collection of children's books were stacked on the floor, next to a humidifier and an ancient tub of Vaseline. Edward had rushed out for a giant box of diapers.

The boy cried, absently and automatically, into the clean sheets. He fell asleep with the three of them huddled in the doorway.

Toby sat with his parents for an hour, in front of the television, drinking stale herbal tea. Edward fell asleep.

"Now we have two of them," whispered Karen.

"Not for long. His mom knows where to find him."

"No one cares what I think."

"If you'd seen that place, Mom."

"These hasty choices, made in confusion, sometimes weakness, they're the ones that determine everything."

"Are we still talking about Hugo?"

"If, if. If someone took me aside, forty years ago, and showed me the future."

"What would you have done, Mom?"

She sipped her tea.

The next day would be busy, as Nahla had received worrisome news about her pregnancy. She was taking at least a few days off, to rest and consider. Karen would handle the morning shift at the Dollard Chien Chaud, and Toby would take the afternoon—with his little helper.

At ten o'clock, he pulled a mottled hunk of foam from the closet and a few sheets from the dryer. Hugo's head was on one pillow and his arms were on the other, so Toby pulled one of his 1990s sweaters from a drawer and folded it into a ball. He lay listening to the boy's gentle breaths, his occasional sigh.

A car alarm woke Hugo. Again, he wanted his mom. The boy sat up on the bed, and there was just enough light coming in from outside to see his eyes shining with terror. Toby climbed into bed with Hugo, careful not to squash one of his limbs, and held him and hushed him until he fell asleep.

Eight

Karen stood in the doorway, dressed for work, the cordless telephone at her ear. At first, she was integrated into Toby's dream about Benjamin Disraeli, who was, at once, Toby. Then she wasn't in the opposition benches of the House of Commons at all. She was in his bedroom, and Hugo was sitting up and peeking over Toby's chest.

"Yes, I understand." Her cheeks were pink. "I *understand* that you, all of you, are slandering my husband and my family. And for what? A few thousand dollars?"

She listened, and pink bloomed to red.

"Who is it, Mom?"

"You'll next hear from our lawyer," she said, and pressed the end button.

"We have a lawyer?"

"Hi, pumpkin." She sat next to Toby and spoke to Hugo. "My name is Karen. I'm so very pleased you're here. Anything you want, anything at all, just ask."

The boy stared at Karen. Karen stared at the boy.

Then: "They're crooks."

"Who are?" Toby picked up Hugo and followed Karen into the kitchen.

"They're hatching a scheme, some ridiculous scheme, to besmirch your dad."

"What are they saying?"

"What do you *think* they're saying?"

Karen tossed cutlery into the sink, and asked rhetorical questions of no one, and cussed. Toby consulted the insurance policy and phoned the law firm of Whyte, Gladstone and Newman. Garrett said he would look into it and phone back, but he was fairly certain the insurance company would consult and act upon the police and fire department reports.

There was another problem. Karen had two last-minute appointments at two different banks, to look at alternative financing arrangements for the shops, and hoped that Toby could mind the Dollard location all day.

"I was going to call the last of my friends today—my 'friends' in the industry. I wanted to follow up on some follow-ups, Mom, for jobs in Saskatchewan."

"Saskatchewan."

"In the summer, apparently, it's lovely. They have rivers."

"It's a day or two, Toby. We're having a crisis here."

"The longer I wait, the more I'm damaged goods. Today Saskatchewan, tomorrow . . . I don't even know. Afghanistan? You have to seem in demand, even if you aren't. And what about Hugo's diaper changes? It's unsanitary."

"Your dad'll be there."

They were in the living room, where the small grandfather clock Edward had inherited donged eight. It was the first Toby had heard from the grandfather clock, which had been broken since 1989. A hunger for coffee arrived with disappointment, as Toby had forgotten the espresso machine in the condo. Then again, if he were to put the espresso machine on the passenger seat, he would be admitting that his retreat and failure were complete. Of course, his failure *was* complete. The condo was officially for sale. He was officially unemployed. He would be officially sleeping in his parents' basement if he were not sleeping in his old bedroom with the two-year-old that was, unofficially, his charge. It was deeper than failure. It was trailer park.

Hugo recovered from the scary clock and played with a set of red and white building blocks that predated Lego, building towers until they were too tall to stand on their own. It smelled as though he had filled his diaper again. Potty training would have to commence immediately. Karen stood behind her rocking chair, arms crossed.

"All right, Mom."

"You'll do it?"

"If you change Hugo's diaper. I'll watch."

"What are you going to do with him?"

"Wait for Catherine."

"If she doesn't come back?"

"She'll come back."

Karen shook her head.

"She has to come back." It had not occurred to Toby that she might not come back. "Couples who can't have kids fly to China to adopt. There's a little boy right here in Dollard. He'll be bilingual by the time we're done with him. They'll jump at the chance."

Karen picked up Hugo, sniffed him. "Now that's a smell only a mother could love."

They were out of white buns at the Chien Chaud, so father, son, and abandoned boy drove west to Costco first. Edward insisted on carrying Hugo on his shoulders from the Chevette through the parking lot. He weaved and wobbled. Hugo gripped his curly salt-and-pepper hair.

"Ouch. Ouch. Third-degree burn there." Edward veered right and placed his hand on the trunk of a red Hyundai Elantra. He leaned toward the back window, as though he expected Hugo to hop off his shoulders and somehow land on his feet.

"Poney!"

Toby rescued the boy and they went straight to the fluorescent-and-concrete bakery section, and loaded the cart with buns. The Chien Chaud was due to open, so Toby turned the cart around and headed toward the cashiers. Hugo, safely inside the cart, with a strap around his belly, slammed the rails and said, "*Plus vite.*"

"See? You can talk."

"*Vite, vite.*"

"We shouldn't run, Hugo. People will think we're flustered, out of control."

"Are you kidding me?" said Edward.

Toby at first assumed that Edward was taking issue with the substance of the teaching moment, and he prepared to defend his philosophy on running in public. Instead, bland suede bomber jackets with an elasticized waistband had been kidding Edward. He zipped up one of the jackets and puffed out his chest, which had always been his manner of judging fit and quality. "Eighty-five bucks, for a *suede*. What do you think?"

"Do you want me to answer honestly, Dad?"

"Hey," said Hugo.

Edward raised his eyebrows. "Hugo loves the look."

"Hugo's two."

"You have two," said the boy, in English, his first sentence in English. Toby bent down and took Hugo's hands in his. Hugo looked away and back, shyly. "You have two," he said again.

"Pronoun trouble, Hugo. Say, 'I am two years old.'"

"No."

"Say it: 'I am two.'"

Hugo did not say it. He pulled his hands from Toby's and rocked from side to side in the cart, like a blind boy playing the piano. For the first time in days, even months, stretching back farther than Toby could calculate, as he crouched near the suede rack in Costco, he was happy. Not *being happy* on camera because someone might be watching, or satisfied after shooting a clever segment on elevator etiquette, or proud to be with Alicia or on a billboard. But actually happy. It didn't last long, but it lasted long enough to frighten Toby. This was not his son. He was not a father. He had agreed with Alicia that someday they might want to have children, but both of them had seen friends with babies struggle with their ambitions, their houses strewn with ugly plastic toys, smelling of mashed bananas and diarrhea, and with each passing year the opportunity to have a child faded without Toby feeling an ounce of angst. He would have to take Hugo in to child welfare. It was wrong, even dangerous, to wait a day longer. For all Toby knew, he could be called to Saskatchewan by the end of the week. The last thing he wanted was for Hugo to become attached to him.

Edward turned around. "Be my mirror. There aren't any mirrors."

Starting with the collar, Toby moved down the jacket, pointing out obvious signs of mass production and poor quality. The style was not garish but non-existent, really, rectangular and baggy at once, as though the designer wanted to avoid making any statement about the wearer of the garment other than, *No, I have not yet given up completely. But I'm close*. Of course, it would melt in the rain.

At first, Edward appeared wounded. Then, curiously triumphant. "Fine," he said.

"Fine what, Dad?"

"I'm just gonna walk right out with it."

"What do you mean?"

Edward leaned in, so only a few inches separated them. The whites of his eyes had been invaded by veins and a yellow tint. "If they don't have the guts, the integrity, to make something nice, with a statement, like you say, I'm just gonna wear it right on out of here."

"You mean steal it."

"I mean walk right out, like I own the place."

"You can't."

"You're goddamn right I can."

Hugo clapped. "Goddamn."

"Please, Dad."

"Don't touch the jacket. Don't touch me. Don't even look at me." He winked. "We've never met."

"I'll buy the jacket. I want to. It's my gift to you."

"You're unemployed," he said, in a mock Toby voice. "You live in your parents' basement. And besides, it's the principle of the thing."

"What principle? What principle do you mean?"

"Pay for those buns and your mom'll get you back. Meet me in the parking lot at oh-eleven-hundred."

Edward walked stiffly into the vacuum cleaner section, and Toby decided not to follow him. He called Karen immediately, for advice and possible rescue, but her phone was off.

The buns were twenty-two dollars. At the checkout, the woman who stacked the buns in a box meant for frozen lasagna recognized Toby from television and asked for his autograph. She was fortyish, with a wedding ring and either a cold sore or a pimple on her lip.

Toby wrote *Love the buns, best wishes* on one of his photos.

"Your son is cute."

"Actually—"

"His mom is lucky." A cold breeze circulated near the giant doors, so she wore a winter jacket with white animal hairs about it. She unzipped it to reveal a tight blue T-shirt and continued packing the groceries. "She must be beautiful."

"I don't know her well."

"You've drifted apart."

"Something like that."

"So you're a single father."

"No, no, no."

"You ever have . . ." She laughed. "You're Toby Ménard. Of course you have no free time. But if you ever do, and you want to grab a pint or something. Or I can get my hands on some weed."

Toby looked at her ring, demonstratively.

"It's a total sham, a disaster. He's an idiot. Believe me."

Hugo pointed to a large woman in the lineup, buying

frozen meat, and repeated a name he had learned from one of Toby's old books earlier that morning: "Humpty Dumpty." Toby didn't know whether to discipline the boy or respond to the checkout woman's offer of sexual intercourse. He imagined rolling around in a bed full of cat hair. At the same time, he expected to see his father, weeping, escorted by a security guard into a small interview room. But there was no sign of Edward. Not in front of the kosher hot dog stand— vile multinational competitor—or at Customer Service, where the brochures and coupons lay.

"Let me give you my number, Toby."

"Perfect."

"Humpty Dumpty!"

Her name was Antoinette, and she wrote her phone number inside a pudgy valentine heart with an arrow through it.

Outside, Edward leaned on the Chevette like Robert Redford.

For the first hour at Le Chien Chaud, Edward and Hugo sat at the table nearest the washroom. Edward read the same four books aloud. Hugo placed his hand on two of Edward's burn-peeling fingers. Six customers came in, all of them looking for coffee. Toby pulled some dogs out of the freezer and placed them on the rotating oven. He wiped the machines and studied the digital cash register. He found the baroque station he liked, on the satellite radio system, and leaned on the counter. Curious George was following some ducks to a lake. It made for a rare sort of discomfort, the possibility of day passing into day with no bite of ambition, no anxiety about progress, or the lack of it. The story turned out well, with everyone understanding that the monkey's curiosity, which had at first seemed troublesome and dangerous, was actually a blessing.

"What if the banks say no to Mom?"

Edward shook his head.

"The house?"

"Leveraged up."

There were no customers until Randall and Garrett showed up together just after twelve thirty to order far too much food—out of charity. Randall was in the same suit he had worn before, even though there were grease smudges on his neck and about his ears. They joined Edward and Hugo at the table nearest the washroom, and everyone was introduced.

"So, you're babysitting?" said Randall.

"Something like that," said Toby.

"Just for the afternoon?"

"No."

"Who's his mom again?"

Toby couldn't bring himself to explain as Hugo stared at him. "A friend. She's on vacation."

"A friend?"

Toby tried to change the subject. Since he was in Dollard, with some extra time, maybe they could start up a Benjamin Disraeli Society. Meetings, a lecture series, fashion shows. It seemed a shame, his expertise going to waste.

"That's a thought," said Garrett. "I've always liked fashion shows."

"What sort of friend?" said Randall.

Edward placed his palms on the table. "He slept with a wacko Québécoise, and she abandoned her kid with him. That's pretty much it, right?"

"Thank you, Dad."

"No way!"

Garrett elbowed Randall, changed the subject. "The legal secretary couldn't find a precedent for an overturned decision on an insurance payout. They're pretty careful, those insurance companies."

To avoid an emotional scene, Karen had neglected to tell Edward that the insurance company had decided to withhold payment on the car. The bank price of the Oldsmobile was seven thousand dollars, which Edward had already characterized as out-and-out thievery. Now even *that* wasn't coming.

"There's been a decision?"

"Mom found out this morning."

"And she didn't tell me? Why?"

"It's not confirmed."

"Garrett's secretary knows and I don't know? It's my car."

"Can we speak about this in the back, Dad, or maybe in the washroom?"

"I'm embarrassing you."

"Dad."

"Oh, I'm *embarrassing* you again, in front of your precious friends. I'm so sorry."

Garrett and Randall investigated their hot dogs with exceptional concentration.

"Who else knows?"

"No one."

"The Moroccan neighbours, surely they know. The mayor?"

"This is inappropriate."

Edward opened a ketchup package and threw it at Toby's face. It hit him in the cheek, but very little, if any, of the sauce escaped. So Edward opened a second package, squeezed some of the ketchup out, and daubed Toby's forehead. The ketchup was warm and fragrant. "How about that? Is *that* appropriate?"

For the first time since Toby met him, Hugo smiled.

"Who else knows?"

Randall slid the metal napkin dispenser across the table.

"Steve Bancroft, does he know? Maybe that's where your mom goes when she's off to the 'bank.'" He made air quotations. "They sneak into the back seat of a sedan at the car dealership in Pointe-Claire."

Toby banged his fist on the table. "Enough."

Hugo started to cry.

Edward stared at the opposite wall for some time, kissed the boy on the top of the head, and walked out of the store, leaving his new suede jacket behind. No one remaining at the table looked at anyone else. Toby stood up, went after him. On the sidewalk, he called out. He apologized. Edward walked determinedly, his hands in his pockets, toward Centennial Park.

Toby returned to studied silence in the shop. In the washroom, he splashed the ketchup off his face and tried to avoid looking in the mirror.

"That was my fault," said Garrett, when Toby returned to the table.

"Nonsense."

"If the police and fire departments are testifying against you, and the evidence can't be examined by a third-party expert, there's pretty much no chance. Besides, the insurance companies will spend triple the amount of the settlement on legal costs, just to crush you."

"But you're Garrett Newman."

"And I get stress nosebleeds. I would advise strongly against the legal route."

Toby pulled a grape juice from the cooler and diluted it with water for the boy. Everyone seemed content to make him the centre of attention for another ten minutes.

"You can probably stop wearing the suit now," Garrett said to Randall, as they walked toward the door. "Toby wouldn't be horrified by your coveralls. Would you?"

Toby declined to answer.

The afternoon faded. He phoned the property management company and learned that the apartment in Pie-IX had been leased to one Carla Bruni. Her forwarding address was No. 1, Palais de l'Elysée. He phoned home, to be sure Edward had not wandered on to the autoroute. At three o'clock, Toby changed the boy's diaper without touching fecal matter or gagging, and celebrated with an Orangina. By three thirty, every book had been read, every game played. Hugo crawled up on Edward's suede jacket, behind the counter, and took a forty-five-minute nap.

Toby was about to toss the remaining dogs in the garbage and shut down early when a gang of teenagers arrived. School had let out. A rush ensued. Hugo stood behind the counter, timid before the teenagers bursting with cusses and cackles and headlocks. Toby appreciated the ubiquity of the phrase *And I was, like* . . .

By five, he had sold twenty-one hot dogs. The boy would be hungry soon, and Toby was not willing to give him another hunk of processed meat and white bread. He called home again and asked Karen if he could shut down early.

"You might as well," she said.

He hunted in his pockets for Antoinette's number. They

were building a particle accelerator in Switzerland that could manufacture black holes. Surely there was a way to have an evening of clandestine sex with a Costco cashier without coming into contact with her cold sore. He could not find the number.

"What am I looking for?"

"What are *you* looking for, Hugo. You."

"You."

"You're me, you see. Or I. I'm you, to you, who is me."

Hugo removed his apron. "I am you."

"No, no, no. You are I. I and me."

"You are I."

Nine

Nahla had learned that the child in her womb had been conceived with a genetic disorder called Edwards syndrome, or
Trisomy 18. She and her husband were opposed to abortion.
The remainder of her pregnancy was to be spent waiting for a
monumentally disabled, or dead, child to be born. She never
did come back to Le Chien Chaud.

On the thirty-first of October, both Toby and Hugo
dressed as ninjas. Hugo's costume was superior; it was
an elaborate hand-me-down from Randall's son, Dakota,
complete with a plastic sword and a pouch of three rubber
throwing stars. Some innovations were introduced to the
store. Toby bought a giant tin of hot peppers. but no one
used them. He offered veggie dogs and sold one, to Garrett, who felt sorry for him and told him so. The diaper
change lost its pique. No one from any television station

anywhere in North America replied to any of his queries. The condo sold for sixteen thousand dollars more than he had paid for it, even though he had invested fifty thousand in the kitchen and bathroom. The espresso machine now resided with Toby on rue Collingwood. November arrived with snow, more snow, and some marathon sessions with a shovel in front of the store. Then the rain came and washed it all away. Business increased marginally. Then more snow, and a melt. A salty, filthy sludge bubbled and foamed along the gutters. For a month and a half, days passed into days, and none of them seemed quite right for bringing Hugo to a child welfare office.

Now that he was finished with the parenting books, Toby turned to informal language classes during the substantial quiet periods at Le Chien Chaud. From time to time, Hugo would become cranky and impatient—tired, hungry, mysteriously moody—and refuse to recognize English. But by the end of November he was speaking his second language in full sentences, without an accent. His vocabulary remained stunted, so he occasionally spoke Franglais—"Honey comes *d'une abeille*"—with such sincerity that Toby wanted to take a bite out of him.

The route from the failing hot dog shop to his parents' house on rue Collingwood took Toby and Hugo past the fire station, on Sunnydale. One cold night at the end of November, as Dollard twinkled with electric snowflakes and menorahs, Toby pulled into the parking lot and shut off the Chevette. Edward was not just marching out into cold streets without his jacket anymore; he was talking to himself, crying spontaneously, waking up in the middle of the night a sweaty madman, uncertain of who he was and where he lived. Then, for several days or a week he would be exactly as he had been most of his life: calm, stable, funny, kind.

Toby carried Hugo to the doors of the fire station, cozying up to the boy, head to head as they walked, as neither of them had hats or mittens. They stopped for a moment to admire the cardboard Santa in the window.

"Do you have an appointment?"

Toby did not have an appointment, but this was Dollard. How many fires could there be? The chief was on a conference call, it turned out, so Toby and Hugo sat in the waiting area and read the *TV Hebdo* together. Two women with the northern dialect of the Saguenay decorated a sad-looking artificial white pine and talked about the premier's hair. The chief arrived, in a fire department uniform, and introduced himself, in English, as Chief Max.

"I watched your show many times, and I know Edward."

"My father's the reason for my visit."

"I had assumed. And is this your son?"

Toby had grown tired of these conversations. "No, actually."

"No?"

"Your name is Hugo," said Hugo.

Toby's most robust failure: he could not crack the pronoun mystery.

"I'm caring for him. He's not mine." Every morning now, Hugo woke him up by calling out "You're awake now!" Toby had purchased a monitor so he could hear the boy from his bedroom in the basement. He would creep upstairs and into the darkness of the boy's room, pull him out from under the covers. Hugo would lie on Toby's chest, warm and docile, and discuss in a froggy voice the night's sleep, any dreams he might have had, and strategic plans for the day—playing, jumping, sliding, eating.

"He looks like your son."

They followed Chief Max through a heavy set of doors and into a large office with a view of boulevard des Sources to the west. Hugo wanted to sit in his own chair, so Toby set him up as the chief opened a file and cleared his throat. There were owls everywhere in the room, stuffed and ceramic. Photographs. Representational art owls, including a legitimate sculpture on a small pewter stand.

"Owls," said Hugo.

Chief Max, apparently pleased not to speak of Edward Mushinsky for another minute or two, described a love of owls that had begun when he was not much older than Hugo. An owl obsession. The cohesion of an owl obsession lasting from age four to age sixty-four transformed Toby's anxieties about his father into a general mortification about death. Once, a lifetime had seemed lengthy.

"I guess you want to know, in detail, how we came to our decision about the fire."

"Want" was not the right word.

"You're a family member. I will assume you have your father's permission."

"I don't."

Max flared his nostrils. "This is important. It's important, I think, what I can tell you about your father. If you have his permission."

"All right."

"Edward was with his friends in the Optimist Club. We've spoken to them. He was troubled on the night in question, and drinking. Desperate thoughts were articulated."

"Like what?"

"Thoughts of ending it."

"Ending what?"

"He left the Baton Rouge after an argument with one of his mates about whether individuals have any control over their own destinies. This is, I gather, a central tenet of the Optimist Club. There was talk of conspiracies, mind control, the American government. Your father quit the club when his ideas were not accepted, and left the restaurant. He stopped at the Ultramar, purchased a jerry can and filled it. Now, that is the last piece of corroborated evidence we have. However, we do have the science. Our investigation of the car showed that the fire started on the surface of the vehicle, with a flammable liquid. There was gasoline on Edward's pants."

"It makes no sense, Monsieur Max."

"Max is good enough. My family name is Gagné." He slipped a card over the desk.

The chief, clearly a father, stood up and fetched three stuffed owls for Hugo just as he began to squirm in his chair. Toby had come to argue with the chief, to demand a more thorough analysis of the fire and a new assessment for the insurance company. Now he sat before the man with nothing more to say.

"This is not good news," said the chief.

"No, sir."

"We were in Kinsmen together. Like I said, I know your father. This is not your father."

Toby was briefly filled with the happy possibility that Edward had been replaced. His real father was being held in a shed somewhere on L'Île-Bizard and only needed rescuing.

"There's really no need to fret about it, Toby."

"Really no," said Hugo.

"All your dad needs is a pill of some sort. This is, by far, the best time in history to have a mental illness. Let me tell you a little story." Max launched into an informal motivational speech, filled with clichés and bons mots about picking ourselves up and getting right back in the game, turning lemons into lemonade, and putting family first. It led, cleverly, to the Lord. Night had fallen and Toby was eager to get the boy home for dinner. Proselytizing had always made him uneasy, as though the defects and deficiencies of his heart were suddenly open, readable, wanting. Max continued to offer advice, encouragement, and the great solace of our Lord and Saviour as Toby carried the boy outside and fastened him in his car seat. It took five minutes to terminate the conversation in the parking lot, and even then, as Toby started the Chevette, he opened the window to hear Max's final piece of wisdom, drawn from Scripture. "'For as the heavens are higher than the earth, / So are my ways higher than your ways / And my thoughts than your thoughts.'"

"So I shouldn't bother thinking?"

Max brought a finger to his lips and paused. "No, no. Just be comforted by the knowledge that someone out there is thinking more effectively, and magically, and just for you."

"Thanks again, Max."

"No, thank *you*."

Rush hour in Dollard was a half-hour affair, from four thirty to five o'clock, as the bureaucrats and clerks flooded in from the autoroute and plugged boulevard des Sources. It was now after six, and the streets and avenues of his hometown, lit blue and yellow and red by the neon signs of the mall, were nearly deserted but for a late-model SUV and a couple of German cars, lawyers who had stayed late. There was still time to become a lawyer. Hugo babbled to himself in the Westchester, about owls. The word in French was so much more fun to say, with built-in onomatopoeia. *Hibou. Un hiboooo.*

Toby wanted to chat about owls, but he was faintly nauseated. The more he tried not to think about his thin, failed, burned-up, loony father, the more he thought about him. A general capacity for illness, as he understood it, was inherited; this gurgle in his stomach and vague pain in and about the left side of his chest promised tragedy. If he survived the gurgling—leaky bowel syndrome—and the chest pain— rotten lung—he could expect, in the vicinity of his sixtieth birthday, to start eating his toenails and arguing with Benjamin Disraeli in the middle of boulevard de Maisonneuve.

The house on rue Collingwood was alight when they arrived. Hugo had left the subject of owls behind and now turned his attention to pooping. He stopped on the brown front lawn and closed his eyes, concentrated.

"You want to poop on the potty?"

"No."

"You're pooping right now. Let's go on the potty."

"No, no, no."

"Right now, let's try."

"You don't want to!"

Toby picked him up, bent over and mid-grunt, and carried him up the steps.

"There he is!" Edward opened the screen door, silhouetted by the light inside. "Come here, Hugo. I have something to show you."

"He's going to use the potty, Dad."

"No!"

The boy wiggled fiercely until Toby lowered him to the platform of the concrete steps. He jumped into Edward's arms. "Édouard."

"Whoops. I think someone went and availed himself."

"I'll change him."

"You sure? I can do it, or your mom can."

"He's my guy."

Toby had intended to hug his haunted father immediately upon seeing him, to declare his unconditional love and a commitment to the spirit of understanding. Instead, he pulled Hugo out of Edward's arms and marched straight into his bedroom. Hugo looked at a book about hippos while Toby wiped him down and took defensive measures against rogue urine. Millions of middle-class men in their thirties had normal fathers. Right now, they were gathered in the dining rooms and restaurants of America, in blue jeans and pressed shirts, sipping wine and arguing about politics, stunned in the warmth of their drunkenness by how like their handsome and accomplished fathers they really were.

Without a sound, Karen appeared in the doorway.

"Were you at the bank again today?"

"How much more can I debase myself in front of account managers who skateboard?"

"I'm sorry, Mom."

"We'll keep trying."

"I only sold—"

"Don't even tell me, Toby. But thanks."

"Hi, Karine!"

"Hello, Hugo. Are you hungry?"

"Yes, yes. You are."

Cream to guard against a rash, a new diaper, the corduroy pants with the bleach stain on the back pocket.

"Your dad picked up some things for Hugo."

Something in Karen's tone, the way she had paused before and after "things," inspired Toby to take Hugo up and follow her wordlessly from the room. Karen led them down the hall and into the living room, where Edward stood rubbing his hands together. On the chesterfield, separated into themes, were miniature suits, shirts, slacks, and ties. In front of the chesterfield, three pairs of leather shoes—black, brown, and more casual white slip-ons. There was a selection of short ties on the arm of the chesterfield, one straight black and three patterned.

"Everything's size three. So it might be a bit big, but it'll last him."

Karen tapped Toby on the arm and slipped him the bill, for $1,927. Hugo's new wardrobe was from a boutique called Alice à Montreal, in Pointe-Claire.

"It's all yours, Hugo. Try it on."

"Yours." He looked up at Toby. "It's yours?"

"Mine. Say 'It's mine.'"

"It *is* mine, yes, Poney, oh yes, it *is*."

Edward stripped Hugo down to his fresh diaper and started with the suits. The collection of boys' clothing had a ring of familiarity about it, but Toby could not see why until he stood behind Hugo in the full-length mirror in his parents' room. Both wore grey suits with white shirts and black ties, black shoes. Edward had replicated the core of Toby's wardrobe, in miniature. Toby straightened his tie and Hugo, watching him, pretended to straighten his own tie. At first it was comical, but the image had a hint of the eternal about it, like man and woman and priest. The fire chief had been right. They had come to resemble one another, if not physically then in other ways. Unless Toby did something quick and brutal, this boy would be his. His temper tantrums, his scary friends, his hormones, his goth phase, his fist fights and heartbreaks and drug experimentation, his pregnancy scares with the first serious girlfriend, his gap year in Asia, his intellectual rebellion. Twenty years at least until university graduation and then the queer slide into whatever it was Toby shared with his own parents, today.

"We need handkerchiefs."

"Hammer."

"Hand-ker."

"Ham."

Karen joined them in the bedroom, and Hugo rushed back to change into another outfit.

"We can't keep these clothes, and it's your job to tell your dad and Hugo."

"These things are beautiful. He was so careful about it."

"Your father and I are weeks away from bankruptcy and foreclosure."

Toby shrugged his shoulders. "In some ways, it's a good deal. I could only buy a suit and a half for two thousand dollars. Hugo now has an entire closetful. And I was somewhat concerned about the clothes he came with. All those giant logos. You don't want him to be a walking advertisement for a chain store. We don't yet understand what that does to a person, psychologically."

"He's two."

"I get that."

"We can't pay our mortgage this month. Do you get that?"

"I'll write you a cheque for the clothes."

"You can't afford it either. I can say this with confidence, as your employer."

Toby stopped concentrating on his mother's worries and wishes, which transformed into a lecture on saving and spending, the nature of debt. She had failed as a mother, as a wife, as an entrepreneur. She broke down, and he hugged her, more satsuma than Old Port tonight. The loose flesh on her back. The rattle in her lungs he could not hear but, only now, feel.

"I stopped at the fire station on the way home."

"Why? Why would you do something like that?" She broke away from him, her eyes red and small. "Why in hell?"

"I wanted to know."

"Wanted to know what? There's nothing to *know*. We're just trying to get through an evening here."

"We can help him."

"How, precisely?"

"By getting him on the right drugs. The chief was saying—"

The boy returned, this time in the navy blue suit with a red tie, an obvious combination that reminded Toby of a bureaucrat dressing up for a meeting with the Minister of Public Works. He could practically see the identification badge around Hugo's neck, the burgeoning pot belly, the fart jokes and fast-food lunches, the minivan.

"You need a different tie with this."

"You do," said Hugo, grimacing and pulling at the tie.

Toby helped him take it off and led him by the hand into the living room.

"We'll be homeless soon," said Karen, behind them. "Real, actual homeless people. This is how it happens."

Toby sat in one of the navy blue recliners his parents had purchased with their modest income tax refunds in 1996 and watched Hugo try on what Edward kept calling "the new threads." Much of it was slightly too large, but Hugo carried it well. The recliner was, traditionally, his father's. It smelled faintly of smoke, but also of Skin Bracer aftershave and microwave popcorn. Before moving in, the last time Toby had spent an entire evening in the house was last Christmas, the night Edward learned that microwave popcorn was killing thousands of Americans. Instead of singing carols around the piano or drinking hot chocolate about the hearth, the Mushinskys drank sparkling wine in highball glasses—they had neither a piano nor a hearth, and only one champagne flute—and watched a repeat broadcast of a current affairs television show, *20/20*: "Killer Fat in Microwave Popcorn." The program had confused Edward, and he had expressed this confusion in a dialogue with himself during a commercial break. Why would the executives of a food company endanger their customers, upon whom they relied for financial success? Yet why wouldn't they, if they also owned pharmaceutical conglomerates and funeral homes? This dialogue had ended neutrally, in the middle of a holiday-themed advertisement for Swiffer cleaning products—"Farewell, feather duster"—and Edward vowed to continue taking microwave popcorn with his prime-time television consumption.

Toward the end of the modelling session, Hugo became increasingly uncooperative. Edward pulled clothes on and off the boy with great care, but Hugo had started to whine. It occurred to Toby that the boy had not eaten, and that a blood sugar–related episode was imminent. So he rushed into the kitchen to heat up a few cans of tomato soup and throw a frozen pizza in the oven.

Karen watched him, leaning on the doorless jamb that separated the kitchen from the living room.

"They're good together, Edward and Hugo."

Toby grated extra cheese for the pizza. The large white frozen chunks that came with the product carried a distinct sadness. He wanted Karen to forget about the money, even if only for half an hour. There was a bottle of red wine on the counter, with a twist cap. He poured her a glass and handed it over.

"Your dad was good with you, too."

"I bet he was."

"No one loved being a dad more. Not that I ever seriously considered leaving or anything, but I remember thinking, *You can't leave this. You just can't.*"

Karen closed her eyes and kept them closed for some time, as she drank and Toby stirred the soup.

"Other people we knew at the time—I mean when you were little—the man was never around. He'd work all day, long hours, overtime, and then go out in the evenings, doing whatever. Seeing his friends. Volunteering. Whatever, like I say. Not Ed."

"What was Steve Bancroft like?"

Karen flinched and sagged, a punctured tire.

"Dad talks about him."

"Does he?" Karen looked away, watched the proceedings in the other room. Hugo was making demands. He was shouting at Edward, in English, about doing something "all by yourself."

"Oh." Karen pulled a square of paper from the front pocket of her jeans. "I forgot to tell you. Adam Demsky called."

Toby abandoned the tomato soup, swiped the paper from his mother. "What did he say?"

"Nothing, really. To call him."

"Jesus, Mom." Toby dialled and stirred the soup. There was no answer, and Mr. Demsky had never burdened himself with a voice-mail service. The unreasonably smooth and coherent tomato soup, staple of any recession, bubbled once. Toby turned it down to simmer and, when the timer on the oven dinged, removed and sliced the pizza. He changed into a fresh shirt and one of his tier-one ties, and kissed Hugo.

Both Edward and Karen objected. "You have to eat something first."

"No time."

"Poney, you want to go."

"No, Hugo, sorry. But I'll be home soon. I'm just running a couple of errands."

"You want to go!"

"*I* want to go." Toby closed the insulated front door and, through it, heard Hugo break into a shriek and then a tantrum. He was tempted to stay and hold the boy, murmur sweetly and rock him back into food-related sanity. Of course, it said in one of the parenting books that one should never give in to this temptation, lest the child learn that throwing a fit is productive. Toby listened for two or three minutes, until the house on rue Collingwood was quiet again, then jogged to the Chevette. He enjoyed jogging in a suit whenever an opportunity presented itself: FBI agent.

It was just cold enough for the light rain that fell on the autoroute to transform, by the time he reached Montreal, into wet snow flurries. He parked on Elm, fixed his tie, examined his teeth, said a brief mantra three times—"Success is mine, for I deserve it"—and crossed the deserted avenue to Mr. Demsky's townhouse. The carvings and moulds in the stone were lit strategically with soft orange spotlights, the tiny shadows of snowflakes darting across them like aphids. Toby removed his glove and touched the doorbell button, noted its smoothness. Somewhere on the continent, a factory in what was once the outskirts of a city, now a realm of suburban development, produced doorbell buttons. Its owner was wealthy and happy, retired in Palm Beach, though the doorbell magnate feared, as he eased into sleep at night, that the industry was changing too quickly, that his children would fail. Toby pressed the beautiful button and a bell echoed within. He didn't smile, exactly. In between smiling and not smiling, shoulders back, casual but alert.

Nothing.

Toby retreated to the Chevette and watched the late-November snow swarm the street lights of Elm Avenue for fifteen minutes. During the desperate cold snaps, Toby often found himself resenting both his ancestors and the fathers of this halting nation, who settled on Montreal as the capital of Canadian commerce and culture instead of, say, the eastern shore of Vancouver Island. But he was not a winter-hater. It was a far more fashionable season than summer, demanding two layers of elegance and creativity instead of one. Scarves alone justified living in a four-season climate. After twenty minutes, hungry and frustrated, he decided to depart. He made the same decision at about forty-five minutes, and at an hour, and at an hour and a half. Then, having invested that much time waiting to speak to Mr. Demsky in person, Toby vowed to stay all night if necessary. He had always kept a book in the BMW, a facsimile of the 1922 first edition of *Etiquette*, by

Emily Post, his progenitor and hero. *Etiquette* was the holy book of his trade, its wisdom and its truths so full and articulated with such authority that it steeled him against all critics and challengers. In his haste and his shame, he had forgotten his copy of *Etiquette* in the BMW when he returned it to the dealership, tucked in a pocket behind the passenger seat. Now, even in the absence of critics, challengers, or an audience of any sort, for two hours and seventeen minutes he longed for its return. He read sections of the Chevette's owner's manual, which he found in the glove box, and thought of Alicia on the day of their someday wedding in St. George's Church on rue Stanley. He had begun to abuse himself, through his slacks, when a black Infiniti M45 with tinted windows pulled up to the townhouse and remained idling until Mr. Demsky opened the door, mid-chuckle, waved, and exited.

Toby knew better than to open his own door immediately, but he was sore from sitting and half mad from thinking. The Infiniti accelerated silently to the end of the block and turned left, into more elevated realms of Westmount. Toby opened his door and called out to Mr. Demsky, who stood directly below the street light. He blocked it with one hand.

"Yes?"

"It's me, Tobias." He walked across the street and noted that Mr. Demsky was looking at the Chevette. Toby walked between his former boss and his current car, to keep them separate. "Terrific evening."

"Watch out!"

The Chevette was rolling slowly backward, down the gentle slope of Elm Avenue. Toby sprinted toward it and opened the passenger door just as the car began to pick up speed. He dove in and his jacket ripped under his right armpit, his third ruined suit in a season. To stave off boredom, he had kept the car in place with the foot brake. Now he pulled up the emergency brake. The gear shift dug into his neck, and the driver's seat, which contained twenty years' worth of ass, was a cushion for his nose. At that moment, if a small animal had been in the vicinity, regardless of its cuteness, Toby would have picked it up and thrown it. He twisted so the gear shift dug deeper into his neck.

"You all right?"

Toby closed his eyes, wiped the moisture away, and waited a moment to speak.

"That was like a movie, Tobias. A really pathetic movie. One of those low-budget jobs from the Midwest."

"Sorry." Toby slid out of the Chevette. "I've surely ruined your reputation with the neighbours."

Mr. Demsky looked around. "No one saw but me, Tobias."

"They might have seen."

"Fuck 'em. How long were you waiting?"

"I don't know. Ten minutes. I was running some errands in the neighbourhood, and since I missed your call . . ."

"Your reel, I packed it up and sent it to a friend in the States. There's no guarantee. All I can really ensure is that he looks at it. But if he calls . . ."

Toby extended his hand for a shake. "Thank you so much, Mr. Demsky. I don't deserve your support."

"Shut up with that shit. It doesn't suit either of us."

Toby wanted to kiss Mr. Demsky, or just make a declaration.

"I'd invite you in, but I'm beat."

"Me too. I was just about to leave."

Mr. Demsky glanced at the Chevette again. "Everything's okay, otherwise?"

"I've had some financial setbacks."

"Right."

"But other than that, Mr. Demsky, everything . . . no, everything's really quite terrible."

"Everything?"

He decided not to tell Mr. Demsky about Hugo.

"Good. Honestly, good, Tobias. You need to touch the bottom of the shitter for full renewal. It's the way I felt after my wife died, like I couldn't get any lower. I did, of course, get lower, on account of a cocaine binge I could have done without and a trip to a singles resort in Aruba for unattached Jewish baby boomers."

Toby leaned against the Chevette, crookedly parked, and wet dust transferred to his forearm. He glanced about quickly, looking for a small dog or perhaps a bunny.

"Your advantage, today, is you have nothing holding you back. No wife, no kids, no job—sorry—in Montreal. The economy and our industry are global now. One of my colleagues in Toronto, for Christ's sake, his son works for Al Jazeera in Qatar. Doha, Qatar, Tobias, and he's not even hardly half an Arab. I'd give anything to trade places with you right now. Even the car, fuck it."

"I don't know, Mr. Demsky."

"Just look over the hill and you'll see a new valley."

"All I see is a hot dog shop."

Mr. Demsky crossed the street again, wiping the snow from his hair and from the shoulders of his black overcoat. "If I hear anything from William, I'll let you know right away."

"William?"

"My friend in New York."

"Thanks again, Mr. Demsky. I can't tell you how—"

"Shut the fuck up."

Toby waved until the door was shut, then inspected the new tear in his suit. The emergency brake debacle and his mini breakdown in the Chevette had been related to his own crisis of low blood sugar, he determined. So he parked a block away and walked east in the slush along Sherbrooke until he reached the Musée des Beaux-Arts. An exhibition of Cuban work was either opening or closing. Men and women in suits and cocktail dresses stood in the foyer with tiny white plates and wineglasses, canapés and South African merlot, Quebec Inc. living the life he had lived up until a few weeks before. Toby walked around the corner, to the side of the building, and looked in. A man with a beard, certainly francophone, leaned in and whispered something to his companion, a tall woman with red hair tied back. In their late forties or early fifties, naturally attractive. Confident. Both of them with wedding rings. The intimacy they shared, close to the window, did not suggest the ease of marriage. Mystery juiced their lips, jumped in the black wool, shone their shoes, seduced them from their well-designed kitchens this cold night. Toby recognized several people in the room, the French culturati, and it occurred to him that Mr. Demsky, as usual, had been perfectly and brilliantly correct. There was nothing for him here anymore. He should have realized long ago that his fake name was not sufficient. These people would never accept him as one of their own. Post-disaster, none of them had sent a note or a card inquiring about his well-being.

There was an unlikely harmony about the neighbourhood to the south, a jumble of nineteenth-century two- and three-storeys arguing with the boxy high-rises built in the misapprehension of hope in 1967—Expo year, Canada's last great year. It was now a tacky student core, full of delis and cafés and bars and restaurants, well populated with young pedestrians like himself wearing improper shoes and outerwear for the weather. It was the unselfconscious Montreal, the free market, unregulated, United Nations of Montreal, a counter-argument for the Québécois boomers, the language police, former hippies nostalgic for an uglier, meaner, rigid and unilingual time; a counter-argument for the pro-something and anti–everything else manic depressives of the English universities.

Once, in his early twenties, Toby had attended an ethnic fair in the foyer of the Hall Building at Concordia University, with a girlfriend whose name he could not recall. Members of the Jewish Students' Association wore folk costumes and played klezmer on a small ghetto blaster, served falafels and hummus. Across the hall, members of the Arab Students' Association wore not dissimilar folk costumes and played devotional music on a small ghetto blaster, served falafels and hummus. One of the Arab student leaders crossed the floor and accused the Jews of "colonizing" the chickpea, and it led to a fist fight.

The wind sneaked up Toby's ripped jacket. In a busy pizzeria, he ordered two slices and a V8, as the men behind the counter hollered and gestured at one another. He sat at the only vacant table, under a yellowing poster of Beirut as it was before any of the recent troubles. No one in the little restaurant recognized him as a television star. Lebanese pop music blared from ruined speakers. Toby was old enough now that he would seem a lost and defeated divorcé, eating alone in a two-dollar pizzeria.

He finished and walked back to the Chevette. On the
way, he stopped at a depanneur on de Maisonneuve to escape
the cold for a moment. He bought a jumbo can of Molson
Export, and the Indian clerk slipped it into a brown paper
bag for him, with a wink. Toby's pants legs were wet all the
way up to his knees and he had no overcoat; for the first time
in his adult life, a stranger had judged him a hobo. There
were several bouquets strewn about near the produce, so
Toby chose the prettiest one.

"I love freesia and gerbera daisies together," he said.

"Yes," said the clerk.

"They're for my wife."

The clerk nodded. "Yes."

Toby finished the jumbo beer just as he reached the
Chevette. He wiped the snow from the windshield with the
sleeve of his jacket. His spirits renewed, he decided to take a
quick tour of Westmount before returning to Dollard; in case
he won the Lotto 6/49 jackpot or was asked to anchor *The
National* on CBC, it only seemed responsible to be prepared
with real estate ideas.

The lights were on inside the house on Strathcona
Avenue, but with snow on the apple tree he could not see
clearly into the salon. The clerk on de Maisonneuve had
wrapped the flowers haphazardly, as he had clearly been worried that Toby, a cultivated vagrant, would steal a chocolate
bar or a lighter if he were left unsupervised. Toby tried to
straighten the paper and add a sense of crispness and gran-
deur to the package.

It was not déjà vu, exactly, for he had walked along her
stone path and up the steps of her porch hundreds of times, in
all four seasons. No, he felt as though he were being watched

by a version of himself, a Toby Ménard of the past or of the future, hiding under the freshly painted steps or in the peeling boughs of the apple tree. Alicia was the most beautiful woman on the island of Montreal, and easily one of the most intelligent, despite the limited demands of her profession. To ignore her, to allow her to escape him was malevolent pride. Alicia had been calling out for Toby, and he had not been listening.

He rang the bell. A deep and authoritative *clong* echoed through the cottage. The noise had always reminded him of the stroke of one in a cathedral—not that he had ever been in a cathedral at the stroke of one. The white button, with a swirl of marble about it, was the same size and shape as the button on Mr. Demsky's townhouse.

A woman he did not recognize, with a round face and frameless glasses, opened the blue door. Foundation caked over a pimple next to her nose.

"It's you."

"Good evening. My name is Toby Ménard, and—"

"I know who you are. Come in." The woman introduced herself, Carrie, as a member of the book club. Several other women sat in an oval of chairs and pillows around a coffee table full of Greene Avenue snacks—hummus, sushi, premium sliced vegetables. Yoga pants, yoga pants, yoga pants. They turned to him and waved, said hello flatly. "Hello." "Hi." "Wet out there?"

Carrie felt obliged to stand next to him, as his guide into the house, but she did not make eye contact.

"Did someone tell Allie he's here?"

One of the women popped up and slid over the wood floor in her socks.

"What book are you doing? Reading, I mean, in your club."

Three of them answered at once, so Toby did not catch the title. It sounded like every other recent novel. Two nouns, mixed up for pretty effect: *The Something of Something*.

"Brilliant choice."

"Oh, you've read it?"

"Yes, yes. Harrowing."

Carrie rubbed her hands together. "You must join us. It would be useful to have a male perspective."

The women stopped chewing and looked at each other. Alicia entered through the swinging door that separated the kitchen from the salon. She strode in a queenly fashion, in a tan dress he did not recognize and black high-heeled sandals, carrying a bottle of wine and a bowl of artisan potato chips.

"He read the book," said Carrie. "We thought he could join us."

"Nonsense," said Alicia. "He doesn't read books."

"Yes, I do."

She placed the wine and chips on the table and lifted a copy of the paperback. It was thick, with a bee on the cover. "What's it about?"

Toby looked at Carrie and the others, shrugged. "Making conversation, you see. But I do read books. I read them all the time." Something about Carrie's expression inspired him to continue. "I was just thinking about a book earlier this evening, in my car. A book that had been very important to me, in recent years."

"Very impressive." Alicia reached back for an artisan potato chip. "Did you come by for any non-literary reasons?"

"I was hoping we could speak in private."

Alicia placed a hand on the mantel. "Where are you living? I saw the condominium in the *Gazette.*"

"Dollard."

"With your parents."

"Yes."

Alicia turned to the fellow members of her book club. They looked down at their books, their small plates filled with snacks, their glasses of wine. One actually snickered.

"What could we possibly discuss, Toby?"

"I thought alone, we could . . ."

"We could what?"

There were several Alicias. None of them was capable of appearing emotionally dependent on the affections of a man. In all their years together, she had never once consented to hold his hand in public. But she encouraged and inspired him, and really never seemed to mind, excessively, that he was from the West Island. Hosting-a-book-club-meeting-Alicia crossed her arms and tilted her head just slightly, like a nightclub bouncer, and didn't open her eyes all the way.

"We left things oddly, I thought, back at the station," he said.

"Define 'oddly,' in this context."

"We had three goldfish together. To this day, and I'm sure it's the same with you, I'm not sure we actually broke up."

She turned again to her utterly rapt book club, then back to him. "We actually, definitely, assuredly broke up."

"I was wondering if that might be negotiable."

"It was non-negotiable. It remains non-negotiable."

"Of course. I just wanted to be certain." Toby pulled the bouquet off the narrow table in the foyer. "These are for you. Just some flowers."

"I see that." Alicia did not step forward to take them.

"Excellent. All right." He put his free hand in his pocket. "I suppose I should say, Alicia, that I wish you the best, all the very best, in your career and in every other facet of your life."

"This is what you came to say?"

"No." He placed the bouquet on the wooden floor. "There's this website. If you upload a digital photograph of yourself and one of your partner, they mash it up and for five dollars make a prediction about what your child will look like. They make a boy and a girl. I chose age three. It's a cute age, I think, and you do have a fairly solid idea of what a person will look like as an adult by age three. The clothes weren't right. I can just imagine, Alicia, how you'd dress up a little girl. Dresses, long coats, boots. Straight out of the forties. I would sometimes browse, you know, real estate websites in Europe. One day, when the kids were old enough to appreciate it, and to learn from the experience, I thought we could get an apartment in Barcelona. Remember, when we were there, how I would go downstairs and bring up breakfast and coffee, and we'd lie there with the shutters open? The sirens of those police cars. That sound still excites me when I hear it. In movies, or on television, what have you."

There was a hint of sympathy in her eyes, and she listened without fidgeting or looking away. It was quiet in the big old house on Strathcona Avenue. Alicia stood and soaked it up, his discomfort and now his humiliation, as though it were a rare replenishing cream. Just when it seemed she would be led into pity, she sighed and gently slid the flowers across the floor to him.

One of the other women, a running partner of Alicia's, a neighbour of a certain age, said, "Can we open the goddamn wine?"

⌒

Traffic was light on the autoroute. The radio in the Chevette cut in, and Toby turned up a scratchy version of Bach's Concerto for Two Violins in D Minor. It was, he deemed, the most beautiful piece of music ever written. With whom in his new constellation, he wondered, might he share this opinion? Neither Randall and Garrett nor his parents would understand. He would have to play it for them and explain, which would only strain his knowledge of baroque violin, history, the philosophy of music, and the human heart. He would have to make things up. More importantly, it would bore the hell out of them. Twice he nearly drove off the autoroute into the shadows of some snowy nowhere.

From the front yard, he heard Hugo crying in his bedroom. The door was not locked, so he threw it open and ran down the hall before he had a chance to answer his parents' greetings.

Hugo spotted him in the faint hallway light and said, "Poney, Poney, you need water, Poney, you *need* some."

There was a small glass of water on the bookshelf. Hugo took a short sip and lay back down, smiling. "I'm home, Poney."

"I *am* home."

For the next long while, he explained to the boy about Bach's Concerto for Two Violins in D Minor. "If there is a God, this is where He resides. Do you understand?" The boy fell asleep holding Toby's hand. The smallness and smoothness and newness and guilelessness of Hugo's hand. It took Toby several minutes to extricate his fingers gently enough so that he would not startle the boy awake.

Karen sat in her blue recliner, watching *Law & Order.* It was an early episode—the young people in a nightclub scene pulled their jeans up too high and tucked their shirts in, beltlessly.

Edward was in his own recliner, staring up at the ceiling. "Where were you just now?"

"I met Mr. Demsky to talk about my career."

"Come to any conclusions?" Edward continued to look at the ceiling.

"I suppose not, no."

"It's ten thirty."

Toby had carried the flowers and a vase into the living room to properly arrange the bouquet. In the car, he had briefly considered presenting the depanneur flowers to Karen, but he did not know when his father had last bought any for her.

"You should be here, with your son, at ten thirty."

Your son. Toby needed to sit. He looked around for the footstool, but it had been flipped over and its underside filled with wooden spoons and three plush chicks. *With your son.* Toby looked to his mother, and she closed her eyes, shook her head. He learned, from this gesture, that Edward had been in a state for some time. "You're right, Dad. I'm very sorry."

Something about *Law & Order* had always comforted Karen Mushinsky; she turned to it for wisdom and consolation the way earlier generations had turned to Wordsworth.

"A crisis is coming. You do know that," said Edward.

"I do?"

"It's upon us. I can feel it."

"What sort of crisis?"

Karen cleared her throat to warn Toby away from this line of questioning.

"The grandest and darkest crisis of our time. Food and fuel are running out. The economic system? A sham. We're in for drought and then for war. The drought war. The crazy Jew-haters are going to bomb New York City, you just watch. It's a six-hour drive. You think the nuclear winter won't float up here, on a nor'easter?"

"I don't know how nor'easters work."

"When I close my eyes, Toby, I see them coming."

"Who?"

"They're so close I can smell them. They're going to sweep through our little house and rip us to pieces, you see? Destroy our human dignity. That's why I want you close, our family close. In case it comes. So we can be together in that final moment. Huddled. Huddled."

Edward's eyes had expanded their dominion over his face. Karen's hands were at her mouth in a gesture of prayer. She was about to cry.

"This is why you cannot, cannot stay out until ten thirty at night. What if it happened while you were away? What if I missed it, missed a chance to say goodbye?"

"Dad . . ."

"Having Hugo here just brings it all back. Our little family, what, thirty-five years ago. You and me and your mom. Three." Edward cleared his throat and sang, his voice weak and wavering. "*Three is a magic number. Yes it is, it's a magic number.*" He stopped singing and turned to Karen. "You remember, my sweet?"

Karen whispered, "I remember."

"Why are you crying?"

"I'm not."

"Are you unhappy?"

"No."

Edward reached down and lowered the recliner, climbed off it, and crawled to his wife; he winced and smiled and kneeled before her. "*Three is a magic number. Yes it is.*"

"Stop, please, Edward."

"*It's a magic number.*"

"Stop."

Edward reached out to Toby. His mother shook her head, *No, stay where you are.* Toby did not want to hurt his father, so he walked to his mother's recliner. He did not know what to do. Stand over them? Touch them? Edward pulled him down, and father and son crouched at Karen's feet. Edward put his arm around Toby's shoulder and sang, "*Three is a magic number.*"

The chair trembled. Toby would leave here, eventually, but his mother would stay. Edward finished singing and remained on the floor, with his arm around Toby's shoulder, a couple of priests considering the divine mystery. Nothing had prepared Toby for this. Not even a word to say. The living room was a desert, and every direction led nowhere. It hurt to kneel. Another suit ruined. He feared his father, what he could do in the night.

"I'm very thirsty." Toby stood up slowly, easing out of Edward's embrace. "Can I bring anyone anything? Mom?"

Karen shook her head, her face streaked with tears.

"Dad?"

"Bring me a brew, why don't you?"

In the kitchen, Toby crumbled two of Karen's sleeping pills into Edward's Labatt 50. He was tempted, as the powder absorbed into the alcohol, to drink it himself. He poured a second beer, and a third for his mother.

Back in the living room, he proposed a toast. "To our family."

"Here here," said Edward. "To love."

The three of them drank, and Toby lightened the mood by talking in a flat tone about Mr. Demsky, who had sent his reel out to a friend. He told his parents about the Cuban exhibition at the Musée. Perhaps they could go, as a family, and introduce Hugo to the peculiarities of Caribbean communism. Twenty minutes after his first sip, Edward faded. Toby helped him out of his recliner and, careful not to bang or scrape his father's still-tender shins, eased him into his bedroom. There was just enough consciousness and energy remaining in Edward to allow Toby to remove his clothes and baby him into pyjamas. Together, in the aromatic darkness of the master bedroom, they sang "Three Is a Magic Number." Edward invented lyrics and, finally, notes. Like Hugo, he held Toby's hand as he fell asleep.

Ten

The halls of the emergency department had been decked with thirty-year-old Christmas lights and garlands, cardboard Santas and menorahs. Edward held an old issue of a trashy current affairs magazine in his hands as though it were spoiled meat; he felt he had been tricked into coming. He had refused to see his family doctor, Dr. Smythe, that morning in Dollard. "A quack with cold hands and vodka breath," Edward had concluded. The lunch rush had amounted to Randall and Garrett, and no one had showed up between one and two, so Toby closed Le Chien Chaud early and suggested they "take a drive, see the sights," which led them to explore the architectural nuances of the Montreal General. Hugo lay silently across their laps.

An hour and a half after they sat down, a gigantic nurse appeared in the waiting area and called out, "Edward Mushinsky?"

Despite Toby's best efforts, Hugo woke out of his doze in the transfer from lap to shoulder. Several women had commented on his outfit, and how darling a boy he was, next to his daddy. Toby nodded to them and followed his father. The nurse, almost six and a half feet tall, with bad skin and the jaw of a man, a fascinating specimen, showed them to a room and instructed them to sit and wait.

"What's wrong with me, do you think?"

"It's a small chemical thing in your brain, Dad. Easy to fix. You're going to feel a whole lot better."

"You remember what I told you, that something's wrong with me."

"I do, Dad, and that's why we're here."

"You know it hurts to piss."

"Right now?"

"Has for ages. And to shit, too."

"Just tell the doctor."

"The doctors know all about it."

"This is a different thing. You need a pill, that's all, and by this time next week? 'Wow,' you're going to say. Just really, 'Wow.'"

"About what again?"

"About how good you feel."

"Thanks so much for this, son. I do mean it."

Toby asked Hugo if he would be all right with Edward, and the boy said he would be. Edward held out his arms, and Hugo shook his drowsiness away and jumped into them.

"I'm feeling so much better, Hugo, now that I'm here," Edward said.

The giant nurse stood in the hall, speaking with a colleague. Toby closed the door behind him and tapped her on the shoulder.

"Yes?"

"May I speak to the doctor before he sees my father?"

"She."

"Of course."

The nurse led Toby to a small office, where an Indian woman of his generation, Dr. Singhmar, sat in front of a computer, an e-mail program open before her. The nurse introduced him as the son of a patient. Toby sat.

"I was just about to join you."

Toby thanked her. "My father has been acting strangely. Very strangely. But I didn't want to tell you about it in front of him."

The doctor asked Toby to summarize recent events, and he did, right up to the sleeping pills in the beer. She sat for a moment, in active silence, a sexy hint of a moustache on her upper lip. It was a small office, with few personal decorations. Some inspirational quotations, in French, about treating the whole being. Dr. Singhmar stood up abruptly and led Toby into the examination room. She introduced herself warmly and dismissed both Toby and Hugo.

The toys in the waiting area of the emergency department were of the broken truck and naked Barbie variety, and Toby worried that they were covered in bacteria and viruses that would attack and harm the boy. Hugo received several more compliments on his smart attire from the women in the waiting area. He thanked them in the language in which he had been addressed, and each time Toby rubbed the boy's head and kissed him.

His phone rang: Karen. She had been to the Chien Chaud, to the bank, and to Garrett's office. It was over. She would be filing for bankruptcy protection first thing in the new year.

"How's Edward?"

"We should be home soon."

"Let's order in tonight, while I still have a credit card."

The big nurse came through in the automatic swinging doors that separated the waiting room from the emergency wing. She beckoned to Hugo and led him into the examination room, saying, "Let's go see your grandpa." Dr. Singhmar stood in the doorway of her office, waiting for Toby.

Her expression was stern. He worried that Edward had complained about the way Toby had acted toward him, the birdwatching, the dope in his beer. A scolding was in order.

"When was the last time your father had a physical examination?"

"I don't know."

The doctor transferred her prescription pad, for the drug that would return Edward to him, from one hand to the other. "Edward is going to have to stay with us. I'm ordering some tests."

"Tests for what?"

"I can't say, exactly."

"Can you say inexactly?"

"I suspect your father is ill."

"Mentally ill, I know."

"His behaviour may be only a symptom."

"A symptom of what?"

"It is my strong suspicion that your father has cancer and that it has metastasized. There are certainly tumours in his abdomen—I could feel them during my examination. It's possible they have spread to his brain, you see, where pressure can cause—"

"You could be wrong."

"I could be."

"They might be benign. It might be nothing. It's nothing. He just needs a pill."

"Would you like to sit down?"

An open box of Pot of Gold chocolates sat crookedly on the doctor's desk. Underneath one corner of the box were a set of keys and a grocery list. Canola oil, yogurt, chickpeas, butter. Five of the chocolates were missing from their plastic moulds. Outside, a siren. A heart attack or a car accident or a stabbing on the north side of the mountain, where the stabbings happen.

"What do people do in these situations, Dr. Singhmar?"

"Sorry?"

"What do I tell him?"

"I tell your father, we tell him, that further tests are necessary."

She stared at Toby for a moment, drew air in, and released it with a faint gesture of uncertainty. Uncertainty or defeat.

In the examination room, Edward and Hugo had pulled out several feet of the paper blanket. They had constructed a fort, using the chairs and stool, and had hidden under it, giggling. Edward whispered something and Hugo peeked his head out.

"Surprise!"

⌒

All the way home Toby and Hugo played the translation game. Toby would say a word in French and the boy would either translate it or ask for help. They had made it through barnyard animals, fruits and vegetables, clothing, and musical instruments. When they were only a few minutes from the house on rue Collingwood, Toby stalled for time by stopping at the IGA. Neither Emily Post nor Letitia Baldrige had prepared him for the conversation he would soon have with his mother.

From the grocery store to rue Collingwood, they concentrated on automotive concerns.

"*Autobus.*"

"Bus."

The cars and minivans parked along the curved streets had acquired an exotic quality. Vehicles *after* one's father is diagnosed.

"Bus. More, Poney."

"Please sit quietly."

They remained in the Chevette, under the dim street light.

"You want to see Karine."

"Just a minute, Hugo."

"Now, please. You want to see her. Okay?" He struggled in the Westchester. "Okay!"

Toby released the boy from his straps. They held hands. Toby walked slowly through the wet snow in the front yard, while Hugo tried to run. In the interests of environmental conservation, Toby had refused a plastic bag at the IGA. He carried the carton of eggs in his left hand, but he did not trust the muscles in his fingers to work, so he cradled it.

The door opened. Karen stood in jeans and a white Juste Pour Rire T-shirt. It was too large for her. Her husband's shirt.

"Where's your dad?"

This was not how Toby had planned it. They weren't even inside yet. Hugo was supposed to be on the floor, playing. Karen was supposed to be in her recliner, relaxed and philosophical. "Back at the hospital."

"What for?"

"Tests."

"What sort of *tests?*"

"I don't know, exactly. Scans and things. He has to stay overnight."

"And you left him?"

"I have a two-year-old here. His bedtime is in an hour."

"You can't leave someone alone in a hospital. You know the condition he's in. He'll be scared."

"I didn't want to tell you on the phone."

"Why not?"

"We should save some things for genuine human contact, shouldn't we?"

Karen pulled a ski jacket from the rack. "This isn't one of those things, Toby. You should make a note of that."

Toby and Hugo remained outside.

"Karine! You are here."

"Hi, baby." She snatched up her purse and stepped outside. "You're all right for dinner? I was going to make a—"

"Soufflé, I know."

Hugo reached for Karen, and she picked him up, hugged him tightly, kissed him. "Édouard and I will be back soon, Hugo."

Karen tromped over the snow to her Corolla. Toby nearly let her go. "Mom."

"What?"

"It's not good."

She stopped on the sidewalk and moved the hair from her face. "What's not good?"

"Dad."

"What's not good, Toby?"

"He's sick."

"But there's a pill."

A plumbing van drove by slowly, the driver squinting at the house addresses.

"You left him there, sick and alone?"

Toby picked up Hugo.

"Did you . . ." Karen rested her arm on the roof of the Corolla. A man in tights and a long yellow jacket jogged down the middle of rue Collingwood, puffing. Days into days. Karen watched him go. "Did you get a second opinion?"

"The tests aren't all done."

"You have to get a second opinion. And you never leave. I would never leave you. Never." Karen stomped around and opened the driver's-side door. She paused and looked up into the cool night sky, its faint glow obscuring all but the brightest stars. She slammed the door closed and walked back toward the house. Toby put the boy down and met her near the cherry tree. She fell into him. Hugo pulled at their jackets.

"What kind of sick?"

"Terrible sick."

"How is he? Is he terrified?"

"He doesn't really know."

Karen cussed all the way to the Corolla, then shouted an apology to Hugo. She honked and held the horn as she sped down rue Collingwood. The jogger veered toward the sidewalk, a strip of silver shining in the headlights.

Hugo stood in the snow.

Inside, Toby sliced vegetables for the soufflé while the boy sat against the warm door of the oven, flipping through an oversized edition of *The Velveteen Rabbit* Edward had picked up for him. In Toby's chest and pelvis, minute tickles and clenches. He was clearly being poisoned by the same forces that were killing his father: tobacco, microwave popcorn, failure. Edward, as they took him away to be scanned, had dished his son a thumbs-up: "Wipe that look off your face. It's a *test*."

The doorbell rang. It was the original bell that came with the house, and part of it had died in the mid-eighties. There was a distinct melancholy about the sound, heralding not the excitement of a new visitor but the miserable certainty that someone else had arrived and would need to be fed. It was the first time Hugo had heard the dying elephant call of the doorbell, and it alarmed him. Toby scooped him up and carried him to the door.

A small man in a black watch cap, an army jacket, and astoundingly thick spectacles, stood clutching a piece of paper. "Yeah, hi, Toby."

"Hello."

The man waved the piece of paper before him. "I'm here for the meeting."

"What meeting?"

He read aloud from the paper. "The first meeting of the Benjamin Disraeli Society, devoted to the art of how to be a gentleman. And in brackets here it says, 'in the twenty-first century.' Hosted by celebrated television host Toby Ménard, of television's *Toby a Gentleman*. And then it says your address."

Snow had begun to fall. Hugo delivered a whispered monologue directly into Toby's ear, in a combination of French and English, about the snowman he would build tomorrow. The man at the door adjusted his eyeglasses.

"I'm Toby Ménard."

"From television's *Toby a Gentleman*."

"Evidently."

"Real nice to meet you. I'm James."

"May I look at your flyer?" Toby noticed right away that James was half an hour early. The military garb, designed to conceal weapons, and *half an hour early*. "This may come as a disappointment, James, but I think you've been tricked. I didn't put these up."

"You didn't?"

"Not at all, and I know nothing of this."

"Oh."

"I mean, I am half interested in starting a Benjamin Disraeli Society, and I'm thrilled to know that interest is out there. Thrilled, so thank you, James. But a meeting: no, not yet. And not here, at my parents' house. And *definitely* not tonight. I can't think of a worse night."

"It's something I want." The man sniffed, looked away. "I want to know how to be a gentleman. It isn't easy, with all those temptations out there."

Toby fetched a pen and asked James to write his name and contact information on the back of the paper. It took some work to convince James to actually leave the property, first promises and, eventually, as James grew both suspicious and ornery about the misunderstanding, sincere apologies.

To ensure his safety and that of his family, Toby walked out and wrote down the licence plate of James's red Trans Am. It was a rear-wheel drive, and it fishtailed in the slush as it growled down Collingwood.

Fifteen minutes later, when Randall and Garrett arrived, Toby was ready for them. He described James as a hulking criminal who was not at all happy to have his evening's plans thwarted. The irony of all this, he explained, is that a gentleman would never do this to a friend: spring a party on him, in his own house.

Randall swung a white plastic bag. "We brought meat."

Flyers had been posted all over the West Island, in restaurants and coffee shops and on community bulletin boards. Garrett had designed them and Randall had photocopied and distributed two hundred of them. The festivities were set to begin at eight. Only two more budding gentlemen arrived, one an old high school classmate who was now a toupee-wearing accountant in Dorval and the other a newly divorced science teacher from West Island College who was so nervous that Toby worried he would faint.

Edward's fate and, now, the repudiation of what he had seen as his life's work, his contribution, were too much to consider, let alone discuss with Randall and Garrett. So Toby entrusted Hugo to them and went outside with a glass of wine. The garden light was weak but ample for his task: lighting the barbecue.

The instructions had faded long ago, but Toby understood the principles. One turned on the propane and the burners. Then one made fire and introduced fire to the propane. It was common family knowledge that the automatic lighting mechanism on the barbecue had worked for one week; thereafter, Edward had used matches. The matchbook Toby had found in the kitchen cupboard advertised the American Hotel in Bethlehem, Pennsylvania. On the cover was a photograph of the hotel, which appeared historic, a couple arm in arm out front, dressed in bell-bottoms and flamboyant hats. The colours were unnatural.

Toby practised with a match. The last time he had lit one was for *Toby a Gentleman,* an episode about how to be dashing around an intended who smokes. The match did what matches are supposed to do, so he turned on the propane and opened the burners. He stepped back and dropped the matchbook into a shallow puddle of meltwater. Toby wiped the matchbook on the grass and pulled off a match. He could smell the gas now. The first match didn't light. Neither did the second. It was decision time: make fire and light the barbecue or turn it off and regroup. Match number three lit, and Toby tossed it into the barbecue. Flames shot up with a *whoomp,* high enough to make the cable line to the house shiver. Something on Toby's face had singed and now smelled.

It did not feel like a winter night, but cold air did rise off the new snow. Toby stood in his Paul Smith suit, the one with the hole in the knee, and stared at the flickering orange and red inside the black barbecue. Through the windows of the house, he could hear Randall and Hugo engaging in the art of medieval Japanese assassination; upon seeing them, Hugo had insisted on donning his ninja costume. Toby gulped his wine and tossed the glass against the side of the garage. It shattered with a high-pitched whisper. He looked around; there was nothing else to throw but the barbecue sauce and smoked gouda he had prepared, so he reached down and slid his finger into the knee hole and pulled up.

Eleven

The young woman wanted the handsome man to leave. Go, she said. It rained outside the stone house, in the valley. Sheep and goats wandered past olive and fruit trees, and there were bells around the goats' hard necks. The handsome man was American, and the woman was Mediterranean, or seemed so. Slim, dark-skinned, large-eyed. There was something primitive about her; perhaps she lacked the capacity to understand political stories in the newspaper. Her fingers were long and thin. They covered her enormous brown eyes because she did not want the handsome American to see her, to witness and enjoy the pain he had caused her. The American smoked a cigarette and looked away. The valley, where he looked, was drunk with green. A gentle fog obscured the hills. Two fighter jets passed overhead. The man dropped his cigarette, stomped it out, winked at the woman, and walked out the door. She fell to her knees.

Toby watched the American reject the woman on a miniature television. It hung over his father's hospital bed from a rotating arm attached to the brick wall. His first coherent thought was that he longed to be in the valley with her, that he longed to be the handsome American just as all Canadian men long to be the handsome American. The smell of disinfectant and pudding faded, the tube below the bed, unhidden by covers, filled with blood and shit, blessedly faded.

Karen walked into the room, holding the ninja's hand.

"Poney! Édouard!"

Toby touched his finger to his lips. It was a vast room in the oncology ward, a recovery area with six beds. Of the four who had been in for treatments, only Edward was awake—and barely. His eyes opened slowly.

"Hello, sweetheart," he said, to no one in particular.

It had begun in his lungs and had spread up and down. In the two weeks since Edward's diagnosis, the radiation treatments had diminished the tumours in his brain somewhat, alleviating the pressure. Already he was more like himself—himself on a fixed diet of morphine. His doctors had warned that the mood changes were unpredictable; some patients in his situation turned petulant and cruel. Others seemed to understand the fix they were in, and in the act of resignation they were more philosophical, more festive and amiable than usual.

It was dark but not late, rush hour on a cloudy day. Cars hummed and honked five storeys below. On the rolling table near the window stood a tall vase of smoked glass filled with yellow freesia. The flowers were from Steve Bancroft, a fact that Karen and Toby had agreed to keep a secret from Edward.

Toby's BlackBerry bleeped quietly in his bag. The sound had become distressingly rare since October.

"Is that your phone?"

"It is."

"Shouldn't you get it?"

He wanted to devour it. "I don't want to be a boor. I'm in my dad's—"

"Go answer the phone."

Toby locked himself in the first private washroom he found and listened to his voice mail. The BlackBerry had been in his satchel all day, where its regular bleeping had apparently been muffled by the four handkerchiefs he had carried since Edward's diagnosis, just in case. There were two businesslike messages from Mr. Demsky's assistant, the woman he had met in the townhouse. The third was more informal. "Adam—Mr. Demsky—really wants to speak to you. It affects his travel plans in the go-forward. Please call at your first opportunity."

Two voice mails followed from Mr. Demsky himself. The first was short: "Where the hell are you? Call me, Tobias, soon as you can. Business hours." The second was more contemplative. "I don't know how any member of your generation can be away from his phone for so long. If it weren't so damned annoying at the moment, I'd admire you for this. But I cannot bring myself to do that, because, frankly, I want to track you down and slap you for leaving me hanging all afternoon. You try to do something generous, and this, this is how you're rewarded. Like a stepchild he treats me."

"Adam," said the assistant, in the background.

"Like a stepchild!"

Toby dialled Mr. Demsky's home office number, and his assistant answered.

"*Bonjour, Madame.* This is Tobias Ménard phoning. I understand Mr. Demsky has an interest in speaking to me."

A moment or two passed. Then: "Goddamn you. God-damn you to hell for this. This uncertainty!"

"I'm very sorry, Mr. Demsky."

"You know what I had to do?"

"No."

"I had to book meetings for you, and a flight. I had to, and I happen to be the semi-retired president and CEO of a small but profitable media company. Maybe the only profit-able media company left on the continent. Do you know why I did it?"

"No, sir."

"'Sir,' he calls me. I did it because I can't help but give. Give and give and give."

"I don't understand."

"My old friend, William Kingston, liked your reel. He wants you to adapt the gentleman business for the Americans. He's not willing to sign on to anything, yet. He wants his staff to meet you first."

Toby pulled down the toilet seat and sat down. He didn't even look to see if he was touching urine or pubic hairs. Mr. Demsky's friend William was *William Kingston,* the president of ABS. He had heard William Kingston speak once, during the industry run-up to Canada's gloomy television awards show. There was that something about him, that easy and expansive confidence, that quality a Canadian who loves his country but hates himself just a little for living in it always recognizes. No amount of money or education could allow someone like Toby to approach a man like William Kingston in style, in poise, in elegance, in authority. Kingston possessed a middle-aged assurance so natural and so healthful it defied easy comprehension. Generations of gentlemen had come

before him, and he himself had absorbed all that he knew—
from private schools in New England and Europe, surely, but
also from his father and his grandfather and from every other
man with several sets of meaningful cufflinks he would have
encountered in his formative years.

"Jesus."

"Jesus can't help you."

"Mr. Demsky. This is the most—"

"Clam up. Just tell me you're free tomorrow at nine
thirty. That's when we fly out."

Toby had been congratulating himself for not having a
job, for having this time with his father. Yet his little black
book of aphorisms only had one entry so far, and it was a
piece of wisdom adapted from Mr. Demsky: beast of ambition.

"Two nights."

"Mr. Demsky, I—"

"Stop."

Mr. Demsky insisted on picking him up in the morning,
and took his parents' address before Toby could invent an
excuse to meet at the mall. The phone silent, he sat on the
toilet and stared at the fading off-white of the washroom
wall. The men who had built the hospital were dead by now.
Its doctors and nurses, thousands of them, worked nobly to
save and sustain human life, to preserve dignity in death—
and all but a few of them were forgotten. Montrealers worth
remembering were remembered for other acts, other trajec-
tories and pointless sacrifices: hockey, religion, movie sound-
tracks, politics.

His shoes clicked along the empty halls of the dinnertime hospital. It was quiet, as ever, in his father's room. A

young woman, hardly older than a teenager, lay in the bed across from Edward's. She reached out to Toby. Her head was perfectly tiny and hairless. "Nurse," she said, in a voice so meek he was surprised to have heard it.

"We already called for one," said Karen, leaning on a heater. Hugo was on the floor at the foot of Edward's bed, flipping through a book, mere feet from the tube of blood and shit.

"Is he asleep?"

"In and out. What should we do for dinner?"

"We could eat here again. Or you could take Hugo home, if you want. I could stay with Dad awhile."

"Could," said Karen.

Toby had planned to tell his mother now. But he could not summon the vocabulary. "You haven't been home much. You need sleep, and a shower."

"True."

"I'll stay with him for a couple of hours. But you'll have to take the Chevette, the way the Westchester's strapped in. I'm sorry."

"It's a car."

Karen kissed her husband and whispered in his ear, took Hugo's hand, and rounded the corner.

For the last several months, Edward had been in ferocious pain—blood in his urine, blood in his stool, headaches, abdominal cramps. In April he had seen the family doctor in Dollard, Dr. Smythe, who had arranged blood tests and diagnostic analyses. Edward had avoided the tests. For the pain, he had been doubling up on over-the-counter extra-strength ibuprofen and mixing it with alcohol. Neither Karen nor Toby could recall more than two or three instances when

Edward had actually complained since the spring, when the symptoms had become—according to Dr. Smythe, who had met them at the Montreal General in a state of defensiveness and regret—unbearable.

Up in Edward's airless room, Toby waited until eight o'clock for his father to wake up. A home decorating program was on, and its level of audience participation gave Toby an idea or two for New York. This show was boring, though, and the host was too loud and too gay.

"You're going home?" Edward's eyes opened slowly.

"Yes."

"Thank you. For being here."

"I'm so sorry I—"

"Think good thoughts."

Toby was stricken with good thoughts, and he wanted to express them somehow, but there were five other patients in the room. The young girl with the tiny head had visitors: her parents and what appeared to be a teenage brother, who guffawed nervously every few minutes.

"Is there anything I can do for you?"

"Come back."

"Done."

"And remember what I told you."

Toby mimed taking notes.

His father sneaked a hand out from the covers, and Toby took it: a dark hand, big fingers, wedding ring, cuticles always immaculately cared for, burn streaks.

He had never liked beets, Edward Mushinsky, despite his connections with Eastern Europe and, more recently, his fractional Jewishness. Borscht, never. He could not smell a pickled beet, lest he retch, but he could eat the mould off a muffin, a piece of bread, a brick of cheddar cheese. On Saturday and Sunday mornings, after he and Karen had been to a party together, or out for a rare meal at a restaurant, Edward would drink a large glass of beer and tomato juice to splash his hangover away. When membership in the Royal Canadian Legion was diminishing, they opened it up to relatives of veterans. Edward joined, and on Saturday afternoons they would go to the hall in Lachine for the meat draw. On summer weekends, he liked to wear shorts. But at the Legion there was a dress code. To conform, just barely, Edward would wear blue short shorts, navy knee-high socks, and a pair of leatherette slip-on dress shoes. At weddings he would dance so vigorously that sweat stains would appear under his arms and in a winged pattern on his back, soaking the poly-cotton blend of his faded shirts. "Hey, hey, hey," he would say, stomping one foot and clapping his hands. Midway through Toby's one disastrous year in organized hockey, in grade six, the team had travelled to Hull for a weekend tournament. Edward and the father of another inferior player, Georges Tremblay, drank a bottle and a half of Bailey's Irish Cream over the course of Saturday, and screamed and danced in the stands. They were quietly escorted out of the evening banquet for spooking some of the children. Christmas was his mother's time. She bought the presents, wrapped them, and decorated the tree. But every year, his father would buy one thing for each of them and present it on Christmas Eve. These unwrapped gifts included flashlights that were also bookmarks, mobile battery packs, laser pointers for corporate presentations, flashlights that twisted like snakes, scissors that were designed to open hard plastic packaging, compact stepladders, sweatshirts that commemorated the Canadian team's participation in the Salt Lake City Winter Olympics, heated seat covers for the car, cordless drills, and flashlights that one attached to one's forehead. Never once had Toby used one of these gifts, but he had kept them, like talismans. When Toby was small and could not sleep, his father would come in and rub his back and sing "You Are My Sunshine" in a soft voice, and he would stay until Toby could not remember him leaving.

If there were only some way to express all this without saying it aloud.

"I'll come back."

"Tomorrow?"

"Yes, tomorrow."

"I am so proud."

Toby was prepared to outline the ways and means in which he had wronged his father, from elementary school all the way up to the previous week. "I'm regretful, Dad."

"Shh."

"When I saw you in the car, burning up, I wanted to pull you out."

"You did. You did pull me out. You pulled me out."

"I was a coward. I am a coward."

"Good thoughts."

Toby kissed his hand.

"You better go."

"I'll stay awhile longer."

"We'll see you tomorrow."

"Tomorrow."

As he walked, Toby stared down at the fifty-year-old tiles on the floor, decorated with squiggles—the fucking squiggle-maker had probably lived to be 104—until he found the washroom. He splashed water on his face and stared at himself in the mirror. There was a rogue grey hair on his left eyebrow, long and kinked. He pulled it out. The counter was riddled with drops and pools of water. Empty soap dispenser. Dirty mirror. An ungrammatical sign urging everyone to wash their hands, singular subject and plural pronoun, to avoid gender-specific language. The secret damage of this.

It was eight fifteen, so he drove first to Boutique Jean-François. He bought three new shirts and a pair of meaningful cufflinks, black and silver. The shop smelled of new fabric unleashed, quality cologne, the latest in cleansers.

When Toby arrived at home, it was forty minutes past Hugo's bedtime. The boy was still awake, sitting up in his pyjamas and babbling. Toby hugged him and kissed him and implored him to sleep, rubbed his back and attempted to sing "You Are My Sunshine." He didn't remember anything after *"Please don't take my sunshine away,"* so he started over and repeated himself until Hugo was asleep.

Karen sat in the living room, a bottle of Alsatian white wine on the coffee table, the glass a small fishbowl in her hand. "Want a drink?"

"No, thanks."

"Your dad and I were saving it for a special occasion."

"No, thanks."

"You went shopping." She nodded at his Boutique Jean-François bag. "How festive."

She was in her white satin pyjamas with a character from the Japanese alphabet on the breast pocket. On the table, next to the bottle of wine, lay a book called *Chicken Soup for the Grieving Soul.*

"Be careful with that stuff, Mom."

"The book?"

"The book too."

She looked down at the glass, swished the wine around, smelled it. Her eyes were gluey.

"I have to go to New York tomorrow morning."

Karen slowly leaned back in her chair.

"Someone wants to interview me."

The room was lit by one faint lamp, loaded with an energy-saving fluorescent bulb that gave the room a pale yellow tint. She stared at Toby for a long time, as though she struggled to recognize him. The old grandfather clock struck six. It was 9:52. She finished her glass of wine quickly, picked up the bottle, and walked out. The sound of the refrigerator door opening and closing. Blowing her nose. Running water to take her sleeping pill. Her feet swooshing across the shag.

Downstairs, Toby washed and ironed his three new shirts and prepared himself for the interviews. He put extra-strength whitening strips on his teeth, clipped imperfections out of his hair, and researched William Kingston on the Internet; the man enjoyed sailing, Tintin books, small Greek islands, and Nina Simone's covers of the hit songs of the 1960s.

Toby practised spontaneity. Pompousness had to be scraped out of his ideas and philosophies, so he repeated them aloud in front of a decorative mirror. Teenagers today are *expected* to cuss on public transit, Mr. Kingston, to spit on sidewalks, to litter, to modify their mufflers, to wear clothes that reveal the colour and style of their underpants. Even the smart ones. Their role models are celebrities who did not finish high school, who speak in artificial British accents, drink and drive, and upload videotapes of themselves performing doggie-style. Books have become irrelevant, and not just for teenagers. Their parents have abandoned newspapers, suits and dresses, symphonies, pleases and thank yous, the library and the voting booth, in favour of Pilates and poker and plasma screens. Media companies are the most cynical of all, and television the most potent force for the erosion of order, but all that can change.

Men have reacted to the challenge of gender equality by elevating their lizard brains—dressing like cartoon characters, carrying handguns. The popularity of no-rules cage-match fist fighting, a weekly festival of televised vulgarity, is the visual culture equivalent of tearing off one's clothes and running into the bush, eating raw meat, and howling at the moon. It is a sign of desperation, the far end of the social pendulum. We have gone as far as we can go. Soon, very soon, gentlemen will be back. And they will want to know whether or not they should remove their suit jackets during dinner.

Never.

Toby would accomplish for his generation what Emily Post had for hers. She had written *Etiquette* for women like herself, well born and wealthy members of Best Society who had a genuine need for guidance about the treatment of household servants. The majority of her readers, though, were regular people, the newly literate yet poor citizens of the twentieth century, desperate for a dream that would lead them from the horrors of the war through technological, social, and cultural transformation, the hopelessness of the Depression. A book that would teach them the rules of the ruling class, that would give them permission to pretend. *Etiquette* was the book most requested by American soldiers fighting in World War Two;

Toby a Gentleman could be the most-watched video segment on YouTube.

He recited all of this aloud, several times, sitting and standing. For the first time in ten years, it took some effort to back it up with feeling. This, he determined, was not so much a crisis of faith as the comforts and consolations of suburban mediocrity seeping into him. He crept up into Hugo's room and gave him a kiss on the forehead. "Tomorrow," he whispered.

The sun came up. Toby paced with his shoes on. He wanted to say goodbye to Hugo before Mr. Demsky arrived, so he faked some coughs and stomped outside the bedroom door. The boy was still sleeping when a silver Town Car parked in front of the house at exactly 7:45. Karen did not speak; she did not even nod when Toby asked her to say goodbye for him and to kiss the boy and to make sure he sat on the potty at least once each day.

The tinted rear window rolled down, and Mr. Demsky's mad scientist hair was revealed. "Hurry your ass!"

Karen stood at the door as Toby hurried down the front stairs with his folding garment bag and small suitcase.

"Good morning, Madame Ménard," said Mr. Demsky.

"Mushinsky," she said.

The driver, a tall man in a black suit and a Siberian fur hat, stood at attention before the open trunk. Toby did not know whether to put his own things inside or to hand them over. So he asked.

"Is your choice, sir. But I take."

Another potential segment. It was endless. He told Mr. Demsky as much, as the driver navigated his way out of the mysteries of Dollard.

Mr. Demsky shifted on the black leather, his own suit at least twenty years old and tailored for a larger man. "What was up with your mom?"

"It's early."

"Here I am, going out of my way to help her son move out of the house, and what do I get? *Mushinsky?*"

"It was a controversial moment in our little house when I became a Ménard."

"Still."

It was the last thing Toby wanted to talk about. "She didn't want me to go."

"Why not?"

"Just . . . family stuff."

"Everything's okay?"

"Beast of ambition."

"And one day, beast, you can have all this." Mr. Demsky gestured at the back seat of the Town Car, at his suit, and began to laugh. A three-minute coughing fit ensued, and Mr. Demsky spat into his handkerchief several times. It occurred to Toby that he had not eaten breakfast. An empty stomach always made him prone to nausea. He retched as daintily as he could manage at the sight and sound of Mr. Demsky's spitting, and opened the window for a blast of exhaust and river.

"How did you hatch from that little house?"

Inside the airport, Mr. Demsky initiated Toby into the wonders of the Maple Leaf Lounge. An emergency phone call from the national sales director freed Toby to read the New York press and take a complimentary breakfast of yogurt, fruit, and granola. For the first time, Toby knew the pleasure of boarding the airplane early, sitting in business class, and making eye contact with the unfortunate as they filed into economy. He suppressed an urge, as the airplane taxied away from the gate, to kiss Mr. Demsky.

A black man in a polyester suit, walking shoes, and a demeaning *chapeau de chauffeur* waited for them in the arrivals area of LaGuardia with a printed sign that said MISTERS DEMSKY AND MENROD. Toby did not allow him to take his bags. He did not allow him to open the limousine door.

"Sir," said the chauffeur, quietly, as he closed the door, "this is my job, all right? I applied for it. Don't let it torment you."

The driver navigated the wide and clogged streets, thick now with rain. The tips of the towers were hidden by fog. In Manhattan, the transition from the symbolic to the actual was noticeably smooth. Arrival came with mild disappointment, like spotting the tour guides of a great museum smoking at the loading dock.

Mr. Demsky slapped Toby on the knee. "What's your problem, Tobias?"

"Nothing."

"What's your key message?"

"My—"

"Don't hesitate."

"The gentleman must return. Etiquette, to the video game people, is more exotic than Burma."

"Rangoon. Say 'Rangoon.' I love that word, and I know I'm not alone."

"They only need a spiritual guide, a Moses."

"Moses isn't sexy."

"I'm completely uninterested in street drugs and hookers, so no one who hires me has to worry about scandals."

"Completely uninterested? I don't think you should say that aloud."

"I'd never hire a hooker."

"Never say never."

"Have you?"

"They never bother you for attention, or ask you to be nice to their mothers. If you want them to sing an Edith Piaf song and dance while they defrock, no problem. It's an extra twenty."

Toby wondered, briefly, if Mr. Demsky was quite the best mentor for a man in his position. The car stopped in front of an industrial brick building with a glass-walled restaurant cut into the first two floors. Silver letters spelled NEW GOTHAM above the entrance. Toby opened his door. Mr. Demsky did not.

"You're not coming?"

"I'm not."

"Oh."

"I'm off to a meeting of my own."

"Oh."

"You nervous, Tobias?"

"Absolutely not."

"Terrific."

"Are you sure about this, Mr. Demsky?"

"I'll meet you back at the hotel."

The driver held a large umbrella for Toby and opened the restaurant door for him. Toby had prepared a five-dollar bill.

"Obliged," said the driver.

The darkness of the autumn rain added an air of noontime romance to the restaurant, designed with a loft aesthetic that seemed a bit tired. Toby had thought New York would know better. Huge windows, white pillars, bamboo floors, exposed brick, an open kitchen hidden behind glass like an exhibit.

A great beauty held his menu. He was not good enough for this place. No, he was. He was. "Your name?" she said.

"Tobias Ménard."

"Mr. Maynard. Welcome."

Toby had expected William Kingston, his hero. Instead, he met a thin, fierce-eyed woman in a skirt and blazer and an uncommonly ugly man, lumpen and either sick or hungover, a dusting of white on the shoulders of his black corduroy sport jacket.

Astrid Stanhope, East Coast director of entertainment, sat across from Harry Bennett, outgoing senior producer of *Wake Up!* Astrid drank Gerolsteiner, while Harry had already finished most of a carafe of white wine. The Americans stood up to shake hands, a peculiar moment as they boldly assessed him: the colour and sparkle quotient of his eyes, the white of his teeth, the blush of his skin, the way a suit hung on his shoulders.

"How old are you?" Astrid replaced the serviette on her lap.

"In Canada, we always begin conversations with a comment about the weather."

"It's a piece of shit out there," said Harry. "Feel better? How old are you?"

"Thirty-seven."

"See?" Harry pointed to his temple, and a pinch of dandruff shimmered into the carafe of wine.

"There's thinking thirty-seven," said Astrid, "and *seeing* thirty-seven."

Harry topped up his wine and splashed some into Toby's empty glass. Two of the dandruff flakes twirled on the surface. "The flight was okay?"

"Lovely. Thank you."

"I like that, you know?" Astrid waved her jewelled fingers at Toby as though she were watching him on television or visiting his cage. "The way he just tosses the word out there. 'Lovely.'" She included him, now: "Our worry, when we hit on this concept, was that we'd get some pretty boy who's spent most of his life rich and silly in Kensington. Or some, sorry, blander-than-maple-syrup Canadian with a stick up his ass."

"Maple syrup is bland?"

"Lovely," said Harry. "Some lovely Canadian."

"Maple syrup may not be bland, but we think it's bland. You see? The very idea of it bores us. You see?"

"I see."

"You gay?" Harry took a drink.

"Not necessarily."

"Smartly put, Harry. You just violated a constitutional amendment. Now if we don't hire Mr. Maple Syrup on a two-year contract, he'll sue us."

Harry stared at Astrid and sighed languidly. On the exhale he whispered, "I'm an unhappy man." He called the server to the table and ordered another carafe of wine.

Astrid tilted her head winningly, renewed by Harry's declaration. It was clear she had once been on television herself. "We treat Canadians like that smelly aunt upstate we never visit but *should* visit. And that's a terrible feeling, knowing she's up there, alone. But we're busy, right? We have our own shit to deal with."

"On behalf of my people, I'm only sort of insulted."

"You see? You see! That's what I'm talking about. Could you get any milder? More sweetly inoffensive?"

Toby scanned the room for exits. The server arrived and interrupted an eight-second silence. It was a simple menu, one long sheet of paper, but every item was complex and needlessly employed French phrases. The words steeled him.

"I'll have the boudin blanc of Saint Pierre," said Astrid, enunciating every vowel and consonant.

Toby didn't really know what it was, but he asked for the Rouelle de Thomas farm squab *avec farcie aux cerises*, pronouncing the French with his best imitation of a Parisian, not a Québécois, accent.

"You said you weren't gay," said Harry.

After lunch, a different driver, also a large black man, squired them to the headquarters and studio, just off Times Square. It was all quite similar, on the broadcast floor, to what he had known in Montreal, only twenty times larger, busier, cleaner, prettier, newer. No one walked, they scurried, as though the stories of missing babies in Arkansas, schoolyard stabbings in Texas, and polygamous religious cults in South Dakota were the glue that kept the United States united. Every stupid little thing was epic. Toby knew that if he ignored or dismissed this simple fact of American storytelling, he would fade into loveliness and maple syrup.

Astrid disappeared. Toby interrupted the tour and extended his hand. Harry took it, and they shook for a moment. "I want to thank you for a fascinating lunch, and for this mini tour," Toby said. "But I'm sure I'm wasting your time."

"You are. You are wasting my time. I could be in my office right now, watching old episodes of *Seinfeld*."

"I can find my way out."

Harry wheezed. Reporters with sheets of paper whirled about them. "You don't want to work here?"

"I'd love to work here. But the maple syrup."

"The what?"

"We just sat in a restaurant for an hour and a half. I didn't say more than three words to you and Astrid. I haven't actually pitched the idea."

"We're pretty clear on the idea."

"How?"

"Our boss, William, was the best man at Adam Demsky's wedding. If you shit the bed, you'll be on the first train back to the sticks. But you have your shot. You're in."

"I'm in."

"I have to call Stanhope. She'll piss herself that you didn't know."

Harry led him to a small conference room populated by three people—two writers and a producer, all women. The final confirmation that this was more advanced than an audition was when the team showed him mock-ups of *Toby a Gentleman,* a daily segment on *Wake Up!* that would, in the producer's words, "Consider fashion and etiquette in the broadest way possible."

"You're basically Martha Stewart," said the senior writer.

"But a fellow," said the junior writer.

The producer rubbed her hands and looked up at the exposed vents and ducts in the tiny boardroom. "You're presenting, and ultimately selling, a lifestyle." With that statement, greased with brightness and confidence, Toby knew two things: these people were smarter than anyone at the station in Montreal; and sometime over the next year or so he would sleep with his producer. "Metrosexuality was riddled with flaws, and that's why you don't hear about it anymore.

We're after something more timeless. Our mission is not to teach effete New York professionals how to dress. They already know how to dress. You're addressing, primarily, the wives and girlfriends of dirt bikers."

"Yobs," said the junior writer.

"Firefighters," said the senior writer.

"Chinos, pulled up super-high."

"Wife beaters."

"Contestants on *The Price Is Right*."

"McDonald's eaters."

"Gamers."

"They have those yellow Support the Troops ribbons on their cars."

"Trucks."

"Goddamn trucks."

"SUVs."

"They take up both armrests on airplanes."

"Hockey watchers, basically."

"Professional wrestling."

"Oh God, yes."

"Are you familiar with our electoral system, Toby?"

Harry Bennett, who had listened while balancing the right side of his face on one hand, stood as abruptly as a man of his age, physical condition, and relative sobriety could manage. "All three of you, please, shut the fuck up."

They did.

Toby's phone buzzed in his pocket. He removed it and peeked at the incoming caller. *Dad—cell*.

"Don't listen to them," said Harry. "Not a word."

The phone stopped buzzing.

Harry walked around the table and leaned on the chair

backs of the writers. "Do not let them strip the dignity from the Middle American. There's nothing clever about it, despite what they think."

"Come on, Harry," said the producer.

The phone began to buzz anew. Again, Edward's phone.

Harry informed Toby that he had only three weeks remaining at the network, that this industry and this city no longer interested him. They were a revolving door, the two of them, Toby in and Harry out. He was off to Connecticut, where he belonged. Books and liquor, long walks in the perpetual autumn, cocktails for the exquisite hour. Eventually, he would hire a very young housekeeper from Russia who would have trouble with his tendency to take off his pants during the exquisite hour. "This is an industry for women now."

The producer rolled her eyes and said, "Here we go."

The phone stopped buzzing.

"What's left for a man to do, really? Let alone a gentleman. Play dress-up? As you said, we're after the wives and girlfriends of dirt bikers. We're *after* them."

The phone showed two voice-mail messages. It began to buzz again, a third call. Edward.

"When's your first day?" said Harry.

"I just learned I had the job from you, a few minutes ago, in the newsroom."

"How attached are you to your name?"

"Ménard?"

"*Maynard,*" he said.

"It's fake."

"What's your real name?"

"Mushinsky."

"Ouch. Seriously, ouch. How about Marshall?"

"Whatever you think."

"It doesn't matter what I think. I'm off to get drunk with my dog, Gretel—real name."

They waited for Harry to leave the boardroom and made plans to meet for dinner and drinks that night, to celebrate. The producer, whose name was Jill, led Toby up the elevator and into the corporate offices. "That was impressive in the boardroom, letting your phone go like that."

The walls of the office were rounded and covered in plates of hammered steel. The floors were oak, stained dark, splashed with track lighting.

Jill introduced Toby to the human resources director and extended her hand for a shake. "I'll see you tonight?"

"Perfect. Perfect."

For the next hour and a half, Toby filled out forms and half listened to an explanation of his work visa. There were several opportunities to excuse himself, to listen to the messages on his phone. He had taken too much sparkling water at lunch; a trip to the washroom was in order. But he chose to remain in the office. He was a man of extraordinary ability, an O-1 visa, like Hollywood stars. The network would take care of it. Two weeks at the most, before he could operate as a consultant. He'd be perfectly legal by February. If he could start officially in early January, the eleventh or so, for a week of planning with his team, it would be grand.

"Any family?"

The phone buzzed again. "A son."

"His name?"

"Hugo."

"Hugo Ménard?"

"Hugo Brassens, at the moment. Maybe Mushinsky, maybe Marshall."

The human resources director swallowed. "Oh. How old is he?"

"He'll be three soon."

"I have a couple myself."

The HR director showed him pictures of her children. The view out the windows behind her was of rain-soaked pre-war buildings. Beyond them, he imagined, Central Park. He would jog there, pushing Hugo in a stroller of some sort. They would stop for lunch, in the summertime, and throw something back and forth. They would leave hockey behind and settle in the land of football and musical theatre. She described the furnished 1,200-square-foot two-bedroom apartment on the Upper East Side where he would live for up to four months. It had a maid's quarters but, sorry, no maid. Cleaning services were once every two weeks. Just off the lobby, what was once a ballroom was now a vast children's play area. But he couldn't stay forever, ha ha. As soon as he was settled, in January, he would meet with an ABS relocation consultant who would find him and his son a more permanent place to live, child care, parking, and anything else he might need.

The phone buzzed. Four voice-mail messages. Five.

Broadway was too noisy to hear not his father's but his mother's recorded voice, so he walked a few blocks east on Seventh Avenue. It was only marginally quieter. Montreal had always seemed a big city to Toby, but next to the ambient roar of nineteen million people, it was a quaint French village.

The first call was Karen, frantic. "Toby, it's happening. Please call back right away. It's happening sooner than we thought. Call me, please, no matter what you're doing."

Businessmen rushed past, their briefcases swinging. Young women dressed like extras in a Madonna video, smoking and waving their long arms like ribbons. Men in layers of brown and green, slathered in filth, mumbling and hooting. The mental illness equivalents of vintage wines.

Karen again, her voice quavering and raw. The extra cigarillos she had been smoking. No longer frantic. "The chaplain's in here, and Hugo. The chaplain's going to pray with me. I asked him not to make it Jesusy, because I know Ed wouldn't like that. It's your last chance to say goodbye to him, Toby, or I love you, whatever. Whatever you can manage. It's like I'm watching myself."

To hear the hospital room, with Hugo chattering in the background, Toby replayed the second message. He turned south on Forty-Ninth Street.

The third message was short, little more than a whisper: "Your dad is dying."

A man danced to music that was not there, unnoticed by the pedestrians. Toby the tourist, the rube, looked him in the eye. The man stopped dancing, abandoned his pile of items, and walked next to Toby down Forty-Ninth Street. "All I need is three dollars. Three or four, to change everything tonight."

Toby gave the man a five.

"Here he is." The dancing man kissed the bill. "A good man! Behold!"

The fourth message was difficult to hear. Toby crossed Avenue of the Americas with the phone on one ear and his finger in the other. Karen and a man speaking in a low monotone. "May His great name be blessed forever and ever. Blessed, praised, glorified, exalted, extolled, mighty, upraised, and lauded be the name of the Holy One. Blessed is He."

He had never been to Rockefeller Center, but he decided to continue past it, to look down and avoid eye contact with the dancing men and keep walking. It started to rain again. The prayer went on for some time, with plenty of interruptions by Hugo. "You're hungry." "What am I doing, Grandma?" This was new: *Grandma*.

Toby did not listen to the final message right away. He waited until the crowds with shopping bags thinned on the other side of St. Patrick's Cathedral.

"Don't bother calling back." He did not recognize this tone in his mother's voice. There were no hospital sounds in the background, no Hugo. A long silence, with a faint crackle.

Toby had never been well schooled on what counted as art deco. He usually pretended. If someone was with him now, in the lobby of the Waldorf Astoria, he would say it was art deco. He stood in the lobby. He did not move. If he moved, he would throw up. A porter stood next to him, speaking. Hector. The name tag said *Hector*. There had been this stop-motion animated show on, when he was a kid, about a bear named Jeremy, and one of his sidekicks had been a raven named Hector. Growing up in Montreal, he could watch the original French version, too. The bear's name, in French, was Colargol. Colargol wanted to travel the world and sing in the circus. But if Toby remembered well, he went to the moon. Somehow, Colargol was also Polish. The summer light harsh on the television, dust in the beams, Edward and Karen talking in the background, making meals, plans, putting on the day's clothes, aftershave, hard shoes on shag, blue smoke hanging in the air. *Have a wonderful day. We love you. See you at—*.

"Excuse me," said Hector, the porter, very slowly. "Are

you a guest at the hotel, sir?"

Hector the porter helped Toby through the check-in process and up to his suite, which had a view of the Chrysler
Building. It looked fake. On the upper floors, the rain had
turned to snow.

There was a message from Mr. Demsky. Toby phoned up
to his mentor's room.

"How did it go?"

"You didn't tell me it was a done deal."

"I wanted to surprise you, Tobias."

"There's nothing I could ever do to thank you properly."

"Just promise you won't fuck it up again."

"I promise."

Mr. Demsky coughed for a while, and took the Lord's
name in vain, and spit into either a Kleenex or a handkerchief. "Are you free for a cocktail in an hour or so? William
and I are going to the opera tonight. He doesn't have a third
ticket, you lucky bastard, but he did want to meet his new
discovery."

Toby nodded.

"Jesus. Are you crying?"

"No."

"You can't cry."

"All right."

"It reflects poorly."

"Of course."

"Five o'clock in whatever the mahogany bar's called.
Bull and Bear, I think, or Bear and Bull. Is that kosher?"

"Kosher."

"You sure everything's fine?"

"I'll wear my best suit."

"Good boy."

PART THREE

Twelve

Furman et Fils was the largest funeral home in Dollard-des-Ormeaux. The hands of the head mortician, who greeted Toby and Hugo at the door, were white dumplings lined with tiny blue veins. Arctic air had installed itself over the island for Christmas, but even so, Wally, the head mortician, dabbed at the perspiration on his forehead. Behind Wally, the funeral home's carpet was thick and soft and white. The smell of chemical lemon filled the foyer. Toby removed his shoes and watched the other Furman et Fils employees. The undertakers wore dark business socks and floated on the carpet like movie-of-the-week prophets in polyester blazers. Wood tables on each side of the minty leather chesterfield twinkled with varnish. Giant vases exploded with white and cream roses and carnations, baby's breath. Wally assured Toby that he was dealing with the head mortician, the principal Furman, because Edward Mushinsky, "a very important man in Dollard," deserved no less. Wally's laboured breathing was audible within a three-metre radius and added to the symphony of softness in Furman et Fils—organ music, the tick of a grandfather clock, distant whisperings of Wally's junior colleagues and, presumably, sons. For a year in university, Toby had dated a woman who followed daytime soap operas. Whenever characters suffered a near-death experience, they seemed to come here, to Furman et Fils, heaven in soft focus.

In Edward's will, he had expressed a desire to be cremated. The document had not been updated since the discovery of his Jewishness, and this had instigated an argument. Toby thought he would want to be buried in Jewish fashion, in a simple box, though he was not Jewish enough to be considered by the burial society. Karen wanted Edward cremated so their ashes might together be strewn, upon her death, from a rocky outcropping at Lake Memphrémagog. The argument had taken Toby and Karen to their own rocky outcroppings, so Toby had allowed his mother her wish.

Hugo had been stricken silent by Furman et Fils. In the urn and casket showroom, something about the products on offer inspired him to hug Toby's leg and bury his face. Toby employed his wine-list strategy: he agreed to purchase the second-cheapest vessel, the second-cheapest obituary notice, and the second-cheapest urn. The polished urns on the mahogany shelves featured engravings of eagles, pine trees, retirees in love, and the American and Canadian flags waving in tandem.

"Do you have a plain urn?"

Wally pointed out the eagle urn. "This is one of our most popular."

"I prefer plain."

"You don't find the eagle suitable?"

Toby picked up Hugo.

"There's no extra cost for engraving. Some folks like a poem or a saying about life's journey. We have some of those in the back that might fit your dad."

"No engraving."

Wally chewed his bottom lip and messed Hugo's hair, absently. He pulled a leather-bound book from the shelf and mumbled and tsked. "Actually, due to the vagaries of supply and demand, the plain urn is a mite bit more than the engraved models we have on hand."

"How much is a mite?"

"In the neighbourhood of thirty dollars." Wally linked his hands. "Thirty-three seventy-five, plus tax, of course."

How does a gentleman negotiate the price of an urn? There were a number of tactics he had learned from Edward, at the farmers' market. The secret was to wait. Wait and then walk away.

"In addition, the plain urn might take an extra day or two to arrive. You see—"

"With respect, Wally, I wouldn't be honouring the memory of my father, paying more for less." The theme of the segment spread out before him: the man of taste is socially and financially punished for an interest in design, in minimalism, in simple beauty. "Do you understand?"

Wally puffed his cheeks and looked up at the ceiling, painted to resemble that of a pink chateau. Nearly a minute passed. "Furman et Fils is happy to absorb the cost for a man like Edward. And we will have it here by tomorrow afternoon, so you can inspect it."

"That won't be necessary, Mr. Furman."

"I appreciate your trust, Mr. Ménard."

"My father would be honoured."

"The honour is all mine."

"You need the potty!"

Edward Mushinsky had been involved in just about every community organization in Dollard, including the Elks, the Kinsmen, the Lions, the bingo and casino associations, minor hockey, minor football, the Dollard Centre for the Arts, and the Optimist Club, so Toby chose the only large public hall available at short notice on the Friday before Christmas: the First Church of the Nazarene.

The event was two hours away and Toby was still not dressed. He sat in the blue recliner and wrote Edward's final requests on a slip of high-quality paper, careful not to forget any of them:

> *Look after Karen*
> *A mother for Hugo*
> *Mushinsky*
> *Find God*
> *Get that fucker*

Toby found several unpopped kernels in the folds and grooves of the recliner. He stared at them for six full minutes in a ray of solstice sunshine, and decided he was unable to throw them in the garbage. Toby had never looked for God. He believed neither in ghosts nor in any of the music video versions of love, but it was clear to him that the dissolved spirit of his father inhabited every item the man had ever touched. Toby dropped the lost popcorn into a clear sandwich bag and vowed to carry it for the rest of his life.

The minister of the home congregation at the First Church of the Nazarene performed an interfaith introduction to the ceremony and delivered a short pitch. He quoted with authority from the packet of background material Toby had provided. He lifted his hand to demonstrate emotional commitment, and pulled at his goatee, flared his nostrils, paused for dramatic effect. Toby saw that in his heart the minister knew as little about the fate of humanity and its hope for transcendence as a men's etiquette commentator.

Rabbi Orlovsky took the stage and recalled his own meetings with Edward, a dutiful searcher, endlessly curious about the most important question that has ever been asked: What is it to be a human being? One of Edward's best and oldest friends, a man who now lived in Seattle, played an acoustic guitar and sang four Cat Stevens songs in a row. The current Exalted Ruler of the Elks lodge compared Edward's death to the September 11, 2001, terrorist attacks in New York City and the Pentagon.

"What the hell is he talking about?" Toby whispered to his mother.

"Don't say 'hell' in here."

Toby had written his eulogy the night before, with a box of Kleenex, a bottle of Beaumes de Venise, a large bowl of Neapolitan ice cream, and a foxed paperback edition of *Roget's Thesaurus*. During the meeting at Furman et Fils, Wally had mentioned that every son regrets it if he does not write and deliver his father's eulogy, and Toby had accepted it as truth. He walked up the steps to the raised platform at the front of the church, with a small stage set up for a band, a jolly version of a crèche, a lavishly decorated Christmas tree, and on the wall a giant blanket with the word "Jesus" in an early seventies font that reminded Toby of the Christian Archie comics in his elementary school library. In normal circumstances, the tacky sweetness of the church would have cheered him—the way kindly fat people in floral-print polyester shirts and unpopular haircuts cheered him—as the contrary of his own existence. But the quality of his discomfort, on the stage, was unprecedented. Acidic, curled.

Public speaking was not among his fears. At the podium, he unfolded his notes and looked out upon his father's friends, relatives, and acquaintances. He looked out upon the lonesome and crumpled in the back row who attended every public funeral in Dollard. Toby intended to begin with a gentle anecdote about his father's interest in trestle bridges, then ease into a litany of resonant facts. For instance, Edward Mushinsky would drive five hundred kilometres to Toronto, in a blizzard, to save three dollars on a jazz album.

The speech, double-spaced and in sixteen-point font, lay before Toby on the blond podium. He looked down at his father's mourners, at their crimes: unkempt hair, Gore-Tex jackets designed for cross-country ski trips, slouching, texting, neckties featuring cartoon characters. In the front row alone, three men had cellphones and pagers attached to belts that held up khaki trousers. Karen and Hugo. Mr. Demsky, instantly recognizable by his hair. Toby wet his lips and, in an instant, the wood and stained glass of the walls and ceiling turned pink and brown. The large waiting area at the back fell away and the First Church of the Nazarene revealed itself as an ancient, echoing cave, steam and bones on a soft floor, roiling in slow rhythm. Old flesh swung and dripped from skeletal beams above and splashed on the soggy tongue between the pews. Toby and his father's miserable friends, relatives, and acquaintances were inside a leviathan, and the beast was dying all around them. And they, too, in Wal-Mart black and tan, were moments away from their own painful deaths. They had already been swallowed.

Rabbi Orlovsky helped Toby down from the podium and eased him onto a bench in a basement hallway. Toby had been breathing through his mouth because the smell inside the whale was a marriage of rotten fish and diarrhea. Once he was alone, and once he could hear the echoing voice of the rabbi reading his eulogy, Toby attempted to open his eyes. He breathed through his nose. A small window at eye level revealed Dollard, a layer of dirty snow upon it.

For the occasion of his father's funeral, Toby wore his only bespoke suit, a classic black designed by a British tailor who travelled through the northeast once every three years. Those in the know met him for one-hour appointments in the conference room of the Hotel Omni on Sherbrooke Street. Karen Mushinsky walked down the stairs one by one in a pair of high heels, holding Hugo's hand. She sat next to Toby. Hugo reached up for a hug and Toby lifted him. The crowd laughed at one of the anecdotes he had written.

"So."

An airplane roared low overhead. They waited for it to pass.

"What happens when I'm old and sick, Toby? Where will you be?"

He examined his fingernails, which needed attention.

"Where will you be, Toby, when I'm dying?"

Hugo's fingers were short, like Edward's. The boy said nothing. *When you die, you sleep. Grandpa sleeps on clouds in heaven.* Karen's fingers were long and thin, a pianist's fingers. Rabbi Orlovsky had an American accent, and cleared his throat right before the funny bits in the eulogy. The mourners seemed to like the jazz-albums-of-Toronto item. Several dust bunnies had sneaked under the bench opposite Toby, where the big brooms could not reach.

"You're all I have now. You and this boy."

"I understand."

"This will happen to you, too, someday. It seemed like a long way off to me when you were Hugo's age."

"The church wasn't a church."

"What was the church?"

Karen coaxed him upstairs and they resumed their places in the front pew. To spare everyone the need to dish him sympathetic looks, Toby avoided eye contact. He concentrated on Rabbi Orlovsky, a tall and thin man, stooped just faintly, bearded without appearing unfriendly. He waved his large hands about as he spoke Toby's words. "My father," he said, again and again, at the beginning of statements, "My father." Hearing it aloud, there was a hint of affectation about it, fear, even dishonesty. Toby wished he had referred to Edward more honestly as "My dad."

My dad mowed the lawn with his shirt off, with bug spray in one hand and a beer in the other, pushing the machine with his belly.

The bungalow on rue Collingwood was too small for what Karen called the "after-party." They had been planning to rent the community centre until Garrett offered up his house in Westpark. He had hired caterers and a bar service, and when Toby arrived on Papillon Street immediately after the funeral, with his mom and Hugo, he sat in the car and marvelled.

"Garrett did say it was big." Karen leaned into the back seat of the Chevette and pulled Hugo out of the Westchester.

It was a two-and-a-half-storey brick-and-stone mansion, four or five thousand square feet, the sort of suburban house that inspired skepticism and suspicion in Toby. One lived in Dollard to save money, not to spend more of it. For two million dollars, Garrett could have bought a fabulously restored historic home in Westmount or Outremont. The house next door and the house next to that were built according to the same design envelope. The style and materials were identical.

What would a single man need with all of this? Toby might have asked Karen, but she was already ringing the door- bell, with Hugo. Garrett opened the door, welcomed them in, and looked over their shoulders at Toby—who opened his hands to heaven. Garrett shrugged.

Inside, a massive red Persian rug led to an open stair- case. The floors were oak, the walls were white. A crystal chandelier hung over the foyer, and the house smelled of pie. "What sort of lawyer are you, Garrett?"

Garrett took Toby's jacket and led him to the salon, where Rabbi Orlovsky and the musician from Seattle chatted with three women from the Optimist Club. Servers in red slacks and white shirts moved through the house with trays of hors d'oeuvres and champagne. A wild-haired young man in a tight- fitting velvet suit played a Schubert sonata on a polished black grand piano. The furnishings were modern, if unimaginative. Hugo ran his hand along the wainscotting and said, "Pretty."

The second floor of the house had five bedrooms. Only one of them looked and smelled as if anyone had slept in it in the past several years. There was also a small library, with two leather chairs and a rolltop bar with Scotches and tequilas. Rather than endure several more embarrassing expressions of empathy from people he barely knew, Toby sat in one of the chairs and told a story of a spy dog, loosely based on *The Bourne Identity*, until Hugo fell asleep. It was three in the after- noon, past naptime. There was no way to move out of the chair without waking the boy, and he could not reach any of the books on the shelves. For a minute or two, Toby panicked. To sit and stare at a wall and think quietly, an activity prior generations had considered essential for mental health, terrified him. The quiet led him to Edward in the burning Oldsmobile, Edward in the final moments of his life, his Black Sea skin the colour and consistency of beeswax. He takes a deep breath in and Toby waits for the exhalation, holding his hand. The fantasy of holding his father's hand. Silver wedding ring, the rough swirls of his fingerprint pads. Somewhere in the hospital, faint ragtime piano. He touches his head to his father's head.

Rabbi Orlovsky appeared in the doorway with a bowl of chips and a small bowl of baba ghanoush. "There you are."

"You couldn't have brought a bottle of champagne, Rabbi?"

There were crumbs on the second chair. The rabbi wiped them before he sat. "I would suggest exercise. Learning. Good works. Champagne will give you more than a headache."

Toby told Rabbi Orlovsky of his father's five requests.

"Be careful with this, Toby."

"He had brain tumours."

"There is great truth in what he has asked of you. Even in the bit about *getting* his enemy. The strength of his feelings for that man. I don't know the circumstances, of course."

"It was an affair."

"Lesser men have acted with less restraint. For the sake of his family, for you, he took a more challenging position. As for seeking your spirit—"

"I'm not capable of that sort of faith."

Together they ate a few chips with baba ghanoush. Toby was careful not to drop any crumbs or dip on the boy.

The rabbi turned in his chair. "We're all capable of that sort of faith."

"Not me."

"Bravado, my friend."

They ate more baba ghanoush.

Garrett led a small procession down the hallway. They poked their heads into the library and he described the room and its contents, the mixture of his childhood books and his parents' books, the books of his adult life—legal thrillers, mostly. The mourners laughed. Someone slopped a bit of champagne on the floor, and Randall wiped it with his sock and winked at Toby.

Mr. Demsky did not continue along with the tour. "Hello, Rabbi."

"How are you, Adam?"

"Perfect. Perfect."

Toby did not bother commenting on the fact that the men knew each other. They were roughly the same age. Mr. Demsky's house was around the corner from the synagogue. He inspected one of the bookshelves, built into the wall.

"You're offering counsel."

"And our young friend isn't accepting any."

"The religious impulse is evolutionary, Tobias, did you know that? It was on the radio. An ironical thing: the force in society most resistant to theories of evolution is a product of evolution. I suppose everything is. Now that I say it aloud, it sounds obvious. But on the radio . . . Anyway, listen to Rabbi Orlovsky."

"I am listening."

Mr. Demsky addressed the rabbi. "I called him up and said, 'I set up these meetings for us in New York.' He said, 'Great!' Then we get home and his dad's passed away *while he's in New York*. Tobias knew the man was dying, and he left him, for a job interview. Part of me admires this. It takes me back to earlier conversations, Tobias, no? But I make eye contact with his mother downstairs and she wants me dead. My face on a pole. I could protest: I did not know. I did not know. I only tried to help. I did not know."

"I see."

"Rabbi, what do I do?"

"You offer your condolences to the widow."

"Yes."

"And you quietly make your exit."

"Yes."

"I'm sorry, Mr. Demsky."

He pointed to Hugo. "And this? Your son?"

"Yes and no."

Mr. Demsky shook his head, bid adieu to Rabbi Orlovsky, and made his way out of the library. They listened to the slow and careful rhythm of his shoes on the stairs. The rabbi stood up and pulled out a card, placed it on the table between them. "I had promised your father. If you have any questions or quandaries."

"I'd stand up and shake your hand, but—"

"Another time."

Toby wanted to ask the rabbi, on his way out, to grab a book off the shelf and hand it over. Preferably one of the legal thrillers Garrett had mentioned. He wanted to ask the rabbi about the First Church of the Nazarene, if a church turning into a rotting whale was normal or meaningful or a sign of encroaching cancer. But what he really wanted to do was find a hole somewhere and crawl into it and stay there for a week or two, eating apple cores and cabbage.

Thirteen

They decorated the tree on the sunny morning of Christmas Eve. Hugo's ninja mask fit poorly and blocked a significant percentage of his peripheral vision, so the boy kept knocking decorations off the branches and stepping on the untangled lights. Toby had tried to convince him that assassins do not conform to the yuletide spirit, but Hugo had insisted to the point of a tantrum. Much of what Randall had taught the boy about ninjutsu was dangerous. The boy was convinced it was his duty to protect the family by foot-sweeping marauders and stabbing them, whenever possible, with his plastic samurai sword. In the absence of actual marauders in the living room, Hugo invented them and swung the sword wildly, injuring houseplants and bruising Toby.

The family tree was an artificial Bavarian pine, from back when plastic and other wonders of the petrochemical industry were considered sensible, not toxic. The lights had always been blue, from the hot twist-in bulbs that had melted several of the needles into aromatic clusters of polyvinyl chloride to the efficient LEDs Edward had purchased one year earlier at the Wal-Mart in Côte Saint-Luc.

They could only be blue. For most of her adult life, Karen had been an atheist. Yet she adored the decorations, the Boney M. Christmas album, rum stirred into eggnog with nutmeg sprinkled on top, the smell of a freshly peeled orange. Blue was her compromise colour, somewhere between respect and sacrilege.

Toby lifted Hugo to place the star, a rare family heirloom, on the crooked top branch. It had been inherited from Karen's grandmother, the family star, a mess of cardboard, sawdust, stuffing and tinsel with red wine stains and a permanent indentation in the middle from the year Toby's maternal grandfather fell into the tree.

All week, Toby had received e-mails from the ABS relocation consultant, with links to possible futures in New York. He discussed them with Hugo, who did not have a strong opinion about living in Park Slope or on the Upper East Side off Lexington Avenue.

"If we live in Brooklyn, we'll have to ride the subway a lot."

Hugo sliced an angel off a lower bough of the tree with his samurai sword.

"If you do that again, you're going to bed."

"You are?"

The phone rang in the kitchen. Karen had started to help decorate the tree, but she kept weeping quietly as some memory or other came to her. She would try to explain the memory and its significance, but each time she would give up halfway through. There was a stricken look about her as she walked into the living room with the black cordless phone.

"Hello?" He expected Alicia.

"It is his birthday." Her accent had transformed. At the end of *anniversaire* there was an *uh* that he had not detected before, a swing that was uncommon in the east end of the island. A faint echo on the line. "Did you know that? He was born on Christmas Eve, almost like Jesus."

Toby took several steps back and sat on a bench that had come with an organ Edward had bought at a garage sale in the early eighties. The hope, of course, was that his son would become a musician. Edward was descended from violin-makers and -players, and Toby—the first son of the first son—had broken his grandfather's heart by showing no interest in the violin. Edward had hoped for redemption in the organ, but there was only further heartbreak; his son had enjoyed only the electronic bossa nova function. The faraway-ness of Catherine's voice was all that kept Toby from selecting a glass ball from the nearest cardboard box marked XMAS and crushing it in his hand. He immediately began devising strategies. He would change the boy's name, his own name. They would leave for New York this very afternoon and spend Christmas in Harlem. Garrett was already at work on securing official guardianship for Toby. It had worked in their favour that she had not called after her son. Toby would lie. He would invent abuses. He would say or do anything.

"Today."

"Today. It is his birthday."

"Where are you?"

There was a siren in the distance, one of those sirens that reminded him of Alicia in a white bathrobe, with *Le Monde* or *El País* and a mimosa. Catherine was outside, in a

phone booth. "He lived here, in the fifteenth, a small apartment with these *people*."

"Who?"

"He was poor, most of his life, did you know that? Then
he was rich."

"What are you doing for money?"

"Let me talk to him."

Hugo had read something in Toby's expression and
watched him now. Karen kneeled down to help Hugo place
another angel on the tree. Nearly all of the decorations were
angels. It had started when Karen was a young mother.
Someone had brought a small angel back from Mexico, a
stout brown-skinned woman with colourful wings, holding a
strawberry, making a kissy mouth. Every year Karen bought
another few until the Santas and candy canes and whimsi-
cal sleighs of her own childhood were altogether replaced by
angels.

Toby walked into the kitchen.

"Let me talk to him."

The refrigerator hummed. Toby leaned on it and looked
at Hugo in silhouette, the lazy winter sunlight in his hair.
The boy reached up to the highest bough, his eyes squinting
in concentration, and hung a crocheted angel. Nothing and
no one had ever been more beautiful than Hugo. The previous evening, before bed, Karen had been reminiscing. Before
she had remembered that she was furious with him, for New
York, both of them had laughed, and cried a bit, and the
crying had frightened the boy. Father crying. Toby remembered clearly one night in elementary school when he had presented Edward with some Valentine craft he had made, with
gluey, silvery shell pasta and some crooked interpretation

of *I Love You*, and how his father had cried. His father's helplessness. A hole in the sky opening.

"I thought, when I arrived here, that people would know me somehow. 'There she is, the daughter of Brassens.' I would be royal. I sought out a man, his biographer, but he did not believe me." She sobbed, and quickly adjusted. "He tried to make love to me."

Toby understood what she had wanted to find in Paris.

"He is my son. Let me speak to him."

"No."

"You will give him a nice birthday? And Christmas?"

"He's decorating the tree right now. Dressed as a ninja."

"A ninja?"

"Halloween costume."

"Three years old. My baby is three."

"Stay in France." Toby presented this as though he were her best and wisest friend, or her psychiatrist. "Your life is there now." There was a beep, an automatic voice warning that her calling card was near its end. "Merry Christmas," he said.

Catherine did not respond, but he could hear her breathing in the phone booth, in the dark. She was about to say something. Another siren, this one closer. A man's voice, a furious knock. "Wait," she said, through her teeth, to the man and to Toby—intimate and frustrated. The dial tone.

Karen continued to decorate the tree with Hugo. She whispered, out the side of her mouth, "What did she say?"

"Today's his B-I-R-T-H-day."

"Oh my God. Where is she?"

"Paris."

"Is she coming back?"

"No."

"What do we do?"

"We get him a C-A-K-E and do it up right on Boxing Day. I'm taking him to New York and signing him up for playschool, and everything's going to be perfect."

"Do you have his birth certificate? Won't he need a passport?"

"Absolutely perfect."

There was an invitation on the refrigerator. It had been delivered during the lunch hour by one of the local courier services. Every year, Alicia had a Christmas Eve party in her house on Strathcona Avenue. On the back of the last-minute invitation, she had written in her florid handwriting, "*It would mean so much to me if you came.*"

He had planned to go through his *Toby a Gentleman* files, looking for items to adapt for the wives and girlfriends of dirt bikers, then browse Montessori playschool websites on the Upper East Side. But Catherine's call had agitated him so much that he sneaked downstairs to iron a shirt; a drink with someone who was not his mother was in order.

The phone was still in his hand, and Karen had summoned the strength to continue decorating the tree with Hugo. Toby watched her, surrounded by her old tables and lamps, the art that was not art. The physical evidence of her life's work would not be worth much in a bankruptcy auction. He pulled Steve Bancroft's business card from the old bureau that functioned as his sock and junk drawer and stared at it for a while. The secretary at the Ford dealership in Pointe-Claire put the call through.

"Mr. Ménard. How are you holding up?"

"Thank you for the flowers, Mr. Bancroft. It was a great comfort to us all."

"We've known each other since you were born. Let's try being Steve and Toby."

An intercom announced, in English, that the dealership would be closing in fifteen minutes. Toby waited. He wished he had prepared the exact words. "I was wondering if you would consider meeting my mother and me for coffee after Christmas."

"Why coffee? Let me take you for lunch."

"That's too much."

"A man has to eat lunch, Toby. As does a woman." The way Steve Bancroft said this, *a woman.* "You like smoked meat?"

It was an honourable notion, to eat a lunch of smoked meat before decamping to New York. They made arrangements for the twenty-seventh, and Steve Bancroft said that his secretary would make reservations for three. He expressed "absolute delight" and ended the call cordially.

Toby and Karen quietly decided that they would celebrate Hugo's birthday on Boxing Day, with his favourite foods—macaroni and cheese, sausage, and freshly sliced tomato. A fog settled over Montreal, with the early darkness of the holidays. Toby put on his funeral suit and drove to the mall. He had already bought several pint-sized Christmas presents: a lead-free watercolour set, pre-kindergarten math texts, and typically American plush animals, like alligators and eagles. For the boy's birthday he did not want anything that would be difficult to transport, so he chose three classic children's books about New York: *Stuart Little, The Little Red Lighthouse* and *The Great Gray Bridge.* They were too advanced for Hugo, but Toby would read them in short instalments, before bed, to help the boy adjust to a new mythology.

The lights of the towers in the distance twinkled and
gleamed as Toby neared Westmount. It had snowed so much
since the funeral that the drifts along the side streets were
taller than the car. Pedestrians on Sherbrooke turned away
from the wind, walking backwards with tiny steps, hands
over their ears.

A black Hummer pulled out from a spot directly in
front of Alicia's house. Parking spots were scarce on Strathcona Avenue. Toby's instinct would usually be to park
several blocks away and walk, to avoid any identification
with the Chevette. Instead, he took the Hummer's spot and
revved the car one last time to—in the words of Edward
Mushinsky—"blow out the carbon." The cloud of pollu-
tion had just about dissipated when he exited the car and
walked to the blue door. A couple he had once known well,
a doctor and a public relations executive he and Alicia had
seen regularly in the early years of the decade, reached the
door at the same time. The woman, Laura, was pregnant.
She lifted her upper lip sourly.

Alicia's cousin, a heavily medicated young woman
whose name Toby could not recall, took their jackets. The
couple immediately detached themselves from him, opening
their arms to hug a dance choreographer Toby had also once
counted as a dinner party friend. Before he could wave hello,
the man looked away. At once Toby decided it had been a
mistake to come here, his decision to accept the invitation
the act of his phantom self—a man, he realized, he no longer
cared to be. It was his boy's birthday.

The sad cousin, who had been a regular in the rehab
clinics of the northeast, had not yet reached the cloak room.
A gentleman always walked—the slower the better—and he

spoke with calm and deliberation; Toby called out to Alicia's cousin and ran to her, his shoes clacking on the wooden floor. The remnants of her drug abuse and recovery had formed a cloud of languid misery about her.

"You're already leaving?"

At a McIntyre family Thanksgiving dinner, shortly after he and Alicia had begun dating, the cousin had been at the lascivious height of her methamphetamine blitz. Back then, her eyes caught the light hungrily and she tilted her head forward as she stared across the table. She strode haughtily about the McIntyre mansion, drinking Moët & Chandon. Every time Toby looked up from his turkey and cranberry, she was staring at him, open-mouthed. After dinner, Alicia had asked him to go out to the Mercedes, where she had forgotten her cellphone, and the cousin, who had been out smoking among the nymph statues, confronted him with an offer to blow him in the garage. When he declined as honourably as he could manage, she had called him a pussy.

Nothing of that remained in her. The flesh around her eyes was dark and had lost its elasticity. Her nose twitched as though she wanted to lift a pair of spectacles without using her hands. The dress she wore was fine enough, but all of her muscle tone had been drained with her spirit. She folded the jacket over his arm.

"Thank you. And Merry Christmas."

"Yeah," she said. "Yeah."

Toby had just about made it to the door when he smelled Alicia. Her perfume, a custom design from a boutique on boulevard Saint-Germain, had a peculiar way of filling a room without being overpowering when one was close to her. He could hear the familiar click of her heels.

"Where are you going?"

He spoke quietly so the pregnant woman and her husband, the choreographer, and others in the salon who had so recently populated his social life would turn back to their drinks and canapés. "I feel funny."

"You don't look funny. You look very handsome."

Toby reached back for the door handle. "And you look—"

"Yes. Yes." She placed her fingers lightly on his chest. Her cocktail dress was new; it had been designed and fitted for her, probably by Andy Thê-Anh. After tax, it was surely worth more than his mother's yearly revenues.

There were gloves in his pocket. If he could remove them and put them on, then maybe he could turn away from her and leave.

"I invited you to congratulate you, and to apologize. I've been absolutely terrible. When I heard about Edward, I guess I realized . . ."

Behind Alicia, the snoopiest of her guests had finally begun to turn away. There was a DJ in the corner, a young Asian man in jeans that were way too small, dark glasses, and enormous headphones. He spun pop interpretations of holiday classics—at the moment, a startling hip hop version of "*Il est né le divin enfant.*" Eventually, Alicia would have her medicated cousin and some otherwise invisible husbands clear the furniture away. She would order her guests to dance. The drunk ones would dance and the others would leave. Someone would spark a joint and that would be that.

" . . . some things are important. Everything else, it's just TV."

"Were you at the funeral?"

"It was at an awkward hour. I had the noon news to anchor that day, but as I said, it really inspired a lot of soul-searching. Dwayne's not here, by the way. That terrible mistake. God!" She crossed her arms and appraised him, top to toe, as though years had passed. "You know me: I wouldn't even ask this if I hadn't been drinking champagne. But do you have any interest, at all, in grabbing dinner some night?"

Alicia did not drink at her own parties.

"I forgive you, Alicia. And I do thank you for the invitation."

"Don't go."

Toby opened the door.

"Wait."

Her voice. Her smell. This beautiful house. He closed the door.

"Just one thing. How did it happen? I mean, did you just send in your reel?"

He wished her a happy holiday and sent his fondest regards to her family. He had just enough oxygen remaining in his lungs to lean forward and kiss her on both cheeks, to faintly squeeze her left arm, to turn and walk out of her house.

Fourteen

Some years before Toby was born, in the sunrise of Edward and Karen Mushinsky's marriage, they moved to the razed forest, the counterfeit prairie, that was Dollard-des-Ormeaux. Bulldozers still sat in the mud when they took possession of a new bungalow on rue Collingwood, with a wrapped willow sapling in the front yard. They had not purchased any of the available extras, like a sunroom in the back or half a second floor. The house across the as-yet-unpaved street came with these extras and more—a trellis and a brick facade. A single man lived there, tall with a blond beard and curiously bright brown eyes.

In 1967, Steve Bancroft was a retired road manager for failed rock bands. He had just come out of an awkward period in upstate New York, where he had fallen in with a former folk singer who had started a charismatic sect of Quakerism that encouraged group sex and strict vegetarianism. Karen and Edward had met and married in Notre-Dame-de-Grâce, in what was then the outer limits of Montreal, and had decided to move out even farther for the cheap land, the

quiet, the Englishness, and a single-car garage. Steve Bancroft
and Edward Mushinsky helped each other level and sod their
yards. Steve's friends in Dollard became their friends. A few
nights every week, they would gather at one of their houses
after work to drink beer, smoke the marijuana Steve Bancroft
always had stashed in a teddy bear cookie jar, listen to the
Rolling Stones, and talk about Trudeau.

From the beginning, it was clear that Steve was gifted.
Edward admitted, when he related all of this to Toby one
night in the late eighties, that he had always wanted to be
around his neighbour. There was a warmth and confidence,
an honesty about him that matched the feeling in the air at
the time. Steve never failed to comment on a new haircut. He
golfed, and offered to initiate Edward into golfing. If anyone
needed help moving or with home repairs or even with a
loan of a hundred bucks from time to time, he was their
man. Like Edward and Karen and all of their new friends in
Dollard, he was in the transitional period between student
poverty and the southern border of lower middle class; the
only reason Steve or Edward and Karen or anyone else they
knew could afford a house at all was the West Island's lack of
a self-sustaining economy and its distance from downtown
Montreal. In the summer that Edward and Karen moved to
Dollard, Steve Bancroft had secured a bank loan to purchase
a bankrupt trucking company in Côte Saint-Luc. He didn't
talk about it much, and when he did, Steve mocked himself
for making such a boneheaded move. Businesses go bankrupt for good reasons, and Steve Bancroft claimed that he
suddenly and painfully understood them.

Edward and Karen knew the truth, that their new friend
had transformed the failed trucking company into a profitable

venture. The economy was improving, and it would continue to improve until October, when Expo 67 was due to close. If he was smart enough to capitalize on the energy and optimism in Montreal, and it appeared he was, Steve Bancroft's membership in the club of entry-level bureaucrats and opticians and nurses and bookkeepers—a collection of perpetual almost-theres—would have to be revoked.

Willow saplings were the extent of vegetation in western Dollard-des-Ormeaux, though city council had voted to create Centennial Park to commemorate Canada's last great year—with artificial hills and a phony lake. In the evenings, when they sat on a plank in the mud or on the precious new sod of someone's backyard, all they could hear were children playing and the sound of an occasional jet. They had left city sounds behind. They said hello to strangers on the sidewalks, walking to or from the IGA. Automatically, it had seemed, everyone in Dollard had something in common. They had come to this place for the same reasons, and they recognized it in one another's facial expressions. Yes, we *were* city people. Now we see the sunset.

There were few secrets among them.

One snowy night in February 1972, when Edward Mushinsky was away at a franchising conference in Toronto, the gang met at Gino's, the deli and tavern that had become their local. The CBC was broadcasting a hockey game, the Canadiens versus the Red Wings. The Mushinsky car, a Pontiac Strato Chief station wagon, had not started at the end of the workday, so Karen had abandoned it. She had walked, in the muscle-twisting wind, from Le Chien Chaud to Gino's, hoping to catch a ride from one of her invariably drunk friends at the end of the night. Toby, still a baby, was with the babysitter, Aunty June, who would shortly reveal herself to be a dominatrix and move to West Berlin. When Karen arrived at Gino's, the only empty chair was next to Steve Bancroft. That day had proceeded remarkably well for him, despite the blizzard. A shipping company out of Hamilton had offered to buy his little trucking business, and he had accepted. The difference between the bank's initial investment and the price he received was more money than he or anyone they knew had ever seen or expected to see. So the drinks were on Steve.

When Toby first heard this story, he had wondered about his mother's role. In Edward's eyes, she had been a passive participant, a victim of liquor and charisma, a mother whose hormones had barely settled from the shocks and rigours of childbirth.

Karen and Steve Bancroft were in their late twenties. She was thrilled to be childless for an evening. They were drinking like marines, buoyed by financial news that seemed impossible. In his self-published autobiography, on sale at every business in the Bancroft Group of Companies for $19.99, including tax, Steve Bancroft mentions the day of the buyout, and even refers to a wild night of celebration. While he doesn't name names in the book, he does name the price. Once he paid off the bank loan, Steve was $495,000 richer than he had been a day earlier.

Edward Mushinsky, who had carefully read the autobiography for incorrect and therefore actionable details, first related the story of betrayal to his son shortly before Toby's high school graduation. They were in the Laurentians, "hunting pheasant," one final attempt to forestall Toby's descent into the depths of sissydom. He was already involved in drama and debating instead of sports, and wearing Polo by

Ralph Lauren—shirts and scent. Tae kwon do never took. Edward had lit upon the ancient ritual of hunting as a way to steel Toby against fruitiness before he entered university, where fruitiness was socially accepted, if not encouraged. The sight and smell of spilled blood would transform the boy into a man, just as it had done for countless teenage savages for centuries. They arrived at the rented cabin with their rifles and binoculars, and father and son sat near the fireplace and drank three bottles of rye whisky over three days and two nights. In one of several heart-to-hearts, Toby assured his father that he was not, and never would be, a homosexual. Edward admitted that Steve Bancroft, who Toby already knew as a scoundrel and a purveyor of the worst sorts of treachery, had fucked his mother one February night in 1972.

On Christmas morning, Toby made blueberry pancakes. Then he took Hugo tobogganing at Bois-de-Liesse. The house smelled of turkey when they returned. Toby was knocking the snow off Hugo's boots when Karen stomped into the room.

"You set up a date for me?"

"For us. For us."

"Why, why, why?"

"I have my reasons."

Karen looked at her small wristwatch. There was a faint quiver about her arm. "When were you going to spring this on me? It's in two days."

"It was supposed to be a nice surprise."

"A surprise."

"Surprise!" said Hugo.

"He just phoned. Just now." Karen stuttered, which was not her custom. "Asking if a high chair would be better than a booster seat for Hugo. Who calls about that, on Christmas? It had just occurred to him to ask, he said, to avoid any, whatever, any scramble in the restaurant on Sunday. I mean, there I was, pretending I knew *all* about our luncheon, humming and grunting like a mute."

Hugo was unaccustomed to seeing Karen like this, and Toby had to talk him out of crying. Incapacitated by grief was one thing. Flustered by a lunch was another. She shouted instructions for taking the turkey out of the oven, strode into the bathroom, and slammed the door. On her bed, several outfits had been laid flat in a continuum from blue jeans to winter dress.

Toby knocked on the bathroom door. "You do know we're going to Abie's for smoked meat."

"Jesus Christ."

"Jesus Christ." Hugo had turned his attention to the German watercolours, and was in the midst of painting the Chrysler Building, which Toby had been telling him about. It didn't look at all like the Chrysler Building. The English pronunciation of the saviour's name was new to him. "Jesus Christ."

"It's his birthday."

"Happy birthday."

"And your birthday, Hugo."

"Happy birthday to you. And happy birthday, Jesus Christ!"

They ate too much on Christmas. Then they ate too much on Boxing Day for Hugo's replacement party, which featured turkey sandwiches, warmed-up stuffing, and chocolate cake. Toby stopped keeping track of the number of times his mother cried.

On Sunday, Toby and Hugo wore their matching suits to Abie's Smoked Meat & Steak. Karen wore jeans and a cashmere sweater, with the most expensive scarf he had ever bought for her. She placed her hand on the entrance door and then released it, backed away, as though the handle had burned her.

"This is crazy."

It was a revelation, her anxiety about seeing Steve Bancroft. Toby was well aware of his father's feelings, but did not know Karen's; he had assumed their affair, nearly as old as he was, had passed into the winds of forgetfulness that blew through the acid-pocked baby boomer mind. He did not know what to say to console or encourage her, so he picked up Hugo and stood silently with his mother as she looked out upon the slushy parking lot.

"You are hungry."

"Shh, Hugo. Just a minute. *I am* hungry."

The boy whined, "You're cold, too, Poney."

"*I am* cold."

He squirmed in Toby's arms. "You want to go home."

"Shh. Grandma's thinking."

"Grandma." Karen turned back to the door. "That puts things into perspective."

Steve Bancroft had secured a table at the back of the steamy deli, a riot of argument and laughter. Most of Dollard, it seemed, had been keen to escape their families. He was on a call when he spotted them, and ended it immediately to stand and greet Karen. They shook hands and awkwardly kissed on each cheek.

"I am so sorry about Ed."

"Thank you."

Steve Bancroft made inescapable eye contact, cupped her hand in both of his. "No, really. *Really.* I was devastated to hear. My heart goes out, Karen."

"Thank you."

Another potential show topic occurred to Toby. How to express condolences gracefully, how to accept them, and how to transition from death to other concerns—such as smoked meat. Steve Bancroft was rather skilled. He turned from Karen at the precise moment that Toby began to feel the sweat of discomfort gathering on his lower back, and introduced himself to Hugo. "I take it you're the littlest Mushinsky?"

Hugo turned to Toby, bewildered.

"It's a real pleasure, Hugo."

"Hi," the boy said, in the spirit of clarification. "It's your birthday."

"My birthday's in June, little fellow."

Toby explained about the pronoun challenges, and Steve led a rendition of "Happy Birthday." The whole restaurant joined in. Weather led the discussions. They looked at the menu. The bored server, in jeans and a black shirt mottled with flour and grease, came by to take their drink orders—sparkling water for the adults and milk for the child. Jewishness abounded in the restaurant, in the pickles and the coleslaw and the mustard; as Steve Bancroft talked about the challenges in the auto industry, Toby vowed to stop being a little bit Jewish. In New York, even in Dollard, one-sixteenth equalled zero; the word "brisket" really meant nothing to him.

It was not a sophisticated menu. They ordered smoked meat, variously, and as they waited for the food to arrive, Toby pulled out the business plan for Bullé Pour Moi. He had recreated the title page on the computer, to replace Catherine's details with his own name and coordinates. He laid it on the table, before Steve Bancroft, and cribbed from the introduction. The wonders of bubble tea. The lightness of Asian cuisine. The new capital of cultural export was China, and here was an opportunity to get in early.

"Isn't bubble tea from Taiwan?" said Steve Bancroft.

"China, Taiwan."

Steve Bancroft listened, quietly and politely, and turned to Karen. "What do you think of this?"

"I don't know what to think." She glanced at Toby, kicked him under the table, and turned back to Steve Bancroft. "It's a time of change."

"My plan, as you've known for some time, was to buy you out. There's a franchise opportunity in the area of toasted hoagies that interests me, and your locations—even some of your equipment—would work quite smartly." He picked up the business plan and flipped through it. "This shows real initiative, and I appreciate that. But I don't know. Bubble tea sounds faddish. Where do you see it in ten years?"

Karen picked at her lip.

Maybe bubble tea was faddish, or plain stupid. Toby had not actually read all the way through the business plan because he did not understand business plans. All he wanted to do was protect his mother somehow, to ensure a source of income for her. At the same time, he could "get that fucker" by having Steve put up all the money and all the risk. If it succeeded, Karen would be set. If it failed, a villain with a perplexingly healthy head of hair would be out a few hundred thousand dollars.

"I'm a car guy. But I wouldn't try to design, manufacture, and brand my own car. That's lunacy. The only way to make any money these days is to play somewhere in the middle, to take something that's made for you and hand it off to someone else for a premium. To keep them coming back. If you want to be a frustrated genius, that's one thing. I prefer to play it safe."

The food arrived, and Steve Bancroft stuffed the Bullé Pour Moi business plan into his briefcase. For the next hour, Karen and his father's enemy talked about the years between 1967 and 1972, when they were young and pretty. They spoke of beards and pants and cars and restaurants. They avoided discussing Edward. Toby helped Hugo eat smoked meat.

That night, Toby and Karen sang "Happy Birthday" to Hugo twenty times, during and after dinner. Hugo lay in bed for half an hour, singing "Happy Birthday" to his stuffed animals, to his bed, to the ceiling, to his night light, to Toby and Karen and Edward, and to several pairs of his pants.

The first sanctioned meeting of the Benjamin Disraeli Society was at La Moufette. Garrett had attempted to invite some young attorneys, but they had all been suspicious of his motives. Randall brought a drowsy man named Mike, who ran a rival tow truck outfit; he and Mike were on friendly terms because, together, they looked like a company big enough to get dealership and Canadian Automobile Association contracts.

For the first half of the evening, Randall and Mike talked about the "fuckheads" they had towed that week. At nine o'clock, the society came to order. Toby officially welcomed their guest, Mike, and told him a bit about the society and its inspiration.

"Yeah, but why him?" Mike had been drinking Irish whiskey along with his beer.

"What do you mean?"

"I mean, if you're gonna have a club, why not make it about Kennedy or someone that folks remember? Trudeau, even? I'm not a big fan of his, but at least I've heard of him."

Toby explained, again, about Benjamin Disraeli, his sense of style in the early years of his career, his courage, the way he reimagined British conservatism. The revolutionary aspect. All that had been lost from North America that could be regained if the spirit of Disraeli were as alive and as forceful today as the spirit of, say, John F. Kennedy. Mike simply stared at Toby and blinked a few times.

"I should add, if you are interested in attending further meetings, that a business suit is the dress code."

Mike looked down. He wore a pair of corduroy pants and an unironed blue dress shirt. "Randall, he said to dress nice."

"It's nice what you're wearing, it is. But niceness, as you know, is subjective. The advantage of a business suit is it's something we can all agree on—as a club and, really, as a people. That's the point, Mike."

"Aren't you moving to the States?"

Randall spoke in a chastened manner. "He is, Mike, he is. But he's still the boss. He thought up the society."

"I just got to tell you guys, this is retarded."

A moment or two of silence passed as Mike finished his glass of Irish whiskey, lifted it, and snapped his fingers at the waitress, who was watching a show about the best police chases on one of the television sets attached to the ceiling. She did not seem to remember Toby from last time.

"So I had this stomach ache last night," Randall said. "I didn't think I'd make it this evening. But I did."

Everyone agreed this was fortunate news.

Toby lifted a satchel onto the table and distributed hand-kerchiefs to the three men. "Tonight, I thought the theme could be handkerchiefs."

Mike held his handkerchief as though it were a gelatin dessert. "See, this is what I'm talking about. The retardedness keeps getting more retarded."

"Do you know how to fold a handkerchief?"

"No."

"Would you like to know?"

"I don't think I've even seen one of these before."

Toby pointed to his breast pocket, where he had folded and moulded a *pochette gavroche* by Hermès, a third anniversary gift from Alicia. "How about beauty? Harmony? Courage? Creativity? Our commitment to perfection, however remote—"

"*Courage.* How do you figure that?"

"Allowing the colour of your tie to clash with the colour of your handkerchief. It takes a daring touch."

"This is what your show is about?"

"Yes and no. If you think about it, Mike, a handkerchief says a lot about a man. It's the small details . . ."

Mike seemed to think about it. "And people are supposed to watch this."

"They're not *supposed to*."

"You know what? I could be at home right now, putting my kids to bed. Or at a movie."

"I have kids," said Randall. "Toby's adopting a boy. Benjamin Disraeli had kids. We're doing this *because* we have kids."

"Actually," said Toby, "Benjamin Disraeli married a much older woman and—"

"I could give a shit." Mike stood up and intercepted the waitress with his whiskey. He downed it in one gulp and accompanied her to the cash register.

"I'm sorry," said Randall.

"Does Mike have a dirt bike?"

"He does, actually. Why?"

Toby stared at the handkerchiefs, piled on the uneven table, as Randall and Garrett consoled him. The life and beauty of the handkerchiefs seemed to drip away into the darkness of the sticky floorboards of La Moufette. Handkerchiefs were as random and as ill-used as stuffed parakeets.

This lasted for some time, until Garrett squeezed his arm. Randall was outside, bidding adieu to Mike and indulging in a cigarette. "You're feeling okay?"

Toby wanted to tell Garrett about the handkerchiefs, or at least about the troubling phone call from Catherine. But since his firm was handling the legal aspects of the eventual adoption, which hinged on abandonment and utter silence from the biological parents, Toby decided it was best to forget it had ever happened.

"Can I talk to you about something?" Garrett turned a hot wing solicitously around with his large fingers. "Something a bit personal?"

Toby only half listened, at first, to the real reason Tracy was divorcing Randall. An emotional drift in there somewhere, a coming-to-terms, and Tracy felt it.

"On the night she first asked him to leave—so she could think, you know—he drove over and we drank a bottle of premium Canadian whisky and watched the *Star Wars* trilogy and fell asleep together on the couch."

"Like high school."

"The next night, I made up one of the spare bedrooms for him, and I was nervous to say it, but I had to say it. I said, 'Or you can sleep with me or whatever.' I wasn't going to *try* anything. Frankly, I didn't know how. And you know him. He said, 'It doesn't matter.' So I said, 'Don't feel you have to,' and he said, 'Whatever, I don't. Either way, really.' But he did sleep in my bed that night. And he still is."

"He still is what?"

"Sleeping in my bed."

"Sleeping or *sleeping?*"

"I love him. Always have, I guess. I haven't said it to him, out loud. But . . ."

Toby finished his beer and poured some more.

"It was me. I ruined a marriage. I shall to hell."

"You're not joking."

"This is a secret. Randall would die if he knew you knew."

"Shouldn't I be the easiest person to tell? I mean, Garrett, look at me."

"What about his kids? That's what he always brings up. Imagine Dakota in high school, on the West Island, with a couple of . . . with parents like us."

"Stairway to Heaven" was playing. Toby had never heard the song outside of a high school gymnasium, with the lights out, a DJ's disco ball spinning cookies of light over the straight coloured lines on the floor, the basketball nets, the pennants of forgettable victory. He was pleased to give himself over to anxious memories of high school—wanting desperately to dance to this song in the dark gymnasium three times a year, with Tiffany or Charlene or Melissa. Never drinking lemon gin beforehand, never hitting the parties afterward, never a fist fight or a B.J.

"I don't know if we had it any easier," Toby said, "and our dads were straight."

Randall returned with his arm around Mike.

"Tell him."

"All right," said Mike. "I'm sorry, man, for calling your thing retarded."

"It's not a thing, Mike. Say it like we planned."

"Your society. Your society."

Toby stood up and shook his hand. "It *is* a little bit retarded, Mike. And I apologize for diminishing your slacks. They're lovely."

The members of the Benjamin Disraeli Society put the handkerchiefs aside and talked about their children. They dispersed just before nine thirty, as it was a Wednesday. Toby had forgotten his phone at home, so he could not call Randall for a tow when the Chevette stalled and died on rue Hyman. He pushed it to the side of the road, tucked in front of a mini-van, and walked home.

It was a fresh but windless night, with a gentle snowfall. Toby cut through Centennial Park, where the artificial lake was nearly ready to emerge as a skating pond. The neighbourhoods were silent but for the whoops and cackles of unsupervised adolescents out too late, shovel on sidewalk, a distant honk. The slices of conversation, mostly about weather, suggested a world he had already relinquished: the moderate, workaday, jean jacket and running shoes, kids-are-in-bed-so-let's-have-a-beer world of mothers and fathers and influenza and credit cards. Knowing that he was leaving this place in a little more than a week made it much easier to adore. Already he felt the way he was destined to feel, like a man from afar briefly visiting the country of his birth—a warm and prosaic and condescending feeling he cherished. His posture was kingly. He briefly pretended, among the aspen trees, hidden from the Christmas lights of the suburb, that it was the seventeenth century, that he was leading a small band of brave missionary soldiers to destroy the godless Iroquois downriver. A stupid mission, but pure and memorable, inspired by perfection, stripped of the irony that threatened to render his own generation pointless and forgotten. His technologies were the technologies of transition. The golden eras of television and cinema were over, yet the digital revolution had not yet begun. None of this would endure like the Battle of Long Sault, in which Adam Dollard des Ormeaux sacrificed his flesh for the ascendance of the European story. Certainly not *Toby a Gentleman,* or whatever they wished to call it in New York City. There was a short list of possible titles circulating through a focus group. *How to Be a Gentleman in the Twenty-First Century* was apparently well loved by William Kingston, who had final approval over everything. Toby had vowed not to be precious, even if they wanted to give it a cumbersome and boring—post-boring?—title. He had been exchanging e-mails with the producer, pretty and thoughtful Jill, whom he would call and court upon his arrival in Manhattan, to discuss the first month of topics—twenty shows. Cellphone etiquette, weeping in public, introducing one's wife or girlfriend at a party, tipping, the trouble with the word "cheers," elevators.

There he is, Dollard des Ormeaux, loading up his canoe with supplies and inspiring his fellow martyrs with a speech about Jesus and his sovereignty. *Gentle warriors of Christ, worry not for your blood. Already I can see it, just downriver, the promise of our reward.*

A taxi idled in front of the house on rue Collingwood, its exhaust system even more harmful than that of the Chevette. The driver was reading *Le Devoir* with the window open. It was slightly below freezing, not nearly cold enough for idling to be necessary.

"Who are you waiting for, sir?" said Toby.

"The woman?"

"What woman? Karen Mushinsky?"

He shrugged and turned back to his newspaper. The car smelled like an alley behind an Indian restaurant.

Toby heard Hugo's cries through the door. It was almost ten o'clock, much too late for him to be awake. A nightmare, surely. From time to time, usually in the middle of the night, the boy would cry out about a dog, or a bear, or his snack, and Toby would lie with him, rubbing his back, until the sobs powered down like an old engine, the intervals between them longer and longer and longer. The first stanza of "You Are My Sunshine" quieter and quieter and quieter. Toby had vowed to learn the rest of the song, in the interest of self-improvement and to enhance the boy's vocabulary.

It was unpleasant to wake up in the middle of the night, sometimes two or three times. Nothing was more pleasant, however, than giving the boy a glass of water and a hug, both of which he asked for as though they were equal commodities, and lowering him to his pillow, a kiss on his warm forehead. In the parenting books, they warned against going into the child's room several times a night, for water and whimsy, but Toby did not see how it could harm Hugo. Soon enough, he would be a teenager—a monster of sleep. Soon enough, Hugo would not need hugs or back rubs or "You Are My Sunshine."

Toby rushed in, eagerly, and nearly ran into her. Her hair was shorter, and she had acquired something in between a suntan and a permanent layer of dirt on her face. It was makeup, he realized. Catherine was hiding something—the largest pimple in the world or, more likely, a bruise.

In the kitchen, Karen stood in front of the stove, ready to collapse. Hugo cried next to Catherine, his new snow jacket over his baseball, baseball glove, and baseball bat pyjamas. His face a mess of tears and transferred foundation. He reached up to Toby, and Toby picked him up. Mid-cry, Hugo sobbed, into Toby's ear, so loudly that it hurt, "You want to stay."

Slowed, perhaps, by beer, Toby did not at first realize that Catherine intended to take him away. Then he did. "*Non, non, je suis désolé,*" he said, as gallantly as he could muster, "you can't take him."

"He's my son. Thanks for babysitting. I'm taking him home."

"No, you're not. What home?"

"Our apartment."

"You don't have an apartment. A strange man lives there. This is Hugo's home now, Catherine. Why don't you come back tomorrow, for breakfast, and we'll discuss it. For now, Hugo needs to be back in bed."

Catherine reached up and pulled Hugo from Toby, who did not fight her off. The boy wiggled his way out of her arms and onto the entrance mat, and stomped next to Edward's winter boots. He was nearly incoherent now, weeping and shouting a mixture of English and French. His eyes were red, he was recently awakened, and no one was listening to him. Hugo tried to make it simple, using his finger to conduct and punctuate each short phrase. *Mommy will live here. Poney will live here. Grandma will live here. Ici, ici.*

"I'm his mother. He's mine."

"Not anymore."

"How about I call the police. I wonder what they'll say. Do you want to be kidnappers, maybe?"

Toby's heart seemed ready to bust out of its cage and roar across the room, throw Catherine out the picture window, and carry Hugo to bed. He understood perfectly, for the first time in his life, the potential solace of a violent act. A delicious slap in the face. All he could do was fall to his knees and hug Hugo and kiss him and whisper to him that he would be back here, home, soon, that he need not worry. He never needed to worry. Toby told him, once in each ear, that he loved him, told him that he would protect him, that he loved him *so much,* and he said it some more, as Catherine protested that the taxi was waiting, meter on. Toby said it ten times, an incantation, as there were no adequate words.

Catherine carried a knitted bag of his items: shoes, a suit, Lammy, the lamb he slept with, whatever Karen had thrown in.

Toby, still on his knees, could hear the boy's cries all the way down the front yard, the sound weakening with each footstep in the snow. Hugo's tears were all over Toby's face, dripping salt slowly into his mouth. Karen walked to the window and watched. He hoped that if he didn't watch, Catherine—in her fucking delusional hooker insanity— would change her mind and bring Hugo back.

With the help of a footstool, Karen lowered herself to her knees and crawled over to him.

"Why did you let her in?"

"She's his mom."

Fifteen

The social worker, Mireille, received Toby on New Year's Eve without an appointment on St. Jean Boulevard, in Dollard. He had accosted the woman outside, in what he took to be a courtly manner, a few minutes before the office opened at nine. Mireille was a large and beautiful woman from Haiti, who nodded languidly as he spoke, and clasped her hands in an official version of sympathy. His grandest worry, his conspiracy theory, which he had presented before she answered any of his questions or concerns—that the government of Quebec could not abide a francophone child adopted by a man with a Slavic-sounding surname—did not faze her. He had business cards left over from his work at the station. Ménard, Ménard. It was not yet a legal name change, but it could be, by week's end, if she thought it would help. Anything she thought would help, it would be done by week's end. "Everything can be done in French, you see? I speak French with him. He will always go to French schools, wherever we live. I am Québécois too." Toby finished speaking and allowed himself to breathe properly again. He had gone on longer than necessary because he did not want Mireille to respond. As long as he was talking, it was reason and truth. Hugo was his. His hands were freezing, even inside. He made a cup out of them and blew into it. The traffic on the boulevard whooshed through the freshly melted snow, as it had warmed enough to rain. A sound that had once comforted him, cars on a suburban boulevard, in the rain. Like the spark of a natural gas furnace.

"It is very difficult," she said, "to take a child from his mother."

"You're on her side."

"I am on no side, Mr. Toby."

"She was prostituting herself in Paris."

Mireille sighed. He had said too much, and angrily. "You have proof of this?"

"She abandoned him, without a word, for months. Is that not against the law?"

"It is."

"Well?"

"She *returned*. It is more common than you think, to go through a corrective experience. You will see this, if she has the means to hire a lawyer." Mireille crossed her powerful arms in defiance. At one point in her life, Toby was certain, Mireille had gone through a corrective experience. The lights in her office were not yet turned on, and in the dimness of the December morning it suddenly felt intimate and awkward in the room. There was no ring on her finger. Anything she wanted. Money, oral sex, film rights. She had not yet turned on the computer. Many kilometres away, on its approach or retreat, a crack of rare winter thunder. "This idea, Mr. Toby, that you would take the boy to New York City before finalizing guardianship is equally preposterous, if you will allow me to be frank."

The electronic ticket had arrived that morning, in Toby's inbox. The ninth of January, two seats in business class, an afternoon flight, dinner provided.

"Legally—"

"It is simple for her lawyer. She left Hugo with people she trusted, sorted herself out on a holiday, and returned. If she does it again, well, that is something. But until then—"

"I can't wait for her to do it again. He's my . . . he's mine." Toby breathed, closed his eyes for a moment. The social worker offered him a Kleenex from a floral-print box she kept handy. "I feed him, every day. When he's scared, I . . ."

Mireille leaned on the desk and looked away from Toby, at a thin and windowless wall. Artificial materials. Two degrees, from the University of Haiti and from Laval. From this angle, Toby could see a tiny splotch of blood in the white of her left eye.

⁓

The Chevette was still dead on Hyman, and Karen had a meeting with Steve Bancroft. Toby filled a garbage bag with toys and clothes and walked to the train station, where he picked up an abandoned copy of a community newspaper, *The Suburban*. All the way across the West Island and into downtown, he read the newspaper with the growing suspicion that he himself was in the midst of a corrective experience. It was an old copy, from the previous summer. Had no one cleaned since then? The top story concerned the international flora show in the Old Port. In the filthy slush, lopsided from carrying a stuffed garbage bag, he had soaked his brown suit to the knee. Another suit ruined. His shoes, a pair of black brogues, were also compromised. The mud and salt had begun to dry and cake off by the time he reached Central Station. Two representatives of the Metropolitan Transit System, passing through the cars upon their arrival, stopped to consider him for a moment—soaked, carrying a garbage bag.

In the underground mall of the station, Toby bought a bouquet and a bottle of champagne. He was tempted to buy a new book for Hugo, but once Catherine listened properly and surrendered the boy, unconditionally, to Toby, he would have all the titles of rue Collingwood at his disposal again. UPS would deliver them all to New York, once they were settled in the temporary apartment on the Upper East Side. He silently practised his speech in the metro, the dirty metro, where a homeless person with a garbage bag was perfectly acceptable as long as he made it through the turnstile. Thank you, Catherine, for everything you have done for the boy so far. But listen to reason. *Papa a raison.*

The apartment in Pie-IX looked as though it were peeling in the cold rain. Somewhere on the island, or retired in a bright condominium development in Boca Raton, the architects of despair huddled over their life's work and quietly mourned this place. From his bedroom in Manhattan, Hugo would see a sliver of Central Park.

Toby pressed the buzzer and began manufacturing a smile. Catherine unlocked the door without verifying his identity, another strike against her; who was to say he wasn't a jihadist? She stood in the doorway, her black eye not black but a swirl of gold and pink and brown. Her hair was short, cut into a bob, and dyed. Behind her, Hugo stood smiling in his brown pinstripe suit, his shirt unironed and his tie a mangled mess. Both of them in brown suits. "Poney." He clapped. "I'm here."

"*I'm here,*" said Catherine, in English. "You made him a snob."

"I taught him some manners." Toby lifted the garbage bag. "Some of his clothes and toys. I brought flowers and champagne. I thought we could ring in the new year."

"I'm all wet," said Hugo. "Come in, come in."

Catherine took the bag, peeked inside, and closed it up. She slid it into her apartment and, without a glance at the flowers and wine or another word, closed the door. As it swung shut, Hugo extended his arms toward Toby and wailed.

For twenty minutes Toby sat on the peeling white lino-leum of the hallway floor. The boy cried for some time, and then he stopped and all was quiet inside the apartment. Toby knocked on the door. When Catherine opened it, her rough little hands folded into fists, he offered the gifts. To trade pretty things for the boy. In New York, they would buy a new bed for Hugo and decorate his room with photographs of animals and planets. On the weekends they would visit the children's zoo in Central Park, the marionette theatre, the carousel.

"I can make him happy. Let me take him, and I'll give you whatever you want. You want money?"

"You're insane."

"My job is in New York."

Hugo appeared in the room again. "New York!"

"Read the latest studies: there is no better place to raise a child."

"You stand in my hallway, plastered in mud, talking about stealing my son. Taking him across a border."

My son, my son. "My suggestion is entirely sane: to give Hugo all the advantages of—"

"All he needs is love. And that's my job."

"You left him."

"I did what I had to do. Now I can be a better mother to him."

Toby did not make eye contact with Catherine. He looked past her, at the boy, who waved Toby inside. The jacket was gone. Now he stood in his deranged shirt and tie, like a tiny vacuum cleaner salesman. "I have to fix his tie."

"No."

"You can . . . come to New York with me. We'll be a family."

"Insane."

Toby kissed her. She pushed him away, shouted, kicked his left knee. "I'm calling the police."

A man in a white T-shirt, a bottle of 50 in hand, emerged from a door across the hall. "Is everything all right, Catherine?"

"Yes, thank you."

"If you need help, just yell." The man lifted his chin at Toby and went back inside.

"You left Hugo with me for a reason."

"Back then you didn't seem crazy."

"I can't just *leave*."

"But you must."

"I want a few hours with him tomorrow."

"We are very busy."

"Catherine. Please. I'll beg."

She looked back into the apartment. "After his nap."

⌒

Toby wandered through Montreal for the last time, past his condominium, his cafés and bistros and miniature parks. For one night of the year, almost everyone was properly dressed. Shortly before ten, he arrived at Sunnybrooke station and waved down a taxi.

His mother and Steve Bancroft sat in the living room, Karen in her recliner and Steve on the chesterfield, a bottle of dear-looking Rioja nearly empty before them.

Karen stood up when she saw him. "What happened to you?"

"I tried to get him back."

"Were you in a fight?"

"No."

"There's probably a glass left in the bottle, if you'd like one."

"Thank you. Hello, Mr. Bancroft."

"Steve, please."

"What did she say?"

Toby sat in his father's recliner. There was no smoke in the air. Neither Karen nor Steve Bancroft said much as Toby flatly explained his attempt to negotiate for Hugo. Karen poured him a glass of wine and opened another bottle.

"You think he should stay with her, Mom?"

"I don't know what I think."

"You know what she did."

"I have a compromise," Steve Bancroft said, leaning forward and clapping his hands. Like a football coach, Toby thought. For an instant he was angry, thinking the clap would wake up Hugo, sleeping down the hall. The wine was good. Steve Bancroft was a football coach with an appreciation of fine wine. "It isn't perfect, but what is?"

"A lot is, Steve, if you care to concern yourself with it."

Steve Bancroft blinked three times. "My business man-

ager, Fred—you don't know him—he looked at your proposal. He did some research. And you know what?"

"What?"

"It checks out. This bubble tea thing has legs. That's
why I'm here. We're going into business together, your mom
and I."

Your mom and I. Toby had not eaten in hours, and the
heat of the wine rose up and turned to gunmetal in his mouth.
"Let's go outside."

"Who?" Steve Bancroft looked around, as though there
were someone else on the chesterfield. "Why?"

"Let's go outside and sort this out, once and for all."

"Sort . . . sort what out?"

"Don't act dumb, Steve. Cuckolder. Prepare to defend
yourself."

"Toby." Karen left her recliner and sat next to Steve
Bancroft on the chesterfield.

"I see what's going on here."

"You see nothing," she said.

Steve Bancroft finished his wine. "I'll leave."

"I'll go with you, and we'll have a reckoning."

"A reckoning."

Toby had never been in a fist fight, though looking back
he wished he had punched Dwayne in his office. How he
would actually *summon* a punch, and how that punch would
be received and reciprocated had always mystified him, but not
now. Now, Steve Bancroft's confusion, his endearing handsome-
ness, his sincerity, only strengthened Toby's resolve. They would
fight on the front lawn, in the snow, like a couple of baboons.

"I don't know if this is a joke or something, but I'm
sixty-two. I don't fight."

"Coward."

"Two years ago, I had an angina attack. Do you know what that is? I could actually be *killed* in a fight."

"That's a risk you're going to have to take."

Steve Bancroft stood up. Toby stood up and punched his left palm. Steve Bancroft said, "Karen, I'm leaving now."

"Just a moment, Steve." She put both her hands on his. "I'm going to take this one down the hall and speak to him for a few minutes. And then we'll come back."

Karen pulled Toby by the lapel of his ruined suit. He dished Steve Bancroft the stink eye on his way out of the room. Once he had started to act the bully, Toby had found it quite enjoyable. Karen led him into the master bedroom, her bedroom, where the smell of Edward Mushinsky continued to linger with the cigarillos and perfume. She closed the door. Before he had a chance to defend himself, she slapped him so hard he fell back against her chest of drawers and sliced his hand on the likeness of a butterfly painted on a sheet of corrugated tin.

"Goddamn it," she said, and staunched the bleeding with a pile of Kleenex. The sound of the Kleenex coming out of the box in quick succession—*floof, floof*—reminded him of his childhood bloody noses. "You are not fighting anyone."

"What the hell's the cuckolder doing here?"

"You invited him back into our lives, if you remember."

"Our *business* lives."

"I love him," she said.

Toby pressed the Kleenex to his wound.

"I've loved him for as long as you've been alive." Her eyes were slow and wet. "I fell in love with him."

"Dad knew? That explains things."

Karen slapped Toby again. Then once more. Then she hugged him. His face hurt, and he wanted to say so out loud, to blame his mother for the suicide attempt on the driveway, for the cancer, for marrying his dad in the first place.

"I loved Edward too. Such things are possible. But I made a decision, for you. We made a decision, Steve and I, to stay away from each other. We sacrificed. And we held to it. Whatever you think he's up to, Cassius Clay, it's beyond your understanding. Everything, *everything* is more complicated than it seems. It might help you to keep this in mind as you . . . as you damn Hugo's mother."

Toby's hand was cut between his thumb and his index finger, deeply enough that the loaf of Kleenex had just about soaked through. There was really nothing he could say. He retired to the bathroom. Over the cold water running in the sink from fixtures so neglected and so clogged with soap scum they turned like antiques, Toby could hear his mother pleading with Steve Bancroft to stay.

"He wants to apologize," she said.

This was incorrect. Yet Toby did apologize, making excuses for his behaviour: sadness, hypoglycemia, confusion, wine, the early stages of a stomach ache.

Steve Bancroft explained his compromise decision. And that night, after some goat cheese and crackers, several more glasses of spectacular Spanish wine, and a bottle of G.H. Mumm with his mother and the man who would be his mother's lover, Toby slept on Hugo's sheets and dreamed that he was still there.

Sixteen

At the top of the mountain, deep inside and far from any worn path, was a secret place, an African jungle, Sherwood Forest, a place of danger and liberation: a boy's paradise. In the warm months, before Toby grew too old to appreciate its magic, Edward Mushinsky would take his son up the mountain, and together they would walk, looking over their shoulders to be sure no one had followed.

Other boys could visit, maps could be drawn, but only if these initiates were brave enough, and true. The secret place was the site of an unofficial stone and concrete monument, built in honour of someone's brother killed in the Second Battle of Ypres in 1915, decorated with a large iron soldier and amateur stone statues of a bear, a lion, trolls and dwarves and dragons, all of it less than ten feet away from one of the best climbing trees in the history of the maple.

At Catherine's apartment on New Year's Day, Toby waited at the kitchen table for the boy to wake up. Unaccustomed to his new nap schedule and apparently keen to ignore Toby's directives, Catherine had not put him down until almost two o'clock. She sat across from Toby, the white teapot a crystal ball between them. He had presented Steve Bancroft's compromise.

"Is there anything you won't steal from me?"

"Are you interested or not?"

Catherine had been in France, and that afternoon she looked French. Tight jeans, a red shirt that fit her properly, a silk scarf. The bruise under her eye had faded somewhat. "I should sue you."

"Go ahead."

"Maybe I should wait a few years, until you are rich and famous in New York, and then I will sue you."

"It's a house, with a yard, and a real salary."

"Thief."

Toby shrugged and poured more tea, organic roasted green, his gift, for Catherine and for him; since learning of the job in New York, he had begun to spend freely with his credit card. Two of the reproductions of Georges Brassens concert posters that had been in her living room were gone now, the rectangles behind them whiter than the rest of the wall. The Chevette was at Randall's garage, so Toby had taken his mother's Corolla; he had stuffed in three boxes of toys, two green garbage bags of clothes, and the animal/space art from Hugo's bedroom. The clothes and toys lay on the chesterfield. Catherine had pretended to be annoyed that her son now had a better wardrobe than she did.

The first rumbling from Hugo's room was sweet deliverance from Catherine and the tea. They jumped up and jostled each other on their routes to the messy-haired boy sitting up in his bed. Both of them knelt on the striped carpet in the semi-darkness, waiting for him to shake the sleep away. Hugo wiped his eyes. "What am I doing?" he said.

"What are *you* doing?" they said, in unison.

⌐

Toby parked the Corolla illegally in the backyard swimming pool enclave of Outremont, exactly where Edward used to park. It was cloudy, and it would not be long before the December darkness arrived, so they walked quickly. The wind roared through the upper branches of a cedar stand, and some snow fell on them.

Toby discovered the entrance to his secret forest and knelt down before the boy. "You must never, never tell your mom what you are about to see."

Just-three, it turned out, was considerably too young for this sort of thing. Hugo cried and attempted to run away. It took ten minutes of calm pleading in the flat, dying light, in both official languages, to convince Hugo to leave the worn path and enter the little forest.

"You want to go now," said Hugo, just as the memorial became visible. Toby carried him the rest of the way.

It was covered with graffiti. All of the small statues had been ruined. Spray paint, layers of it, already faded and chipped, covered everything that had not been destroyed. A lesser artist had grafted a bolt to what had been the lost soldier, the dead brother, leaving him with an enormous boner. Liturgical Québécois curse words had been scratched into the rock. It was yet more proof that God was either an imbecile or did not exist.

Crucial branches were missing from the climbing tree,

ravaged by an ice storm. Toby scanned the forest floor for hypodermic needles and used condoms, then put Hugo down.

"You're hungry. You want a snack."

Toby had forgotten the granola bar and water bottle in the Corolla, a twenty-minute walk away. He gamely tried to interest the boy in what remained but Hugo did not see the dragon in the dragon. Painted and smashed, none of the creatures resembled what they had been made to represent.

"Look, look." Toby climbed the tree until he reached the level where the branches had been stripped away. "Look at me."

To Hugo, who had no memories of this place, it was just another spooky and desecrated corner of the city—as charming as a downtown alley. Toby worried, in the end, that the soldier's erection would haunt the boy into his teen years.

There was a smooth indentation in the big rock where, in Toby's day, children had left offerings of marbles, Super-Balls, candy necklaces, Silly Putty, and Lik-m-aid. Toby climbed down the tree and introduced Hugo to what Edward had called a portal into a better world, with prettier weather, no war, and very few class distinctions. This, apparently, was why the children had left candies and toys: to convince the pagan gatekeeper that they were true of heart. On one of his first trips here, Toby had swiped a Matchbox Camaro from the collection of offerings. Each visit, Edward would make a big show of trying to open the "door," but Toby knew he was not true of heart. Just as his father had explained it to him, he told Hugo about the portal. He didn't want to give Hugo a complex about winter or discuss war or socioeconomic disparity, so he just said it was a door to Cuba, where they had beaches and marlins.

Toby pulled out the sandwich bag of unpopped corn he had gathered from the corners of the blue recliner. "My dad left these."

"My dad," said Hugo.

"Your dad."

"Your dad."

"Yes, Hugo. That is exactly how you say it."

"Your dad, Poney."

"My dad."

The sky, and the temple of secrets and wonders, turned a shade darker. Toby pressed on the portal and it did not budge. All the time and opportunity he had wasted—bong hits in university, shopping trips to malls in downtown Toronto—when he might have struggled to know his father. Toby decided to make it easy on Hugo by expressing himself thoroughly and honestly, the dad-and-boy mysteries continually unfurled, but Hugo was shivering and staring numbly into the distance. Snowflakes hung from his eyelashes. Toby emptied the bag of unpopped kernels.

"What are you doing?"

"Good pronoun, Hugo. Excellent. I'm enormously proud."

And Toby prayed, though not to any person or being or imbecile in particular. He did not ask for anything, not protection or even wisdom. With one hand he held the boy close. He pressed the other on Edward's kernels and concentrated, as hard as he could, until Hugo squirmed out of his grasp and declared, firmly, that he was starving.

Rituals did not come naturally to Toby. It took some work to convince himself that he had not just littered.

Hugo refused to walk, so Toby carried him. He had to change arms every minute or so. At the boundary of the park, on the concrete path, they came upon a dead squirrel next to a shrub. It had been freshly killed by something—a park vehicle, perhaps. Hugo insisted that Toby put him down, and he inspected the animal carefully without getting too close. Even in snow, the blood had dried on the animal's ears. It lay on its back, looking up at Hugo, its mouth open just slightly. Toby lacked the training and insight to discuss the fate of the squirrel with Hugo. He did not want to tell the truth, and he did not want to lie.

There were no questions. From the squirrel to the Corolla, a five-minute walk, Hugo said nothing. He did not complain about the snow or whine about his hunger. At the car, Hugo looked Toby in the eye and said, in English, with a tone of finality, "That squirrel wants his mommy."

Toby plopped Hugo into the Westchester, gave him a granola bar, and tightened the strap. The snow settled on the windshield. Snow in New York would be much wetter, and it wouldn't stick around as long. It would last about as long as Hugo's memories of him. Toby did not want the cold, wet boy to finish eating. He wanted to stay like this, trapped in his mother's car in Outremont, until they came for him.

Back in Pie-IX, Toby was reluctant to take Hugo inside, even though the boy desperately needed a warm bath and dry clothes. First, they ran and slid on the sidewalk. Then he cajoled the boy to walk ten paces away and run toward him for a hug. And again, and again, *encore une fois*. After what was probably the fifteenth hug, Catherine appeared in the snow.

Toby held the boy.

"Inside." Catherine kneeled down and Hugo ran to her. She looked up at Toby over the boy's shoulder. Mother and son walked hand in hand up the sidewalk, into the building.

"Where did you go, my darling?"

"To the mountain. No mommies."

⁓

It took Toby an hour and a half to get to Dollard, as there was fresh snow on the roads and he had joined the five o'clock traffic. The signs on the Chien Chaud had already come down, and the arts and entertainment pages of *La Presse* covered the windows of the Dollard location.

Randall and Garrett were in the auto shop, drinking beer, Randall in overalls and Garrett in a grey suit, loosened tie, blue-black bags under his eyes. There was a small television in the corner, with rabbit ears. The local CBC news was wrapping up.

"How is she, doctor?"

"She's gonna pull through." Randall gestured toward the aromatic garage, where the Chevette sat among other unfortunates. "But there isn't much life in her. That engine—"

"Don't tell me. I can't take it."

They sat on hard plastic chairs with tall bottles of Maudite. It was a cozy inside joke. In high school, the first time they got drunk together it was on Maudite, a doubly rebellious act as it was not just beer, but Satan's separatist beer.

One of Garrett's wealthy local clients was being sued over a land dispute. The Maudite break represented his first moment away from the file, apart from a few hours' sleep here and there, since the holidays began. He spoke slowly and precisely, and when he wasn't speaking, his mouth remained open. Toby worried drool would sneak out.

"I put off turkey and cheap wine," Garrett said, "but when this case pays out, in February I hope, we're heading south."

The men looked at each other several times, and Toby asked if anything was up. Randall shrugged. "He told me he told you."

"About what?"

One giant index finger pointed at Garrett, the other at himself. "And we have something to tell you. We're telling you first."

"We're gonna make it official," said Garrett.

"For the kids' sake," said Randall. "Stability and that stuff. So they know it isn't just sex or whatever."

As a child, Toby had often stood in his backyard, looking up at the stars. The idea of an endless universe, endless and timeless, was impossible to comprehend. He had always assumed that when he grew to be a man, he would stop enjoying cartoons and start understanding endlessness and timelessness. But it had not worked out that way. *A Charlie Brown Christmas* continued to move him, and he still didn't get the universe. It was equally difficult to fathom Randall and Garrett having sex, let alone getting married. The word, sure, even the ceremony, but the rest of it—shopping trips, dinnertime, parenthood, weekends at the family cabin, Disneyland, good-night kisses—did not scan.

"Congratulations."

"You think it's crazy?" said Garrett.

"It's gorgeous."

Randall delivered a speech he had clearly been mentally rehearsing for some time. Marriage was a flawed institution. "Me and Tracy are Exhibit A!" But if he and Garrett wanted to be a family, wanted to care for Dakota and Savannah, wanted to have a loving and caring and responsible relationship, what better way? Besides, the party would be in Puerto Vallarta.

"So who asked whom?"

Garrett pointed to Randall. "Negro got on one knee."

"We have to wait until the divorce is all settled up."

They hugged and clinked their Maudites and sat in contemplative silence. Toby considered the dusty racks of snacks: gum, potato chips, chocolate bars. Their chairs were arranged in a triangle, as though they were contestants in a game show.

"You all right?" said Garrett. "All packed up?"

"I can't take much with me. Clothes. My laptop."

"Where will you live?"

"A temporary apartment in the Upper East Side."

"That sounds so New York!" said Randall.

"I don't have to worry about babysitters and daycare and parks and schools anymore. So that'll be awesome."

Randall crossed his arms. "Bullshit."

"What's bullshit?"

"You'll be miserable."

"Are you on H?" Garrett leaned over and cuffed Randall.

Randall finished his Maudite and snarled. The last sip of a Maudite had been nasty in high school, and it was nasty today. "If you ask me, you have two options. We kidnap Hugo and smuggle his little ass down to the Lower East Side."

"Upper."

"Or. Or you stay here. You stay with the boy."

"You know I can't."

Randall stood up and walked close. He stood before Toby, transferring his weight from one foot to the other like he had to pee. "You can't give up the kid."

"She's the mom and I'm not the dad. Legally—"

"I don't care about legally."

"Sit down, Rand, and shut up," said Garrett.

"You'll regret it forever. You will."

"It's the job of my dreams. I'll be—"

"Toby, I liked your show when it was on. I learned about clothes, and being good, and not spitting so much, and using a capital *I* in e-mails. Lots of little things. But still, it's . . . Garrett, what's that word for surfacey?"

"Superficial?"

"You're smart. You're handsome. You're talented. If all the people like you in the world didn't do fashion and celebrity shows and reality TV, imagine. Just imagine the shit we could do. There'd be solar panels everywhere. No poverty. What about the fucking Gaza Strip?"

"Don't listen to him." Garrett stood up and guided Randall into his chair. "You can't stay. *That* would be your great regret, not the boy. You're not a hot dog guy, or a bubble tea guy. You're not a Dollard guy. Every *second* you stay is another insult to God."

"Yeah," said Randall. "God has a plan. He's been waiting for us to get married since junior high. If you want to be like that about it, we should leave too. This really ain't the place for a gay tow truck driver and his gay lawyer fiancé, not by a long shot. But Dakota and Savannah are here. I'd eat shit, actually eat actual shit, if it meant being close to them. Fashion doesn't matter. Etiquette doesn't matter. It really doesn't matter. If it did, you wouldn't have to make a show about it. You know what matters?"

Toby turned away.

"Great. Now you made him cry." Garrett cuffed Randall again, apologized on his fiancé's behalf, and declared him drunk and mentally unstable.

Only Randall chose to have a second Maudite, and in the ensuing twenty minutes Toby felt as though he had already left his friends and this place, this particular oil-smelling spot in the constellation of snack racks.

~

The next morning, one week before his departure, Toby packed two suitcases and three large cardboard boxes to be picked up and shipped by UPS. He sent flowers of congratulations to Randall and Garrett. He had been calling Catherine, and finally she phoned back.

"Have you considered it?"

"You stole my idea."

"How's Hugo?"

Catherine breathed through her nose. "He talks about you. He says English words I don't know."

"I'll visit a lot."

"He'll get over it."

The lukewarm coffee Toby had just finished turned to acid. "In time, yes. He'll forget all about me."

"As for your proposition. Your mother and that man . . ."

"Steve Bancroft."

"I wrote down that you said $45,000."

"To start as manager. And you live rent-free."

"This is charity."

"We don't know the bubble tea business like you do. It's

only fair. And Hugo . . . there are big parks here, lots of room for him. Not so much traffic."

"It sounds like I would owe you something."

"You do. But that's not what this is about."

Karen sat on the chesterfield and listened as Toby spoke to Catherine and paced the short length the phone cord would allow. Her hands were clasped. Karen's French was imperfect, but she understood most of what Toby was saying. Her eyes brightened as the conversation progressed. Toby tried not to look directly at his mother; news that she was moving hastily o'er into the bed of King Claudius did not settle well with him. Especially since he was the one who had pushed the sacrificial lovers into the same room again—Abie's Smoked Meat.

"Toby, can I speak to your mother?"

"I suppose. But slowly."

Toby handed the phone to Karen, who said, "*Bonjour, Madame,*" and nodded as she listened. "*Oui,*" she said, a number of times, and "*Non*" once or twice. "*Je voudrais très heureux d'avoir toi ici.*" Then she laughed, as Catherine would be laughing.

The Chevette may have been fixed, but Toby did not trust it. He borrowed his mother's Corolla one final time, because he did not want to be late. By the time he arrived at the bright restaurant on the Plateau, designed to look like a pub in Trois-Rivières, five minutes late for their reservation, Mr. Demsky—always a gentleman—was already drinking a gin and tonic and tucking into *cromesquis de foie gras.*

"I thought you'd be late," he said. "Actually, no, I didn't. I was just hungry."

Mr. Demsky had chosen the restaurant because it was the height of Pepsi-tude, an homage to meat and fat unlike anything Toby would find in New York.

Toby sat and Mr. Demsky pulled out a present for him.

"Come on." Toby shook the wrapped tube. "Like you haven't given me enough already."

"Open it!"

Six sesame bagels from Fairmont, in a Scotch container. "Thanks."

"I don't know if you realize this, but the bagels in New York are shit."

"Really?"

"It's difficult to imagine, I know, because you're Canadian, but there *are* a few things we do better: wood-hewing, water-drawing, and, it turns out, bagel-making. Here, have one of these dumplings."

Mr. Demsky insisted on ordering. First, the appetizers: onion soup, bison tartare, *poutine au foie gras,* and, of course, roast piglet. For his main course, Toby would enjoy the most exotically Canadian dish on the menu, the *plogue à Champlain,* a monstrous helping of pancakes and bacon with both maple syrup and foie gras on top. Mr. Demsky went for duck in a can.

"Isn't that maybe too much food?"

"Eat your *cromesquis.*"

Mr. Demsky apologized for being incommunicado since the funeral. It had hurt, the way Toby had kept things from him. A debriefing had long been in order. "I'm selling."

"Selling what?"

"Oh, everything."

Toby assumed at first it was a set-up for a joke, but there was no slyness in the president's eyes. The wine arrived and the server opened it. Mr. Demsky smelled the cork, smelled the wine, tasted it, and sent it back. "You must have had the bottle sitting in front of the heater. Bring us something serious, *câlice*. You think we're a couple of homos from Toronto over here?"

Diners at several nearby tables looked over, and Toby's core body temperature rose by approximately nine degrees.

"That was your *real* present," Mr. Demsky whispered, over the table.

It was difficult to imagine Mr. Demsky without his stations. In books and articles about Canadian media barons, Mr. Demsky always merited a chapter or a paragraph. He had grown up poor and had become wealthy and powerful in his late forties. Mr. Demsky had not overreached in recent years like most of his contemporaries; Century Media remained private and carried no debt. When Catherine had arrived to steal Hugo away from him, this had been Toby's consolation: he could become Mr. Demsky. That is, work on-camera until his receding hairline became uncomfortable, then move into management, executive management, and ownership.

"This is supposed to be a terrible time to sell anything."

"It's not going to get any better. Not in my lifetime."

"That doesn't sound like you."

"I'm wretched. I've been wretched for years. I'm tired. I have no heirs. The only person in the company I actually liked . . . I had to fire his ass. Turns out he was a racist."

"Sorry."

"Planning a careful succession, with Dwayne or someone else, the idea makes me want to hide in a closet, naked, with a small tub of magic mushrooms."

"You'll retire."

"I'm a baby boomer, Tobias. This was never supposed to happen. I can't believe I got old. I can't believe this is happening to me."

A new bottle of wine and the appetizers arrived, and it was already too much food for a couple of small men.

"There must be a place in the world for a gentleman of my humours and appetites to, whatever, live out my days in peace and comfort. My needs are modest. What do I want? Warm weather, good food and wine, access to legal and illegal drugs, and beautiful whores who speak foreign languages. I don't even care *which* languages."

The onion soup was rich and cheesy. Toby supplemented it with bites of foie gras poutine and roasted piglet, Mr. Demsky bogarting the bison tartare as he outlined the pros and cons of each possible retirement hot spot: Saint-Tropez, Haifa, Buenos Aires, Sydney. The wine, a Saint-Émilion, was worth more than the Chevette. It was one of those nights when the wine tasted better and better with each sip, and provided a clearer and clearer view of the truth. The bottle was finished before they had made it halfway through their appetizer bacchanal, so Mr. Demsky ordered another.

Toby had not thought to bring a notepad, but:

"Forget, first of all, that there ever was a country three hundred miles north of New York City. You were Canadian, but that's over now. When you say *us* and *we*, they have to know you mean it. No one cares where you came from. You might win a literary award in Toronto for mooning over your origins, but you won't get laid and you won't get paid. Not in a real country. Now. These people want to be entertained. What's your name gonna be?"

"Toby Marshall."

"Good. And what about that boy?"

"Finished."

"And don't fuck around with marriage."

Toby had made a number of profound errors in the past month, but advice from this man had led him to leave Edward for a trip to New York City. If he had been honest with Mr. Demsky, the interviews with ABS could have waited a few days, a week, but he had not been honest. "You loved your wife, Mr. Demsky."

"I did."

"Then how can you say that?"

Mr. Demsky did not answer for some time. He tucked into the bison tartare and took a last spoonful of soup. "She died and left me alone, didn't she? Now I have no one, and I'm too old to make any new friends, let alone find a new wife, like some of my contemporaries. Men in their seventies with thirty-year-old brides. Losers! Clowns! I knew, when she got sick, that I'd never have anyone else. Anyone who'd know my heart, who'd know me without my having to *explain* everything. That simple thing she did. She was . . . she knew when I was shit, when I was frightened and angry and hiding it, when I wanted to get the hell out of here. I'm not an easy person to live with, hour by hour, Tobias—you can probably sense it—but she rose above all that and saw me, the *real me*, better than I did. She started loving me—why, goddamn it?—before I had a penny. And she never stopped."

"You don't regret any of it."

"It's not so simple, Tobias. Regret and not regret. Each minute I've had away from her eats up days, weeks, months, years of our life together. And I'm a fuck-up. Do I sit around remembering the good times? No, I obsess over all the time I *didn't* spend with her, when I was travelling for no good reason or working late in that ugly box on René Lévesque. I cheated on her for a few years, after I started to make a name for myself. Mr. Big Shit. And who cares, right? A little ass on the side? If she knew, she never said a thing. An angel. And I was weak and stupid and selfish and scared of getting old and ugly. *I was supposed to die first.* I mean, look at me. I'm a drunk. What do I eat? Fat! Salt! Do I exercise? Fuck no. Her getting sick—if I believed in God, I'd see he was a genius. He crafted the ultimate punishment for my many sins: eleven years without her."

"Why didn't you have kids?"

Mr. Demsky dropped his spoon in the soup, cold now and forlorn. "That isn't up for discussion."

"I'm sorry."

"Don't apologize! That's another thing. When you get down there, enough with the *sorry, sorry, sorry.* You might as well wear a badge: *I'm a Canadian dope from the outer suburbs of Dopetown.*"

The restaurant was bright and boisterous. The servers took the plates away and the main courses arrived. Mr. Demsky did not say *merci* or even thank you. When the server asked if everything was going well, Toby answered that everything was magnificent, and the server paused for a moment, looked down at Mr. Demsky. A slight finger wave, signalling, *Fine, go away.* When they were alone again, he winked at Toby. "That just tears you up inside, doesn't it?"

Pancakes for dinner. When Toby was growing up, on the few occasions when Karen did not make it home by six o'clock, Edward tended to make breakfast for dinner: cereal, fried eggs, fried egg sandwiches, scrambled eggs, or pancakes. They never had maple syrup, even though they might have tapped a tree down the street. All they kept in the house, all they could afford, was sugar water—a generic version of Aunt Jemima's, butter flavour, which made butter unnecessary.

Foie gras and maple syrup initiated a salt, sugar, and fat battle so intense that Toby had trouble concentrating halfway through the second bottle of wine. Mr. Demsky was talking again, about the medical advantages and disadvantages of his various retirement options. A glow around that white nest of hair, quivering just slightly, Toby's nervous system beginning to fail. Too much fat. The music was so loud, suddenly, along with the crashes and clanks of the cooks and servers. It occurred to Toby, as he pretended to listen, that he was sweating. He dabbed at his forehead and continued eating, eating, drinking, drinking, half listening, willing it all away. In the morning he would be gone from this place, all this fat. The fat had occupied him. His liver was under siege, desperate to detoxify even as he shovelled in more fat, more sugar, more salt, more sulphites.

Cognac.

A man of his time. No, *the* man of his time. His specialness, that locomotive of instinct and certainty, even during the darkest and quietest nights on rue Collingwood as he prepared to see himself as merely regular. His destiny: to talk on television about cutaway collars, the correct thing to say in a receiving line, money talk, sex talk, religion talk, getting old talk, talk talk. Mitigating anxiety and discomfort. Meaninglessness and mattering. To matter.

Toby had never been able to see himself in Edward Mushinsky. But his future was clear in Mr. Demsky: that life

of happy unhappiness, of travel and legal troubles, of only
the best sulphites. Being slightly—please, finally—more.
Being written up in a real gossip column. Some time later,
looking back on his night at Au Pied de Cochon, his final
night in Montreal, he would recognize it for what it was: a
spiritual night. A night with God the Imbecile. Toby had only
one life, and it was already more than half finished. There
was no room for error.

Cognac. "I'm not going."

"You're not going."

"To New York."

Mr. Demsky was as drunk as Toby. He rocked from
side to side, just slightly, and blinked. For a long time, long
enough for the couple at the adjacent table to get up and
leave, Mr. Demsky stared at him. Then out the window, at
the quiet, filthy neighbourhood. Mr. Demsky's sleepy gaze
plowed through the three-storey walk-ups of the Plateau,
where generations of the forgotten had considered the right
furnishings for their time, and had died.

"I've been around. In this business."

"I know."

"What you're saying, it's not unprecedented."

"It's not."

"You're not one of those people."

"One of those people."

"It's a painful business, as you know, and fickle and
fucked. The rewards, as you also know . . ." He paused to
burp. "The rewards can be spectacular. You could be banging
serious models by this time next year, and you know it. But
sure, shit, you can give it up. *People have done it*, and they've
disappeared into their weird quiet delight, I suppose, or their

regret. That's what I see for you, knowing you as I do: regret. I guess you've convinced yourself there's something better, but I suspect you're just raw right now, and a bit spooked."

The cognac glass was ridiculous. Toby twirled the half-ounce in its giant roundness. The taxi home would be fifty dollars, and then he would have to come back here tomorrow for the Corolla, in the cold, his head weighing two hundred pounds and quaking.

"You only get one or two of these." Mr. Demsky's voice had gone down an octave. The unheeded warning in the opening minutes of a horror movie: *Get away from this place.*

"These?"

"Decisions. Decisions like these, Tobias."

"I want to stay with Hugo."

"His name is Hugo?"

"Yes."

Mr. Demsky took a deep breath and slowly shoved his cognac to the centre of the table. "Is he yours? Your kid?"

"Yes."

"Why can't you take him with you?"

"He's mine, but he isn't *mine.*"

Mr. Demsky placed a hand on the table, to brace himself. "We can never take them with us. I don't even know why we try."

Seventeen

A gentleman removes his glove to shake hands. A close-up of the preparation, and the shake, had once opened a segment of *Toby a Gentleman*. As one says goodbye, he slowly removes the glove. The hand must not be bare until precisely before the shake. To pull off the glove too early and render oneself asymmetrically gloveless for the final seconds of a conversation is clumsy and inelegant. One's companion will feel obliged to end the conversation, to shake immediately and walk away.

Mr. Demsky arrived at the Dollard location of Thé Bubble in the middle of a blizzard. It was the fifth of March. Many of the guests had already arrived. Toby was outside in his overcoat, shovelling the sidewalk so the door would continue to open and close. Nine days of blizzard. Mr. Demsky removed his glove for a shake, and Toby leaned his yellow shovel against the glass of the bubble tea shop. In his haste, he shook Mr. Demsky's hand with his glove on.

Separated by a thin layer of calfskin.

"Well," said Mr. Demsky.

"Let me try that again."

"Well, well, well."

"It's cold. You rushed me."

"Amateur!"

"Let's try it again."

"Next thing you know, you'll be whistling at flight attendants."

"Never."

"Mixing up 'seen' and 'saw.'"

"Oh God."

"Wearing white after Labour Day."

"Actually, Mr. Demsky, it's interesting: there are circumstances—"

"You know I don't give half a fuck."

"It means a lot that you came."

Mr. Demsky removed his hat, and his hair bloomed. "I can't believe I flew back for this. You know what the temperature was in Palm Beach yesterday?"

"Thank you."

The front windows had fogged. There were a few spots where guests had leaned against the moist glass, and the crowd was visible inside. "You're going to work in there? All the time?"

"I'll hover between the three locations until they're settled."

"Then?"

Hugo was at the door, his face pressed against the glass. Both men crouched and waved.

"This is going to make you happy, Tobias?"

"Something like happy."

Snow was beginning to gather in Mr. Demsky's hair. "Get me a drink."

Inside, the guests drank spiked bubble teas—vodka, gin, tequila—and ate croque monsieurs. Some had heeded the invitation and dressed semi-formal. Most did not. Hugo wore the world's smallest tuxedo.

"I am wearing a smoking," he said to Mr. Demsky.

"Excellent work, Hugo," said Toby. "*I am.*"

"No, you aren't," said the boy. "That's just a suit."

Toby picked him up and together they escorted Mr. Demsky to the counter. The croque monsieurs, in classic and modern variations—*croque Provençal, croque Auvergnat, croque tartiflette*—were cut up into squares and labelled in French and English.

Behind the counter, Steve Bancroft and Karen Mushinsky wore black Thé Bubble aprons and berets over a new brown suit and a green dress, respectively. Toby and Catherine were slated to take the next shift, in an hour. The music, French cabaret. It had taken Toby a period of research and experimentation to find the perfect volume, a matter on which many experts disagreed.

"Mr. Demsky," Karen said, shaking his hand.

"Please call me Adam. You must be very proud of your son."

Karen's eyes watered up.

"I'm guessing vodka," said Steve Bancroft.

Mr. Demsky extended his hand. "You must be the Amazing Kreskin."

Toby left Mr. Demsky to speak with the Amazing Kreskin and Karen. Hugo asked to ride on his shoulders so he could be the tallest boy in town.

In the final stages of design and brand-creation, Steve Bancroft had hired Catherine as a consultant. There were three reasons for this. Number one: she had a legal claim on the business plan that Toby had not been honest about, and it was a wise idea to placate her lest she sue them. Number two: she had some debts that needed clearing up. Number three: she had a damn good idea. For the Thé Bubble sensibility, they had tossed Taipei and Paris into a blender and come up with art, paint, music, food, and non-alcoholic beverages that suggested both capitals. Toby had added one element to the Dollard location: a black diorama filled with an Edward skeleton dancing to a skeleton band—"Hey, hey, hey."

The room was as full as it could be without contravening fire regulations. Randall and Garrett sat at a corner table, surrounded by potential members of the Benjamin Disraeli Society. The topic: back pills. Randall explained that they had rented several Frank Capra films one Sunday in February and had enjoyed "a Percocet Valentine's Day."

Catherine stood in the middle of the room, in a red dress, speaking to no one.

"I want to get down now."

Toby carefully lowered Hugo, and he adjusted his suit.

"How is my tie, Poney?"

"Perfect."

"I like perfect." He wiggled away, toward the counter and another croque monsieur.

Catherine walked over and stood next to Toby. Their arms touched. It was rare to be this close to her, even though they had lived in the same house for two months and had prepared the grand opening together. A woman from the swimming pool, who had a girl Hugo's age, approached them and began talking about her daughter—who kept choking on the tapioca balls. Toby had been watching the door for special guests. Two people were now outside the shop, tiny people. Toby excused himself.

The Brassens, Denis and Josée, shuffled on the sidewalk in bulky snowmobile jackets. Denis carried a small gift bag.

"*Vous êtes Monsieur Mushinsky?*" said Denis. His head and hands were enormous, not unlike a Taiwanese puppet's, and the skin on his face seemed collapsible. His eyes were small and green, and gave the impression that he was about to explode into laughter. Toby had expected a large man with an unfortunate stoop.

"It's an honour to meet you. And the beautiful Josée."

Josée handed the small bag to Toby. "This is for Catherine."

"Oh, you should give it to her."

The Brassens looked at each other.

"Come in, please."

"We do not know," said Denis. "Now that we are here, we do not know."

They had not been difficult to find, as there were only two Brassens in the phone book for Matane, a town on the northern coast of the Gaspé Peninsula. Denis worked in a shrimp plant of some sort, and appeared every year in the Festival de la Crevette in a shrimp costume. Josée was a short-order cook in a hotel restaurant specializing in seafood. In a twenty-minute phone call, with both of them on the line, Toby learned all this and plenty more. They lived in an attached townhouse on the hill that led down to the *grand fleuve*. This is where Catherine had grown up, from whence she had fled at seventeen. As a child, she had liked to swim, to sing in the choir, and to camp in the Chic-Choc Mountains. Both Denis and Josée had cried on the telephone when they learned they were grandparents.

"Does she know we are here?" said Denis, in a powerful accent Toby associated with taxi drivers.

"It's a surprise."

"She may not like this surprise," said Josée. "I do not think she will."

Toby escorted the Brassens inside and took their jackets. Their glasses fogged. Hugo sat on the counter, surrounded by Catherine and Mr. Demsky on one side, Karen and Steve Bancroft on the other. Toby picked him up and asked Catherine to come along. She spotted her parents and stopped, dished a colourful stew of church-related curse words. Hugo placed his hands over his ears, much too late.

"What are they doing here?"

"I put them in that Hilton by the airport."

"Why? Why did you do this?"

"Poney," said Hugo, "why?"

Toby handed the boy to his mother. He expected another curse word or two, or at least a frustrated sigh. Instead, Catherine looked up at Toby for a moment. She wore eyeliner and lip gloss. The dress was crooked on her shoulders, from carrying the boy, so Toby adjusted it for her. She walked across the floor of the bubble teashop.

The first couple had departed and a small crowd was eagerly gathering at the mess of long winter parkas. His father's friends and the friends of Steve Bancroft, Karen's friends, many of them astounded into silence by the new couple's coming-out party. Women Catherine had already met at the library and at moms-and-tots swimming lessons, who talked about nothing but children. How they ate, slept, played, prayed, talked, battled colds. Most of them wore clothes no one in the city would dare put on outside a private residence.

Toby had convinced himself that he would wake up one morning, in this new century, and stop noticing.

Mr. Demsky held a giant cup of bubble tea before him like a bowl of spoiled milk. "You gave up network television for *this?*"

Toby did not respond.

"These people are your friends?"

"I lost my friends when I became a racist."

"Of course."

Together they looked out on the polyester suits, khaki pants and no-iron blue shirts, the croque monsieur grease, the photos of French bicycles and Asian bicycles, tiny white skeletons in a black box, the blizzard out the window.

"I think I'll be going, Tobias."

"My friend."

"Congratulations."

They shook, gloveless this time. "And congratulations to you, Mr. Demsky."

Over the speakers, "*La Mer*" was just reaching the end point, where Charles Trénet calls out resolutely, "La vie-uh."

Hugo took Toby's hand and pulled him through the crowd toward the corner, where Catherine stood weeping with her miniature parents. A gentleman carried two handkerchiefs, one as a pocket square and the other for practical concerns—tears and other emergencies of the heart. This afternoon, in his haste, Toby had forgotten to sneak a square of white linen into the inside pocket of his jacket. So he pulled out his yellow Hermès, the most perfect thing he owned, and presented it to the mother of his son.

Acknowledgements

I would like to acknowledge the generous support and encouragement of the Canada Council for the Arts and the Alberta Foundation for the Arts.

Equally supportive, generous and endlessly inspiring—my family: that great northern beauty Gina Loewen and my two children, Avia and Esmé Babiak; my mother, Nola, and my brother, Kirk; Alan Kellogg and Liz Nicholls.

Thank you to Martha Magor and Anne McDermid, of the McDermid Agency, who offered thoughtful commentary on many, so many, versions of this book. And to Tobias Webb: *courage, mon ami.*

To Jennifer Lambert, my insightful editor and trusted friend: kids!